D0231383

James Stevenson has been a spare-time writer for many years. *Dartmouth Conspiracy* is his first novel.

DARTMOUTH CONSPIRACY

September 1942: Luftwaffe pilot Karl Deichman must bomb the Royal Naval College in Dartmouth, despite knowing his cousin and childhood friend is resident there. Yet his orders give him no choice — the attack must proceed . . . After the war, Karl returns to England, haunted by the thought: *Did I kill Andrew?* His quest leads him to a former secret agent, a wartime spy, and an ex-RAF Spitfire pilot; but as he uncovers the secret of the Dartmouth Conspiracy, he is drawn into a lethal trap. And it will be more than sixty years before the final jigsaw-piece falls into place . . .

JAMES STEVENSON

DARTMOUTH CONSPIRACY

Complete and Unabridged

ULVERSCROFT
Leicester

First published in Great Britain in 1999 by
Friars Goose Press
Devon

First Large Print Edition
published 2007
by arrangement with
Friars Goose Press
Devon

British Library CIP Data

Stevenson, James, 1934 –
    Dartmouth conspiracy.—Large print ed.—
    Ulverscroft large print series: adventure & suspense
    1. Dartmouth College—Fiction 2. World War, 1939 – 1945
    — Aerial operations, German—Fiction 3. World War,
    1939 – 1945—England—Dartmouth—Fiction
    4. Suspense fiction 5. Large type books
    I. Title
    823.9′14 [F]

    ISBN 978–1–84617–826–9

Published by
F. A. Thorpe (Publishing)
Anstey, Leicestershire

Set by Words & Graphics Ltd.
Anstey, Leicestershire
Printed and bound in Great Britain by
T. J. International Ltd., Padstow, Cornwall

This book is printed on acid-free paper

Then Herod ... was exceeding wroth,
and sent forth, and slew all the children.

St Matthew 3, Verse 1

Part One

1

Maupertus, France — Thursday, September the 10th, 1942:

Leutnant Karl Deichman was suffering from an almost overwhelming sensation of guilt as he settled himself into the cockpit of the most powerful fighter aircraft in the world.

In spite of this his actions were quick and deliberate. In the cramped space he checked his harness and put his left hand on a familiar curving handle to begin the starting sequence.

He said the drill out loud, emphasising the settings — it helped him to concentrate: '*Both fuel tanks:* **on.**' He dropped his hand to a switch: '*Fuel pumps:* **on.**' With his right hand he moved a lever projecting from a horizontal slot in front of him: '*Engine ventilator:* **one third.**' He grasped a round knob just in front of the wireless jack-plug: '*Operate fuel-primer:* **up down, up down, up down.**'

Was it loyalty or treachery that drove him? Nobody knew what he was about to do over the course of the next forty minutes except himself. A reconnaissance mission — just routine — that's what his comrades believed. He looked over his left shoulder and signalled to Feldwebel Ederbach, black-overalled and standing in the wet grass beyond the left wing-tip. He thumbed a spring-loaded switch to start the flywheel: the whine was low at first, then rising . . . wait for it to reach its highest note then press a button, bottom left of the panel: **'CONTACT'**.

There was a loud bang as fourteen dormant pistons kicked into life and exhaled a gigantic breath of oily smoke — making it suddenly dark in the cockpit. Deichman listened to the big radial engine — critically — waiting for it to settle and purr.

The mechanic raised a hand to signal that he was disconnecting the accumulator trolley from its plug on the outside of the fuselage and the pilot pushed his throttle forward. Burning exhaust gas torched back, spiralling an arch of flame over the cockpit of the single-seater. A dozen needles trembled on their dials. He eased the throttle back: the engine smoothed to a slow throb. *Oil-pressure . . . oil-temperature . . . fuel-pressure . . . fuel-contents*.

Karl gave another signal: *chocks away* and manoeuvred out from under the trees, steering with wheel-brakes, swinging the fighter freely from side to side on its

4

broad-track undercarriage to see his way forward, winding a big handle with his right hand to close the sliding canopy.

Bumping over the grass, he glanced down quickly, took his hand off the throttle and pressed the flap-control button with his left index finger: '*Down ten degrees;*' the elevator trim switch was next to it: '*Neutral.*' His hand went back to the throttle-grip and his thumb curled onto the propeller speed-control switch: '*Kommandgerat:* **auto.**'

He turned the Focke-Wulf to face a wind which was already showing its strength and direction by flattening a wisp of smoke from the cookhouse chimney. He pulled back the control column to lock the swivel on the tail-wheel and pushed the throttle lever up to the safety-gate.

A trembling needle on the extreme left of the fascia swung across its dial to register *2700 revolutions per minute.* The supercharger gauge flickered at the required *1.6 atmospheres of pressure.*

Gathering speed across the grass he applied rudder against an anticipated swing to the left and glanced quickly at the airspeed: *170 kilometres per hour.* The ground-rumble stopped suddenly — and he was flying.

Karl cleared a row of elms on the far side of the field, turned onto a heading of 311 degrees magnetic and saw beaches and bright houses racing under the wing. The Cap de la Hague peninsular showed itself under a light sea-mist, pointing its crooked finger at his target on the other side of the Channel — a target which lay exactly 160 kilometres north-west of his home base on the Cherbourg peninsular.

Thirty minutes for the outward leg: plenty of time for Karl Deichman to contemplate an act of treachery against his own comrades that would put him in front of a firing squad if it were ever discovered.

He was low: he had to climb to miss the houses in Braye Street — all of six stories high and overlooking the rusting metal beach defences on the coast of Alderney Island. He pushed down to sea-level again with the airspeed needle nudging 530 kilometres per hour.

★   ★   ★

Before take-off, Oberleutnant Erich Boxhammer, leader of the staffel, had put his hand on Karl Deichman's shoulder: 'Deichy, my friend, you are the only one amongst us with prior knowledge of the target. I'm relying on you. I don't imagine that you'll ever become a famous photographer after the war but that doesn't mean that I don't expect you to do a good job today. The Photographic Unit have given us pictures taken from heights of over 3000 metres — from you I want low-level stuff.'

★　★　★

Karl leant back until he could feel a reassuring shield of steel — twelve millimetres thick — behind his head. Yes, it was true, he knew the Dart Estuary. When he was a boy his English cousins used to say that he knew the river so well that he could have sailed a dinghy from Kingswear to Dittisham on a moonless night — blindfolded. But that was long ago — in peacetime — and it was boys' talk.

Droplets of spray were turning to a fine dusting of salt on the Focke-Wulf's windscreen. Karl took a quick look at the Rolex that Helga had given him — more reliable and easier to see than the dashboard clock, half obscured behind the angle of his right knee. *'Twelve minutes to go.'*

White foam; curling wave-tops.

What was it that Feldwebel Schieverhüfer from the Photographic Unit had said while bolting his apparatus to the mortar launchtube under the right wing of the Focke-Wulf?

7

Please, Herr Leutnant: sea-water is extremely corrosive — if it gets inside my camera it will be ruined for good.

Why did that man always say *my* camera?

Then — the Mew Stone: upended layers of rock in front of the mainland cliff, slightly distorted through fifty millimetres of bullet-proof glass. As a boy he had leapt onto that slippery stone from a swamping dinghy, scrambled up its tilted strata — with his English cousins close behind him — to plunder the nests of seabirds. All those hard-won eggs, pierced and blown, stored and labelled under glass in an upstairs room of a pleasant house in Plymouth — a house set in a leafy street on the northern edge of the town.

As the rocky island edged into the centre of Karl's *Revi* gunsight, he pressed the shutter-release and took the first of Boxhammer's photographs.

For his second shot he put the Focke-Wulf into a steep turn and pointed the aircraft at a fifteenth century castle at the entrance to the harbour — which responded aggressively with a long squirt of tracer — *fifteenth century?*

Then over Kingswear peninsular, jutting from the opposite bank . . .

The sky exploded. *Orange flashes, brown smoke, bucking, shuddering, harness-straps cutting the shoulder, muzzle-flashes under the smoke.*

He flew across the railway-station, turning tightly to photograph ships in the river. A geyser of steam jetted vertically from a locomotive to spoil the picture but Karl didn't care because now he was correctly placed to carry out his own personal mission.

He gave the handle three quick turns; the cockpit cover slid back — a narrow gap. He reached for the brass cylinder hidden in the top of his flying boot — then another quick photo of mullioned windows rearing in front of him — Boxhammer would curse him for that: wrong angle — too low: *below the clock — Christ!*

Torrents of air swirled into the cockpit; the streamer unwound itself — it was caught on something — tug violently without looking down. Khaki figures through the blur of a spinning propeller, running towards a Bofors gun — get down low, and lower over that D-shaped parade ground . . .

In one continuous movement Karl pushed his carefully prepared cartridge case out through the gap, closed it quickly, pulled up sharply, missed the roof and made an urgent turn for home.

Tight turn over the college — one more photo: the Noss Shipyard, Boxhammer's *secondary target*. Slam the throttle through the safety-gate, claw up the high ground on the eastern side of the estuary; enemy artillery pounding the slope, earth and grit splattering the windscreen.

From 500 metres the sea looked flat and calm. Looking down to check the pencilled heading on his knee-pad he saw the streamer; it had torn away from the cartridge case and now lay in a tangled heap on the floor of the cockpit.

Even if enemy radar were following his progress, Karl knew that the RAF possessed no aircraft fast enough to catch him as he flew back across the Channel.

He trimmed for level flight and remembered something that he had once said during one of those summer holidays in England. He had said it to his cousin after their boat had capsized in a sudden squall.

'*It's time you stopped tipping your crew into the water, Andrew, the Royal Navy will never accept you if you can't sail a dinghy.*'

Could that have been in 1938, the summer of English achievements? Ian had been obsessed with Len Hutton's record 364 runs in a cricket match against Australia, and the news that Imperial Airways had extended their flying boat service as far as Darwin. Andrew's passion had been the Cunarder,

Queen Mary, crossing the Atlantic from America to England in less than four days. That was the year when newspapers were forecasting war: the threat to Czechoslovakia; the British effort to build a thousand fighter aircraft.

At home in Munich at the end of that summer holiday, Karl had heard his parents asking each other — in whispers — why their Jewish friends should be forced to leave their homes and wear the Star of David — *in the ghetto*. Then, in October — the same year, Germans marched into Czechoslovakia and a month later, during the night in the Jewish quarter of Munich — shops were looted and smashed. When a lawyer complained to the Gestapo about a swastika daubed on his neighbour's front door, he was beaten and made to walk barefoot through the streets with a placard around his neck: *I will never complain about the Nazis again.*

Was this a worthy cause to fight for — would Father have given his blessing to this if he were still alive?

★   ★   ★

In the cottage assigned to the only married man in the staffel, Karl lay next to Helga and stared into the darkness. He was thinking

11

about the message that he had just dropped on Dartmouth: he had hidden it carefully inside that cartridge-case but the red streamer, designed to make it visible as it fell, had become detached. Now that message might never be found.

It could be anywhere: caught in a gutter on those endless roofs; in a tree; buried in a vegetable plot next to the parade ground or — maybe — lying submerged in water.

2

On days like these the walls of the crew-room sometimes showed patches of damp. Today — for good measure — there was a faint smell of cows exuding from the whitewash, enough to remind Karl Deichman that maybe, one day, the bloody business of war would end and this building at least might resume its peacetime function.

All three *Staffels* of the *Gruppe* had been busy since Karl's photographic mission over Dartmouth one week ago. As usual Hauptmann Boxhammer's staffel remained on top of the list with three allied merchant ships sunk and four Spitfires destroyed on the ground during a spirited attack on the RAF fighter base at Exeter. Cost: one Focke-Wulf shot down over the Channel — pilot picked up.

Karl felt uneasy. Waiting for the *Staffelkapitaen* to arrive was different when you knew what was planned for the following day. There was the usual chatter: hits and misses; girls bedded in Cherbourg — it helped hide the

13

fear — but Karl sat apart from his fellow pilots, staring at the walls: Weiss's cartoon of Winston Churchill had turned yellow and was curling at the edges. The photograph of Marlene Dietrich, with its fake signature, crooked and abandoned behind the piano.

Sparks fell from Hauptmann Erich Boxhammer's cigar as he bustled through the door. He crushed the stub into an ashtray made from a Rolls-Royce piston-head and opened his map-case. The boss was short and thick-set. He pushed a stubby hand through black hair cut like a brush. Hardened in combat — that's what he claimed — while flying Messerschmitt fighters in the *Marabou Staffel* under Oberleutnant Lützow during the Spanish Civil War but he always insisted that the experience had *not* made him invulnerable to the enemy. A tough talker, full of bravado, but he had a concern for the safety of his pilots that he felt with almost the same intensity as his hatred for the enemy. Today Boxhammer's whole demeanour heralded news of something big as he took papers and diagrams from his map case.

'Tomorrow we have an important job to do, gentlemen. As you know I am not a religious man but I have named this mission *Operation Herod*.'

Karl recognised some of the photographs as his own.

'Gather round, gentlemen. Today we are concerned with an English harbour called Dartmouth, situated on a river estuary on the south coast of England. I will concentrate on distinguishing features first before we look at Operation Herod's specific targets.'

He held up the first of Karl's pictures. 'Here we have a small island with sloping rock strata, distinctive as a criminal's fingerprint. It is marked on your maps as the *Mew Stone*. This rock is important to us because it is situated just outside the river mouth and it will serve as a marker — help to guide us into the harbour.'

He looked up from the table and took out a fresh cigar. 'Our mission is the result of a direct request from Bremerhaven. They have asked us to visit a certain building situated on the west bank of the River Dart, one which the *Kriegsmarine* intends to use after the forthcoming collapse of the Allies. Not very often, is it, that we are asked to kill the occupants of a building and, at the same time, cause minimal damage to the structure? But this is what we will do tomorrow, my friends. Not very easy you might think but I have consulted an architect on this one.

'Last week I gave Deichman the day off.

He took a trip to his favourite holiday resort — and like all tourists he returned with some interesting snapshots — but not of English *bathing belles*. I asked him to go over there because our official photographers have lost their appetite for low level flying. Deichy was given an English welcome but I'm happy to say that he did the job rather well: we now have information about some new anti-aircraft batteries. Juicy pheasants need to know these things before sticking their beaks up Mr Fox's arsehole!'

Boxhammer pointed his cigar, still unlit, to a photograph taken from high altitude: *Dartmouth Hafenanlage GB 45158*. Areas on both sides of the river had been outlined in red with specific targets numbered and listed on a key below. Although Karl could easily recognise the Royal Naval College situated to the north of the town, he was pleased to see that it had been omitted from the target list; it kindled a flicker of hope that there might have been a last minute change of priorities.

'Our reconnaissance people took this aerial photograph in October 1940. On the lower border, almost cut off at the bottom of the picture, and close to the river mouth, you can just see part of an ancient castle — full of not so ancient ordnance: probably a British 3.7 inch Mark 111A concealed in a battery

16

designed to blend in with the rest of the ruin, and a pair of Lewis guns on the castle roof. On the opposite bank of the river is Kingswear railway station. Follow the railway line along the east bank for 2600 metres and you come to the Noss Shipyard — again, heavily defended. Deichman has taken low-level shots of all these places so make sure you look at them, get them clearly fixed in your heads.'

Karl felt his last thin strand of hope slip away when Boxhammer's cigar came to rest on that familiar D-shaped parade ground. 'This is our main target, gentlemen, *Britannia*: two mobile Bofors and several Lewis guns on surrounding high ground so we will have to be careful. Britannia is a college: the Royal Naval College — it is where cadets are trained to become officers in Tommy's navy.'

Karl wanted to close his ears to it: *just another target — that's what Britannia was to Boxhammer and the rest of the staffel. This wasn't murder to them — the breaking of a pact — the betrayal of a friend . . .*

Boxhammer took a step back from the table. 'I want you to think about what our *Kreigsflotte* has been doing recently. Since the beginning of this year our U-boats and warships have destroyed five million tons of enemy merchant shipping in less than nine months. It is a wonderful achievement but, unfortunately for us, Tommy is still alive. The bulldog can feel the noose drawing tight around his neck but he survives. The six of us are going to help tighten that noose — because it is actions like these that will one day ensure the dog squeals for mercy. Efforts by the British Navy to hamper the destruction of Allied shipping must be crushed; that is why our target for tomorrow morning is this college. Remember that from this place a steady stream of trained officers emerge to man Mr Churchill's ships.

'Tomorrow is Friday the 18th of September. The agent who works for us in Dartmouth tells us that 634 cadets will assemble in the college at 11.30 in the morning; we are also reliably informed that it will be the first day of their Christmas term.'

Boxhammer looked at his pilots in turn. 'Remember that it is Grand Admiral Karl Doenitz who has chosen us to do this work; we must not disappoint him. Last week we had firm proof of the friendship that exists between this *gruppe* and our naval colleagues — no one knows this better than you — Awak . . . yes, I mean you, but why the crew of that *Schnellboot* didn't throw you back into the sea when they saw what a miserable fellow they had fished out of the water I shall never know. Perhaps another hour's swimming in the Channel might have taught you to take more care.'

The response from Karl's friend was his usual cool, blue-eyed and disarming smile — the one that never failed to give him the pick during dances hosted by the Officers' Mess.

Boxhammer shook his head. 'It is not only our friend Awak that I worry about — all of you give me headaches. I know some of you think you are good pilots — and others think they survive through luck but war is not and never will be a game of chance. It is each man's responsibility to make sure that he stays alive — *and there'll be trouble for anyone who doesn't!*'

He raised his voice above the laughter: 'I have chosen Leutnant Deichman as our leader tomorrow. He used to go sailing on the river Dart when he was a boy, isn't that right Deichy?'

There was no response from Deichman apart from a barely perceptible nod. Boxhammer continued, using his cigar to point at the chart: 'Here is the college, it has a tall clock-tower. In the outskirts of the town, on the rising ground to the south-west of the clock-tower there are two more towers: here, and here. Now take a look at these.'

Karl took a step closer: Boxhammer had produced two more photographs that were certainly not his — *they had been taken from the ground*. Who could have done it, where had they come from, who was the agent?

'The three towers should appear dead in line as we run in for the attack. The middle tower is a church, and the far one is built against the west wall of a school at the highest point of the town.' Boxhammer's cigar traced a wide arc across the survey. 'If we fly behind these hills we will be invisible from the town until we breast the ridge. At this point we will cross the railway line. If we are positioned correctly, we will make our final approach to the target on a heading of 228 degrees magnetic with the three towers in line ahead of us. We will be keeping radio-silence throughout the operation; we will be flying very close together — close enough to see Deichman's hand-signals.'

Boxhammer took another document out of the map-case and spread it out on the table. 'This is a copy of the original ground-plan of the building; as you can see it is signed by *Aston Webb* the architect — notice the date, 1901, here on the bottom. The assembly hall is in the middle of the building — just here — marked *Great Hall* on the plan but known as *The Quarterdeck* as if it were part of a ship: this is the place where the British cadets will assemble — and because they are British we expect them to be punctual. They will gather here at 11.30 tomorrow morning but they won't stay there for ever. We will allow them five minutes to settle before we drop the roof on their heads.'

Hauptmann Boxhammer spread his hands and smiled as if he were already celebrating a great victory. 'Have any of you ever heard of an Englishman being late for an appointment or — as they say over there — late for his own funeral?

'Now for the attack: we will each carry one SC500 bomb. Bombs will be fused so that they explode only when they hit the floor after penetrating the slates and wooden beams of the roof.'

Boxhammer took out his lighter, applied a long flame and looked at the architect's floor-plan through a cloud of smoke. 'The quarterdeck roof extends in a northerly direction from the clock tower. Its roof is supported by four stone arches set on eight stone pillars, *here* — *and here*. Our bombs will destroy these pillars. It calls for accurate flying — *and* punctuality. Do the job properly and we will bury six hundred young men and their instructors beneath the wreckage of the quarterdeck without damaging the rest of this

— and I have to say it — magnificent building.'

Karl put a hand to the edge of the table, sweating. How had it been done? Plans of the college; photographs taken from the ground; the exact number of cadets; their movements inside the building . . .

'I believe that we can do this job with just two bombs. Deichman will attack first, and I will follow him. If we fail the remaining four of you will finish the job before the cadets have had time to disperse. Secondary targets: Awak and Weis to sink ships in the harbour; Sperrle and Geisler destroy the Noss Shipyard which we are told is producing motor launches for rescuing enemy pilots from the sea.

'So remember to follow Deichman; watch for the Mew Stone; attack at low level; smash the quarterdeck and kill those cadets. It is all perfectly simple.

'Any questions?

★ ★ ★

Karl lay in bed thinking about his English cousins — and *the pact* made during an English thunderstorm before the war. That year the river Bovey had been swollen by freak rains; river banks had given way; floods

22

had spread unchecked. At Becka Falls the din of water had been louder than the exploding clouds overhead. It had been Ian's idea to swim under the heaviest part of the waterfall — so it was he who went first. Racing crawl; disappearing under that great curtain of water; bobbing up fifty metres downstream; finding his depth, wading out onto the far bank. His younger brother went next. Andrew: twelve years old — a strong swimmer. But the current took him, rolled him under and swept him away with nothing but a frantic hand breaking the surface to show his progress. Karl ran, cutting his feet on sharp rocks — outpacing the current; he had found a footing in the centre of the channel from where he could grab Andrew's wrist as he came swirling past.

After that it was Ian who decided they should make the pact and swear the oath — something out of a book that he had been reading: a treaty to bind them together and guarantee their friendship for ever — even if the promised war should come. Wet and shivering, the three boys joined hands and shouted above the storm: '*All for one. One for all until death. We swear it before God!*'

That was five years ago. Andrew would be seventeen now, about to start his final year as a naval cadet at Dartmouth. If the message inside the cartridge case had not been found Andrew and his fellow cadets would be inside that college now, unaware of the danger that awaited them on the quarterdeck at 11.35 tomorrow morning. Feelings of guilt were making him sweat again. *All for one. One for all until death. We swear it before God!*

But here was the dilemma; if the message had been found, the enemy would have made preparations which meant the six Focke-Wulfs would be flying into a trap in the morning . . .

Helga stirred beside him. 'What is it, Deichy, bad dream?'

He kissed her and smoothed her straw-coloured hair. 'It's nothing, Sweetheart, go back to sleep.'

3

Karl finished shaving and glanced out of the bathroom window. The sun was not yet up but there was enough light in the sky to show that an unbroken ceiling of cloud had crept across the sky during the night.

He looked towards the airfield. Conditions were still good for Operation Herod but, looking across the dew-laden grass, the familiar feeling that he may never see his comrades — or even himself — return to base at the end of the day was stronger than ever. More important even than that was the impending fate of Andrew Gatting.

In the dining room of their mess in the Hotel de Fleuve, pilots were already at breakfast at the long table. When the staffelkapitaen caught sight of Karl, he poured him a cup of coffee and gestured to the vacant place opposite.

'Have you seen it, Deichy? Have you noticed that we have granny's grey sweater wall-to-wall?' He leaned forward. 'The met man calculates this shit stretches all the way

25

to Scotland, it's low so we can turn it to our advantage. If we stay hidden underneath it Tommy's Spitfires won't be able to dive down on us to join the party. *Stealth*, Deichy — that's what it's called. With a bit of stealth — and if we watch each other's backs, as we always do — the six of us will be there and back before Tommy has had time to roll off his woman and put his trousers on.'

Out in the field, six Focke-Wulfs already had their engines running as mechanics prepared them, like war-horses, for battle. The pilots walked towards their aircraft. Boxhammer spat his cigar stub into wet grass where it died like a spent firework.

He gripped the back of Deichman's neck, then playfully pushed him away. Warm wind, driven by an idling propeller, lifted the collar of his flying suit. 'When we've squashed those boys under bricks and stone we'll drink a bucket of beer together. Cutting your teeth as leader on this soft target is only the beginning, Deichy. After today I will be calling on you to lead us more often.' He looked away. 'If ever I were to lose an argument with Tommy the boys will need a new boss. You are my choice, Deichy. After my death you will be the one to take my place.'

The staffelkapitaen searched the sky as he

spoke: 'The Reichsmarshall replaced our Messerschmitts with Focke-Wulf One-Nine-Zeros because he wanted to give us the fastest, best armed fighter in the world. The British can only catch us now if we let them dive their Mark Fives onto us from above — and they can only do that if they catch us by surprise.' He looked into Deichman's eyes again and put a hand on his shoulder. '*You would never let them do that; even in clear conditions you wouldn't let the Tommies do that to us, would you Deichy?*'

Karl looked at him, dumbly, wondering for a moment if Boxhammer knew something . . . but no, he could see it now: somewhere behind the staffelkapitaen's brave exterior was a tiny spark of fear . . .

Boxhammer strode over to his aircraft, patted it like a favourite pony, put his foot in the entry-stirrup, reached for the hand-hold, kicked his left foot into the upper-step and swung his leg over the side of the narrow cockpit — all in one smooth movement — something he had done a thousand times before. If he was afraid he wasn't showing it now. His expression was one of eager anticipation — like a terrier contemplating a rat-infested barn.

Karl tried in vain to expel every distracting thought from his mind as he squatted down to check the ETC501 bomb-rack, trying to concentrate on the four curved attachment hooks to check that they were correctly engaged in their corresponding recesses on the bomb's casing.

He climbed into the cockpit. Feldwebel Ederbach was standing on the wing-root to help his pilot with parachute and harness-straps. Karl asked him: '*Have you lubricated the bomb-release mechanism? Has the switch been checked?*' He knew perfectly well that Ederbach was the best mechanic in the staffel and would have attended to these things already in his usual manner, but checking details was part of a pilot's pre-take-off drill — and release mechanisms were important because nobody had yet tried to land a Focke-Wulf 190 with half a ton of unshed explosive still attached.

But now . . . even the simple act of tying the life-jacket tapes, and waiting for Ederbach's adjustments to the kapok-filled buoyancy-collar behind his neck, was triggering fear — not for himself, but for the safety of a seventeen year old English cadet who was, at this moment, inside the target building.

But that was not the full extent of it: as leader of Operation Herod the lives of five German comrades were also in his hands — and Karl knew that Boxhammer was wrong to refer to the Royal Naval College as a *soft target*.

Six Focke-Wulfs, six bombs and six men lifted their combined weight of twenty-three metric tons over the elm trees. They had already agreed to abandon the usual battle formation of three separate two-plane *Rotten* flying line-abreast, and were soon skimming the Channel in a long line, one behind the other, keeping low to stay under enemy radar.

Karl brought the formation down to sea-level; his propeller whipped the occasional scatter of spray onto the windscreen.

Flying low like this made him think about his friend Awak — flying third in line behind him — the man who had once failed to deliver his bomb to Portsmouth dockyard because it had been ripped away by a rogue wave on the way over. He thought too about Awak's return from the convoy-strike last week after crashing into the sea: Boxhammer had been drinking heavily that evening, blaming himself for the loss of a comrade; but the indestructible Awak had turned up unexpectedly after dinner like a bedraggled ghost with his knitted rabbit peeping from the chest-pocket of his flying overalls. Awak: very wet and very cold but fit enough to face Boxhammer's wrath and share his brandy.

Exactly on schedule the South Devon coast

appeared as a dark line behind the breakers. Karl searched for the mouth of the river but could see no Mew Stone. He led the staffel towards the shoreline, saw a curving beach backed by a line of hotels and houses, a pleasure pier, a railway line tracing the coast. Too low to get an impression of the coastline's shape — but he knew it wasn't Dartmouth. He turned seaward again, keeping low — so low that entanglements of rusting barbed wire coiled above the tide-line threatened to ensnare him as he led the staffel back to sea.

Right or left? He chose right, and flew south with his five comrades strung out behind with throttles pushed to the limit. Across a smaller harbour sheltered by headlands; sea-washed boulders; sloping rock-walls; grassy fields; a froth-ringed rhinoceros-horn poking up from the sea — *but no Mew Stone.*

Helga's Rolex: 11.31 — and there it was . . .

Far ahead a cloud of white confetti was resolving itself into a mass of whirling seagulls.

11.33 by the Rolex.

Karl banked steeply over the Mew Stone and entered Dartmouth harbour. His right wing-tip was pointing directly at the castle.

Tracer-shells, like lazy fireflies, rose towards him from a destroyer entering the river — curving in the air — then streaking past and away like toy rockets.

The six Focke-Wulfs roared over a neat pattern of allotments at the back of Kingswear railway station, bumping in turbulence, twisting in each other's slipstream, hurdling hedges, turning towards the river. Women straightened their backs and gestured aggressively with garden tools. A horse bolted, toppling sheaves from its cart.

The clock above the college showed *11.36*. There was the square tower of the church — and the third tower, a stub on the horizon . . .

Working like a robot, Karl thumbed open the guard covering his bomb-release. He made a flat dive towards the target, trying not to think of the person who was in there, stomach twisting, feet like lead on the rudder. Boxhammer was still directly behind, watching his every move.

Through patchy cloudlets of exploding shells, Karl could see the overlap of slates on the quarterdeck roof. His grip shifted on the control column; he could feel the bomb-release button under the ball of his thumb. He swerved out of line, pressed the button — and felt a jerk as the bomb-load fell away.

A hedge was speeding towards him from rising ground behind the college. He pulled back. Too late; the hill was steep. A green flash, then a blinding screen of foliage flattened itself for a split second against his windscreen. He had no time to thank God that he was still flying — Boxhammer was screaming into his earphones: '*Achtung Sie Kommen! Sie Kommen! Spitfire, Deich . . .*'

A hail of steel dashed itself to fragments against the bullet-proof armour behind Karl's head. A blizzard of kapok blew out of his life jacket; fragments of armoured glass were in his face. A gale inflated his cheeks; a curtain of pink mist obscured his vision. He was blind. His neck was numb.

In a strange moment of calm he could hear Helga's voice — reading slow words from the back of the lucky photograph in his pocket . . .

Pink changed to brown as engine-oil rippled over his goggles; he pushed them onto his forehead, tried to focus on the enlarging blur of a church tower racing towards him. He lifted over, missed its spiky projections, and dived down on the far side to shield himself from the following Spitfire for a vital, life-saving second. Bedroom windows level with his wing-tips, children on the ground below with upturned faces like a scattering of handkerchiefs.

He wrenched back on the controls. The flat-topped bulk of the third tower raced back under the cowling.

Then he was staring wide-eyed into inky darkness — which flashed into sudden brightness to reveal farm workers, unfocused, distorted, hurling themselves to the ground as he powered through a storm of flying straw between narrow rows of corn-stacks.

Following the hill's contour Karl gathered precious speed until he was forced to flatten the dive to stop himself plunging into the sea.

Now he was in a desperate race: a damaged Focke-Wulf against a determined Spitfire; the blazing guns of a small grey ship marked the start of it: a race across the Channel that Karl knew he would have to win if he were ever to see Helga again.

★   ★   ★

Out over the sea, Karl's Focke-Wulf still had a valuable edge of speed over the enemy fighter. Strange processes inside his head were running out of control but he was still able to focus through the rear-view periscope: the pursuing Spitfire was falling back — already it appeared to be out of range. The level of adrenaline in Karl's body was falling too, allowing logical thought to re-establish.

If Andrew Gatting had been in the college this morning he would now be dead — or buried alive — along with six-hundred of his fellows. Karl knew that his own bomb had fallen wide of the quarterdeck but, although he hadn't seen it, Boxhammer flying immediately behind must surely have scored a direct hit with his.

Where was Boxhammer now? Where was Awak? What had happened to Sperrle, Geisler and Weis? He pulled his goggles down against a freezing wind that was battering his head through the jagged edges of a broken windscreen. He throttled back in an attempt to restore rhythm to the damaged engine. The spill of oil no longer spewed back into his eyes but when he peered at the dial below the engine ventilator he could see the reason for it: barely enough pressure to lift the needle off its stop.

Again, his concentration was drifting. Again he could hear Helga, slowly reading her favourite words from the back of a photograph . . .

Karl felt his head turning, and turning. He could see boys lying in sleeping-bags in a peaceful orchard on a hot summer night before the war. Ian Gatting was looking at the sky, wishing he was piloting one of the new Imperial Airways' flying boats to the far extents of the British Empire: destination Singapore in the Short Brothers' latest S-23 'C' Class Empire flying boat, the handsomest aircraft ever flown, rolling out of the Rochester factory, two per month, each capable of carrying twenty-four passengers and five tons of mail; bigger, faster, more powerful than any aircraft yet built. Under orchard trees, Ian was telling them: *Canopus* the prototype, unsticking its eighteen tons from the Medway river after only seventeen seconds at full power; *Centaurus, Caledonia, Ceres, Centurion, Connemara, Challenger.* The whole route — he knew that too: *Lake Marignane* in France; *Lake Bracciano* near Rome; *Phaleron Bay* in Greece; *Mirabella* on the coast of Crete; *Alexandria; Galilee*; a desert lake somewhere in *Iraq; The Persian Gulf*; the sacred lake at *Raj Samand*, the reservoir in *Gwalior* — Ian knew them all — every night-stop and refuelling station along the route to Singapore. Andrew was in the orchard too — saying nothing because his passion had always been ships.

Karl could hear his engine faltering again. He eased the throttle forward and the spluttering tempo gave way to a smoother note.

He could taste plums; he could see himself climbing in the branches of a tree. Ian and Andrew were there again. An old lady was standing under the tree, speaking in that strange Devonshire way: '*A little higher, Karl, three beauties right above your head!*'

Now he was in a boat — two buckets of fruit wedged in the narrow angle of the bow where Ian was sitting. Andrew was at the tiller, worrying that the results of his recent eye-test might not satisfy standards set by the Royal Naval College. A sudden squall capsized the boat. How many times had they upset that dinghy in the River Dart on the way back from Dittisham — and righted it by standing on the centre-board and pulling on the shrouds, and climbed in again to continue sailing up the river as if nothing had happened — with the big canvas triangle drying in the wind? And how many times had they crept, unseen by adults, soaking wet, in through the back door of the Gattings' holiday cottage in Dartmouth?

Karl wanted to sleep but the life-saving bite of a freezing wind — *thank God for it now* — and the deafening clatter of oil-starved machinery were driving away a creeping languor that threatened to sap away his will to survive. *It is each man's responsibility to make sure he stays alive . . .*

36

Helga: he could see her — pigtails, green eyes — and hear the hint of a stammer that he loved so much. That chance meeting in Bavaria: he could see that too; a dreamlike summer before somebody's axe fell across Europe. The wedding: *Mutti*, the only member of the family who could attend; three off-duty nurses as bridesmaids; Erich Box-hammer downing looted Calvados; Helga called away to spend the entire night tending a dying pilot in the dressing-station.

A violent vibration brought Karl out of his dream. He told himself, aloud: '*Concentrate on flying a damaged Focke-Wulf back to France.*'

Friendly Channel Islands and Normandy beaches showed themselves, grey and flat on the horizon — but the engine was no longer responding to the throttle. Below the numbness in his neck and shoulders, Karl could feel a scratchy shell of drying blood encasing his back, cracking and crumbling with every movement of his body.

The church of St Pierre Eglise, under a long gap in the clouds; a glint of sun on its rain-wet spire. *Search for the elm trees — try to move your head.* His eyes were near immobile, sticky in dry sockets.

The flat hectares showed themselves. Karl turned cross-wind and dropped his left hand

37

onto the button-studded shelf under his elbow; his little-finger touched a vertical seam of aluminium to orientate his hand; his index finger found the undercarriage control. He had to force his whole body round to look for the indicator-rods on either side — yes, in spite of the damage — the rods were sticking erect from both wing surfaces to prove that both wheels had lowered and locked down safely.

The engine was dead now; he could hear the *whick-whick-whick* of an idling propeller.

He was too high — the moment he crossed the boundary fence he knew it. Too late to side-slip, no engine to take him round for a second attempt. Karl's last squandering glide sucked him in towards the line of trees that by rights should have been cut down six months before.

Tall elms held out their branches to gather him in. A weak sun blinked its last light through a leafy canopy — before the darkness came.

4

Karl Deichman opened his eyes. He could hear something, and through the blurry bars of his eyelashes he could see, clearly enough, that he was still in the shadow of trees. It was a shadow pierced with many points of light but he knew that these were not elm trees because there was pink blossom on the grass.

The voice seemed to start in the middle of a sentence, but he couldn't make out the words. His eyes were still trapped in their dry sockets but he managed somehow to turn his head very slightly. Helga was sitting next to him on a wooden seat; she had her glasses on and was reading aloud from a book.

Karl's mouth felt dry when he opened it to speak and at first his tongue would barely move. Then he managed: *'This is not the airfield.'*

Helga froze on a half-spoken word, her eyes flicked from the page. Several seconds — and then she said his name, repeating it in that attractive stammer of excitement: *'Karl . . . Karl? . . . Are you awake?'*

39

He moved his head and saw a tree. He tried his voice again — and this time it was easier: 'The orchard ... why are we in Mother's orchard?'

Helga dropped the book and flung her arms around his neck. 'Deichy — have you come back to me now?' And then with head tilted: 'You've been away. Eight months is a long time ... '

He gently tested his grip on her hand. 'What has happened to me?'

She pushed his wheelchair across the grass, down the path towards the house. 'You always said this war is no place for you — and now, while you are here with Mutti and me, you are out of it for a few months, thank God. Shell splinters in the head, broken bones — you've been in hospital long enough, that's what I told the doctor. When you came out of the coma and started to swallow normal food again I persuaded Dr Schaffen to let me bring you here and nurse you back to health.'

The elm trees at Maupertus flashed points of light through a tangled canopy of leaves — but before that ... 'The Spitfires came from above, they were — *diving*. The Tommies were ready for us. *How did they know?*'

Helga leaned over and kissed the top of his head. 'You must try not worry about it now.'

'Is Andrew Gatting here?'

Karl could feel the smooth head of an electric button under the ball of his ungloved thumb — but what had happened *after* he had dropped his bomb? *Plums* . . .

'We were picking plums in Dittisham; we lost them when the boat capsized. Ian told us all about the route to Singapore. Where is Awak and Boxhammer?'

Helga: concerned now, stammering again: 'I don't know anything about these things and you, you must not worry about them . . . nobody has told me anything. All I know is that the other pilots in the staffel . . . ' She stopped, leaving the sentence unfinished; then, 'But you are not to worry about it. Dr Schaffen told me that you must not be allowed to worry about *anything* once you had properly woken up.'

'Were the British waiting for us?'

She smoothed his hair. 'So many questions. Mutti and I will look after you now. Do you remember the photograph? I knew you would be safe because of the photograph — they found it in your pocket when they cut you out of the wreck; do you remember what I wrote on the back of it?'

She brushed her cheek against his ear and whispered five words and Karl knew then, for certain, that he was no longer dreaming . . .

No, he was no longer dreaming: there was something else. A premonition? Some bad news? There was a message trying to come in from a place far away that would not identify itself.

Helga tipped the wheelchair and turned it towards the house. 'Your mother has been worried to death but at least it has helped take her mind off Aunt Gerda over there in England. She worries so much about her sister; sometimes she wishes that Gerda had never met Mr Hugh Gatting, especially as it is impossible to get any news of them these days.'

Karl's eyes were hurting but he kept them open. He recognised the long shadow of the cedar tree as they crossed the lawn, and the low roof of the house as Helga manoeuvred the wheelchair down the shallow steps that led to French windows.

She wheeled him into the house: '*Mutti, are you there? Somebody has come back to us!*'

Karl's mother ran in and snatched off her glasses. She dropped her knitting; a strand of hair fell across her cheek. She stooped to look into her son's eyes. 'Are you awake now, Karl? Can you see me, can you talk?' She took his face between her hands and kissed him on the lips.

Helga stood back. 'I'll telephone Dr Schaffen; he said to let him know as soon as there was any change.'

★ ★ ★

After Dr Schaffen's visit to the farm, Karl began a good recovery. Knowledge that he might never fly again boosted his optimism but, sitting in the garden in the lengthening evenings of summer, he still dared to think about the aftermath of Operation Herod: *Had his warning message been found by the British? How could the presence of an enemy squadron be explained? Spitfires circling above cloud, over the exact spot, at the precise moment — with cadets assembled in neat rows within the fragile structure of the quarterdeck. Andrew dying under that fallen roof? Awak? Boxhammer? Brave comrades killed — by whom had they been betrayed?*

On nights when he couldn't sleep Karl would sometimes imagine he was talking to his father: Oswald Deichman, now dead — who had been schooled at *Wahlstatt* from the age of eleven and had always claimed that it was there, in that place of hard military upbringing, that he had acquired the unflinching patriotism and sense of loyalty that was to dominate his life. At the age of seventeen Father had progressed to the Royal Military Academy at *Lichterfelde* where these traditions had been implanted even more firmly, and where he had learned how to become an officer.

Karl could recall, in the clearest detail, all his father's stories of life in the cavalry: carrying messages under bursting shrapnel; wild boar hunts behind the lines — and later — landing a damaged *Halberstadt D.11* in a muddy field within sight of the enemy and running away to the shelter of a wood. Yes, Father too became an aviator. *Flieger Ersatz Abteilung Nr 7* was where he had learned to fly, later serving under Baron Manfred von Richthofen himself. If prompted and persuaded, Father would sometimes describe the thrill of a dogfight or what it felt like to be seen as a shining symbol of chivalry by German soldiery stuck in the mudholes below; but slowly that thrill had died — soured by his unchanging and unending contact with death. In Father's time it had been the same as today: *kill, kill, kill.* The slaughter had been carried out in more primitive style, with *Albatros* and *Fokker Triplane*, barely one-hundred horse-power each — *but deadly* with twin *Spandau* machine guns geared to fire forward through

44

a spinning propeller — just like a modern Focke-Wulf.

Karl enjoyed thinking about these things: his father used to tell the story of how he once damaged a British *Sopwith* and watched it put down in a field near his home camp. He had landed near it, drawn his pistol, claimed his British prisoner for the allowed twenty-four hours. A party in the officers' mess had followed, with the best looted champagne, and the reluctant English pilot as guest of honour.

There was chivalry on the other side too: a military funeral organised by the British for their arch-enemy in the small graveyard at Bertangles: twelve enemy riflemen firing a salute in honour of the Red Baron.

After the war, the continual presence of those memories of death turned Father into a pacifist — gradually — like the slow progress of cancer already inside his body. In spite of this reversal of faith, however, Father always had plenty of good advice for his son. *In war, always regard the lives of your comrades more precious than your own. Set the example and they will do the same for you.*

Karl knew that once he had been passed fit he would be sent back to the war so he used the precious interval to rest and enjoy the peace of this quiet backwater. With Helga's help he learned to walk again. Every day he ventured farther until he was able to walk to the station, board the train unaided and make his first unaccompanied visit to Dr Schaffen's surgery.

On the morning of Friday, the 23rd of July, Karl carried Helga's suitcase onto the Hamburg train at Mülheim station. As the train pulled away from the platform he could see her leaning out of the window, blowing kisses and waving.

But, after the train had left the station, the sight of a red handkerchief, crumpled on the track, revived an inexplicable feeling of ruin and doom that stayed with Karl for a long time.

★ ★ ★

Helga closed her eyes. The train beat a muffled rhythm. The long-awaited letter had finally arrived from the Appointments Board ordering her husband to take a new job: *Present yourself at Abwehr Headquarters, Hamburg, on Monday the 6th of September. Bring your medical clearance from Dr Schaffen . . .*

After months of inactivity Karl seemed to have become impatient to start this new job, hoping that while working for German

Military Intelligence he might uncover the aftermath of Operation Herod. It seemed to Helga that Karl was beginning to believe that things had been deliberately *hushed up*. She tried to tell herself that it was probably just the result of his imagination, overworked by all the inactivity. He had told her that he would probe — and search out for the truth. Helga had never seen him so obsessed. 'One day the war will end,' he told her repeatedly, 'On that day I will go over to England, take the train to Uncle Hugh and Aunt Gerda's house in Plymouth. If I have killed their son, Andrew Gatting, I will not be afraid to confess it.'

Helga thought about Aunt Traudl who lived on the outskirts of Hamburg — she would help find somewhere for them to live, ready for when Karl took up the new appointment. But there was an uncle too — who lived in the heart of the city — a man that Helga hoped she would never see again for the rest of her life.

The train arrived under the high vault of *Altona* station in melting heat. Helga bumped her suitcase onto the platform and, almost immediately, heard a human shriek, loud enough to compete with the guard's whistle. Great Aunt Traudl was running down the platform with arms raised — a hefty female

47

porter was chasing her with an empty barrow.

Traudl caught Helga in a powerful embrace and daubed her cheek with sticky kisses. She was excited and happy: 'You look lovely . . . what a big girl you are . . . prettier than ever . . . I've had such a time persuading a porter to hold the pony . . . '

Traudl was a happy woman, a good-looking woman in her sixties though her body had been inflating steadily over the past two decades; her flow of conversation was punctuated with loud gulps for air. 'Your Karl has had a terrible time . . . I know that . . . and his Aunt Gerda over in England . . . what she must be going through . . . sometimes I wonder why the world has so much anger in it . . . '

Outside the station an elderly man in railway uniform was nervously holding the pony's bridle, trying to stop the steel rim of the buggy-wheel backing into a parked *Hispano Suiza* as the animal tugged against him.

Traudl rambled on: 'Perhaps you will decide to go on living here when the war is over. It won't be long now. The British are done. The Americans have no heart for it; so much immigration into that country means that half of them are German anyway. Hamburg is lovely . . . quaint little corners, centuries old . . . when you are settled you will be able to visit me every day. The *Terror-fliegen* sometimes call on us but that devil Churchill is only after our oil refinery — and the Blohm and Voss yards . . . but Winston is not so clever, half his bombs drop in the lake!' Traudl paused for breath. She took the pony's reins while the porter heaved suitcases into the buggy. 'Your Uncle Herman will be pleased to see you too.'

Herman: just hearing the name was enough for Helga to remember depraved fingers, like sandpaper on the skin of her thigh, probing and pushing under elastic. He had held her in his arms in the sea — pretending to teach her how to swim during summer holidays in Wismar but . . .

Traudl flapped the reins. 'Tomorrow I will show you our beautiful city, after that we will have cakes and strudel at Max's *Konditorei.* We will go to Herman's for supper. When I told your uncle you were coming he insisted that we both spend the night in his house. Herman is a lonely man now, too old to attract all those girls who used to keep him company! He has room there for you and Karl, there is no need for you to look further.'

Traudl cooked supper and — after it — continued the torrent of conversation into the night, not realising that Helga was too preoccupied to listen.

★ ★ ★

On Saturday morning they woke late, the taxi was waiting and they only just caught the city train.

Hamburg sun was fierce but Traudl continued, full of energy, and lost no time in starting her walking tour of the city. By the afternoon their feet were hot and tired and their shoes sank into cushions of molten tarmac whenever they crossed the road.

They sat at a street-table outside a café in Alkserkamp, not far from the Abwehr Central Office, and washed down Max's best strudel with long glasses of chilled lager. Traudl was glowing — proud of her wonderful city and, in spite of her exertions, she again demon-strated a tremendous capacity for one-sided conversation. 'Hamburg is an ancient town . . . before the Third Reich it was a separate state — like Venice. It looks like Venice don't you think? — all those canals threading through the streets . . . '

Helga could remember making a whispered pledge of secrecy when she was eleven years old . . .

'We have a lake-harbour for sea-going ships

but it is many kilometres from the sea. Herman once told me that it took his ship five whole hours to get from here to the Alte Lieb pier.'

Herman: that name . . .

'Who would have thought such a big lake could result from damming a river as small as the Alster? The lake helps us to protect our city from invading armies you know . . . '

Coming into the bedroom for the first time — the smell of his breath — his mouth on hers, the first probe of Herman's tobacco-stained tongue, deep into her throat . . .

'We are peaceful folk — we don't like to fight other countries, we prefer to trade with them. Our men set an example to the world; battles and fights are bad for business . . . Hamburg is a city of traders. Wait till you see the inside of Uncle Herman's house: carved idols, native drums, African masks, strange head-dresses, all brought back to Hamburg when he was a ship's captain.'

The unspeakable act — too shaming to tell — even her own mother would never have believed it . . .

'In 1842 there was a terrible fire that destroyed half the city but you would never know it, would you? Even now — one hundred and one years later — we're still proud of how our city was reborn after the fire.'

They caught a tram which creaked along the edge of the great lake where children paddled and swam. A group of old men sailed model boats. Traudl and Helga walked beside Nikolaifleet, a narrow canal with busy river-traffic bordered by an uneven row of wooden warehouses where men loaded barrels into barges decorated with gaudy paintwork. An ornate spire pointed above the roof-angles. Traudl said the church was St Katharinkirche; inside it was an organ once played by Johann Bach; the big crown halfway up the spire was made from gold found hidden in the hollow mast of a captured pirate ship . . .

And so the commentary continued until they were standing in front of Uncle Herman's house: four narrow stories; plastered brickwork and warped timber in a medieval terrace of taller, shorter, steep and steeper roofs; houses that leaned so far forward that it looked as if they might one day topple into the canal. Aunt Traudl had her hand on the body of a brass mermaid, the knocker on Uncle Herman's front door.

In spite of the happy reunion that Traudl orchestrated on the pavement — engulfing her brother in a suffocating embrace — the sight of that man filled Helga with feelings of revulsion and dread. Traudl unstuck her lips from his cheek: 'This is Helga — Gerhard and Lilo's girl. You remember her, don't you, Herman?'

The old man finally turned his hairless, freckled head to look at the girl. There was a well-remembered look of unsmiling lust in those cold eyes but he addressed his remarks to Traudl. 'She is a woman now. She makes her own decisions in life. She is no longer the girl I once taught to do the crawl and dive from the pier.'

Inside the house little had changed since the day it was built — apart from gas chandeliers that hung from every ceiling. The interior walls were panelled with wood. Furniture appeared to date from the Middle Ages. On every flat surface, and hanging from every wall, were the treasured possessions of a man who had spent a lifetime at sea: ships in bottles, carved walrus tusks, African carvings of every shape and size.

Aunt Traudl lowered herself into a high-backed chair in the hallway and sat there panting while Uncle Herman led Helga up a squeaking staircase hung with dust-laden pictures of foreign ports.

When they reached the second landing Herman put a hand on the banisters to steady

53

himself and spoke to her at last. 'There are two bedrooms up here.' He showed her into the larger room at the front of the house. 'This one looks down on the wharf. The other bedroom faces the church. I do not think that your aunt or I will feel a burning need to pray — except to ask God to kill the English.' His eyes were like steel.

Helga could think of no reply — nor felt inclined to interrupt the hostile torrent that followed. 'If you and that man come here to stay in my house, don't you expect me to speak to him.' He spat the words between discoloured teeth. 'The only reason I'll take him in here is because my sister has asked me to.'

Helga could remember the day she bit him — the unexpected scream for mercy as her teeth began to cut his revolting flesh. She remembered the doctor looking at her strangely as he was leaving the house — and the feeling of triumph she felt when she realised that she would never be molested by him again . . .

Aunt Traudl cooked kidneys in beer sauce — talking happily about everything that randomly invaded her mind: 'Karl will love this house, Helga dear, you'll see. This war can't be all bad if it brings the family together . . .'

And so it went on — while her brother sat in staring silence until gathering darkness on the other side of the window made him get up to draw the curtains. Lowering himself back into his chair he said: 'This is a cowards' war. If they want to make war with us let them come here in their ships and anchor in our harbour — let us see them try to march along the streets of Hamburg — then we would teach them a lesson not to come meddling here.' He was speaking to the wall. 'But what do they do instead? Tell me, tell me what they do? Cast a few handfuls of bombs on us from above the clouds — kill a few children, that's what they do — wound a few old women, knock the roofs off our houses — that's their idea of fighting — those are the kind of people we deal with now!'

During supper Helga could not eat but Traudl continued her babble between forkfuls while Herman scowled from his end of the table.

★　★　★

In her room on the second landing Helga slid between damp linen. The feather mattress was lumpy. She lay on her back, closed her eyes and thought about Karl even though she had already promised herself not to worry about the things that Dr Schaffen had tried to explain . . .

But it was Uncle Herman who dominated her thinking — the man who had once been so friendly towards her — treating her like the daughter he never had — during happier times when she was too young to arouse his lust. *But that one final act of depravity had forced her to act decisively against him.* She would never know how her victim had managed to explain such an injury to that doctor who came hurrying to the house to staunch the blood.

In the middle of the night Helga found herself suddenly awake. Bluish moonlight from the open window flooded the ceiling. Far away she could hear the faint hum of aeroplanes high in the sky.

Then a sharply detached sound: the creak of a floorboard under pressure — *and the soft click of a wooden latch lifting to clear its slot.*

She jerked her head, clearing her ears from the pillow. The latch fell again, almost silently, and now she could hear a rusty pin screwing in the knuckle of a medieval hinge . . .

★   ★   ★

Seven hundred kilometres to the south of Hamburg, Karl had returned to his mother's farm after his final visit to Dr Schaffen. In his pocket he had the medical clearance he needed to start work.

Mutti had prepared his favourite *Königin-pastete*: diced meat and home-picked mushrooms — but Karl ate his supper in silence. The doctor had chosen bland words to describe Karl's state of health but the truth was plain enough . . .

He finished his meal, and when Mutti asked the reason for his mood he refused to tell her.

5

The Wing Commander smoothed one side of his moustache. His voice was higher pitched than usual and today his vowels were distorted by the importance of his announcement.

'*Operation Gomorrah*, gentleman: a ninety-six hour operation which will exterminate the largest shipping port in Europe. For those who haven't been to Hamburg before let me tell you that it is the main centre of U-boat manufacture in Germany and — if you don't know already — the battleships *Hipper* and *Bismarck* were built there. There are oil refineries, aircraft factories, a multitude of engineering works — in fact the Jerries have a lot of nasty stuff there which we are going to deprive them of.

'Tonight marks the start of a four-day operation. The key to success is *saturation*; this means creating a steady stream of destruction over the city. We are pulling out all the stops on this one. Our air-armada will

58

consist of 791 heavy bombers drawn from every operational squadron of Bomber Command — that means we will be in the company of aircraft from as far away as Middleton St George in the country of Durham, to Wratting Common in Suffolk. You will be part of a team of over five thousand men carrying two-and-a-half thousand tons of high-explosive and incendiary into the heart of Germany's proudest city. We will remove Hamburg from the map. We rubbed out Cologne in May last year, tonight we will do the same to this place — and the Stirlings and Lancasters of our own *Three Group* are to be a vital part of this two hundred mile stream of aircraft.

'The United States Air Force, based here in East Anglia, pressing home our advantage in the intervening daylight, hammering them again while we are re-arming, will help bring about the total and complete annihilation of Hamburg during the coming four days and nights.'

A muffled shift of flying-boots and a few whispered comments were enough to demonstrate some mistrust amongst the assembled crews. Flight Lieutenant Ian Gatting, skipper of Stirling bomber *P-Popsie*, shifted his tall frame in an uncomfortable *easy-stak* chair. He was a believer in the RAF motto: *Per*

Ardua ad Astra — but his personal translation from the Latin had always been: *Bullshit Baffles Brains*. Eight-hundred bombers, milling about over the target, diving — climbing — under fighter attack — jam-packed together along a narrow route — struggling to get back into overcrowded circuits and bases — short of juice — shot up. Too far fetched; *a shaky do*. Hamburg was closer than Berlin, easier to find — but Hamburg was the most heavily defended city in Germany: 278 anti-aircraft gun emplacements; twenty-four searchlight batteries; heavy night-fighter presence — Ian knew it all; and he knew the risks involved in getting 791 heavy bombers safely there and back. The Air Chief Marshal was probably under a lot of strain but it looked as though he had finally burnt his fusewire. '*You will be making history, gentlemen . . .*'

The briefing-officer started as he always did: flak, searchlights, landmarks . . . Ian Gatting was listening even though he knew it already. He knew about Berlin, Nuremberg, Cologne, St Nazaire, Essen, the Skoda works at Pilsen — and a dozen other targets. He also knew how to plug a chest wound using a standard first-aid kit and what to say to a dying man; how to word a letter to a bereaved mother without telling her what he had seen

60

or what he had heard.

'*We have something new for this raid: it's been under wraps until now. You will be carrying it with you tonight.*' An elderly civilian — grey hair, stooped, creased tweeds — accompanied by a zealous service police sergeant — had a smile on his face that emphasised the furrow of an old bullet wound. He delved into a briefcase. 'This strip of silver paper is your secret weapon, gentlemen. I thought of the name myself — *Window* — but it isn't like a window at all because the enemy can't see through my window — that's the whole point. It's made out of aluminium foil — ten inches long and just under an inch wide as you can see.'

This provoked another sceptical murmur.

'*When I drop it, watch what happens.*'

The metallic strip spun over and over, strobing a reflection from the ceiling light as it fell onto the old man's shoes. 'I'm quite sure you know this already, but radar-beams reflect off things in the same way light does. Jerry's radar is going to bounce all over the place when it hits this stuff — it will give him a great deal of utterly confusing signals. If every plane drops several thousand of these tonight — as long as they are in radar range of the enemy of course — the resulting reflective cloud will blot out his radar-controlled systems: anti-aircraft guns, searchlights and night-fighter control.'

The briefing officer took over again. 'Window comes in bundles of 2200 strips like this one here. Crews will cut the strings and release them through their flare-shutes at the rate of one bundle per thirty seconds while you are on the target run.'

★   ★   ★

Ian had all four throttles of Stirling bomber, *P-Popsie*, cradled in his right hand. This was to be his twenty-seventh operation; three more trips to Hamburg after this one and then a spot of leave followed by a change to the more civilised role of flying instructor. In front of him he could see *A-Alice* gathering speed for her take off into the last light of the summer sky, her tail gunner waving to the usual knot of well-wishers gathered on the grass at the side of the runway.

While he waited for the green aldis-lamp from the control tower to give him the signal, Ian ran through the inventory in his head: *thirteen canisters of incendiary; one 2000 pound high-explosive bomb; 2,500 gallons of high-octane petrol; 12,000 rounds of ammunition; eight Browning machine-guns; seven assorted men, some of them large and some* of them small — oh yes, and *fifty bundles of silver paper called Window*. Thirty-one tons was the maximum permitted all-up weight but nobody could remember anyone actually *weighing* a fully-laden Stirling. The wind-sock hung flaccid from its pole at the edge of the field, heralding another dangerously long take off run in still air. A Geordie voice crackled into Ian's headphones — because from his place in the upper gun turret, Sandy had the best view of the control tower when Popsie was lined up on runway two-seven.

'Green light, Skipper, and many happy returns!'

Saying it that way had brought them luck so far — like Napier pissing on the tail-wheel before every op. Ian clenched his left fist and showed a thumb to the well-wishers. He slid throttles smoothly up until he had 2000 revolutions per minute on all four engine-speed indicators. He released the brakes, held the control column back with his left hand and lifted the throttles again, this time to the top of their quadrants, making sure that the two right-hand levers travelled slightly ahead of the others to counteract the starboard swing as the aircraft began to move.

Duckworth, sitting on his right, put a hand under the throttles to stop them slipping back with the vibration. Ian gripped the wheel with both hands as the aircraft gathered speed, then eased it forward to lift the tail. Duckworth called out the speeds as they rumbled down the flarepath. *Seventy — eighty — ninety.* At 105 miles per hour the Stirling was still rumbling and, for a moment, it seemed certain that they would smash into the dark line of the hedge that was enlarging rapidly in front of them.

Then Popsie lifted. For the twenty-seventh time Ian found himself muttering the same old words through clenched teeth. *I am half German — why am I doing this? Surely the family has first call on my loyalty. I have a German uncle and aunt — and a German cousin called Karl . . .*

He wound the trims forward and glanced at Duckworth who had just retracted the wheels for the twenty-seventh time — and noticed that he was actually smiling, probably at the thought of going on leave. Yes, the flight engineer was a pessimist by nature and seeing him happy was unusual. Duckworth had been a magician in civvy street — hard to imagine it because the man was ugly and rather boring until he had two or three pints inside him; but without any doubt he was *still* a magician and Popsie was a temperamental female who needed a magician like Duckworth to keep her Bristol Hercules engines spinning their four big propellers for eight hours on end, sometimes with carburettors full of ice, sometimes with different kinds of liquid spewing from bullet-holes in the cowling.

With airspeed nudging 150 miles per hour, Popsie settled into the long climb to her allotted altitude which for this operation was 15,000 feet. Two nights ago she had only managed 14,400, which supported Duckworth's theory that the air ministry had ordered a dozen feet of wingspan to be lopped off the original design so that Britain's first heavy bomber would fit a standard RAF hangar. *And what was that original design based on?* Ian could hardly bring himself to think about that. The S-23 'C' Class Empire flying boat: a nobler species — same manufacturer, same number of engines, similar cruising speed — but a buoyant hull instead of a bomb-bay and wheels. If it wasn't for this bloody war . . . one day he would perhaps work the most romantic passenger route in the world instead of flying a brick, a death-trap; no promenade-cabin with seats for eight first-class passengers; no elbow rail along the port side observation windows; no forward lounge; no after-cabin with crisp bed linen; no kitchen; no cabin trim of green leathercloth; no comfort, no luxury. What a war!

Dad Latter started his instructions almost as soon as they were airborne. At thirty-six, he was by far the oldest member of the crew: his hair was grey; some of his less tactful colleagues were already calling their navigator *Granddad*.

'Steer zero-eight-seven magnetic, Skip. ETA Hamburg one-o-five.'

Ian eased the bomber onto the new heading.

Window might, after all, improve the odds for survival on this trip — the drill was to drop the stuff during the last dodgy ten minute run to the target. There were fifty packs of it so there was plenty to spare; but Ian had never been a great one for *the drill* and had already decided to save his Window for the return when the opposition from fighters was often a lot fiercer.

'Steer zero-eight-zero, skipper. There must be quite a cross-wind up here.'

'Zero-eight-zero it is.'

Another conjuring trick: Popsie had climbed to fifteen thousand feet in thirty-one minutes and forty-eight seconds, and, wonder of wonders, Duckworth was grinning as he made the first fuel check and scribbled the result on his knee-pad. Ian levelled the aircraft and let the speed build to 160 before easing back the throttles as the Stirling droned on across the North Sea.

Ian Gatting stared into the darkness, waiting for his navigator to pinpoint the turning point fifteen miles north-east of Heligoland for the final run in towards the coast over Cuxhaven. Dad was using some newfangled radio detection apparatus for the first time; he now claimed he could find that elusive turning point over a featureless sea and — using a cathode ray tube illuminated by a rotating, clock-like finger — could see the curve of a coastline in darkness or the shape of a river below a blanket of cloud. *Well, well. Bloody marvellous!*

Ian was thinking of what lay ahead. The Yanks would be over there with more incendiary and HE in the morning; RAF again with another 2000 tons the following night. Day, night, day, night — four nights and four days. The scale of this raid was enormous when compared to that one on Plymouth two years ago — but the raid on Plymouth had killed both his parents so nothing could ever be as bad as that. Ian would be thinking about his German mother and his English father again — even though they were dead — once he was over the target.

From fifty miles away they could see Hamburg already burning like a beacon. As they came nearer, the metal interior of the aircraft took on a glow of orange. By the time P-Popsie was on her bombing run, a visible suspension of carbon had risen almost three miles to the height of the aircraft. Countless blazing fires merged below, orange and flickering under the smoke.

'Bomb doors open.'

Blaney was already lying prone with his head over the bomb-aimer's window, looking through the bomb-sight, trying to find that elusive bit of black amongst the flames. 'Left . . . left . . . a bit more . . . steady . . . right a bit . . . ' How many times had he heard Blaney say that? *Twenty-seven.* Then he should have said, '*Bombs gone!*' But he never did — because nobody saw the silhouette of a Messerschmitt 110 against the blaze below. Nobody knew that there was an enemy night fighter in close attendance, directed by radar from the ground.

★   ★   ★

Karl Deichman was lying awake in his mother's house in Mülheim, wondering if Helga had managed to find somewhere in Hamburg for them to live.

★   ★   ★

Helga was sitting up in bed, legs drawn up to her chest, staring in horror at the naked figure standing in the doorway of the bedroom. Moonlight glowed on every slack contour of Uncle Herman's body — and caught a metallic glint from something in his right hand. He stood quite still. His voice made a choking sound before the words came.

'*What do you see in that man of yours? You know what he is, don't you? Do you know that his aunt married an Englishman? I know all about Mr Karl Deichman and his English connections. I'll teach you to go with traitors!*'

Helga was out of bed — backing away as he spoke — hands out — fingers spread. She stumbled against furniture, regained her balance — retreated further until her back was against the wall. Herman advanced towards her with the knife held out in front of him. Under the folds of his wrinkled belly she could see evidence of his intentions. He was close to her now: she could smell Aunt Traudl's garlic soup on his breath.

The first bomb dropped. A dazzling flash — *WHUMP* — a blizzard of glass from the window.

Out of the snow-blindness that followed, Herman's body emerged again: strips of flesh hanging from his face; blood splashing rivulets that twisted into the creases and folds of his body. His lips were moving — but there was no sound except a high whining inside her ears . . . Then he was gone.

From the street outside there was a continuous roar. At the shattered window Helga raised a hand to shield her face against the heat. A speeding wall of fire was devouring the far bank of the canal.

She ran choking down the smoke-filled staircase, along the orange-lit corridor, burst into Aunt Traudl's bedroom and screamed: 'Everything is on fire!'

Traudl was already half out of bed — her beautiful face distorted, flickering and yellow — holding up her hands, palms outwards. Her lips were moving, but the din outside the window smothered her words. Helga ran back, the staircase was heaving under her feet.

Half-dressed and halfway down to the first landing, a fiery blast from below threw her onto her back. She groped through smoke, found the ground floor, clambered over beams from fallen ceilings, ducked under a plume of flame hosing from a ruptured gas pipe. The lintel over the front door collapsed onto her head as she left the house, and her hair caught fire.

It was like walking into a furnace.

She ran towards a dark tunnel in the wall of flame, beating at her head — and heard the crash of masonry above the roaring.

* * *

Karl woke suddenly — but from a nightmare in which he had heard words repeating themselves over and over again: *All for one. One for all. We swear it before God.* Before dawn showed itself through the thin curtains of his bedroom window — there was birdsong in his mother's orchard.

* * *

P-Popsie, once the pride of Austin's car factory at Longbridge, had a cave-mouth where the front gun-turret and bomb-aimer's plexiglass blister had been. The bomber was barely responding to the controls as Ian turned for home.

There was an urgent exchange going on over the intercom: 'We're losing juice, skipper!'

'How bad is it, Ducky?'

'Grim. We're running on numbers two and four tanks — gauge two is unwinding like hell. There's a leak on the starboard-inner judging by the drop in boost. No fire yet.'

A large piece of metal broke off from somewhere outside the aeroplane and slammed noisily into something else.

'How long have we got?'

Duckworth was pessimistic again: 'I could tell you if we had a Stirling to fly. If we can maintain height with boost in M-gear and throttles set to one pound we'll have around two and a half hours' flying time — that's if Popsie decides to keep on flying on three engines with all this extra drag. The starboard inner has had it.'

Ian adjusted the pitch control so that propeller blades on the crippled engine aligned with the airflow; the windmilling engine stopped — no longer hampering their progress. Airspeed was down to 140. Judging by Dad's corrections on the outward journey, Popsie was now tackling a strong headwind.

And thinking of Dad . . . 'Sandy, are you there? Leave your turret and get down here. Something must have happened to the navigator, see what you can do for him.'

Ian waited for his gunner to report back. *How could an aircraft fly with so much of it missing?* Then Sandy's voice in his earphones telling him that Dad had been hit: arm blown clean off, not even a stump for the tourniquet.

'Give him a double morphine, put a wad of

lint over where he's bleeding, strap him with the four-inch bandage, use his shirt if you have to. Button his jacket over the top of everything.'

Sergeant White's voice crackled in: 'I'm sending to Mildenhall for an update on wind velocity, nothing back yet — duff set more than likely.' Ian wanted to make a joke about ordering extra stocks of beer for the homecoming but decided against it.

A gale was swirling around in the front end. Over the toe of his right boot Ian could see oblong islands, moonlit, marking the boundary of the Zuider Zee. He gave Duckworth a signal to take the controls, unstrapped himself and turned his back on the wind. At the navigator's table he knelt in blood and shone his torch into Dad's face. Flickering eyelids — probably numbing into sleep from the morphine; but his voice was still working: 'Tell the boys to bale out, Skip, they'll stand a better chance.'

'Don't be mad. We're over the sea and I'll be relying on you to navigate the dinghy when we ditch. If there's any wind down there we'll be using the sail. I ditched a Boston in the Channel last year and got away with it.' He looked up at the gunner. 'Sandy, do you remember how to work a Dalton Computer?'

'Course I do, Skip. Dad taught me.'

'Then work out a heading for home and tell me where we'll be two hours from now at an indicated airspeed of one-forty. Assume that the wind is two-fifty degrees magnetic at thirty mph.'

Dad again: 'I'll be okay, skipper. Go and fly Popsie, you know what a rotten pilot Ducky is!'

At the front end, Duckworth had his goggles down and had already wound back the trims to take pressure off the controls — for a flight engineer he was doing a good job of flying what was left of Stirling bomber P-Popsie. At the nav table Sandy must have pencilled the wind's speed and direction onto the perspex disc of the *Dalton* and turned the knurled ring to give him a heading for home because he said over the intercom: 'Two-five-seven degrees, skipper.'

Ian fought the Stirling into a turn. 'Now tell me where we'll be two hours from now.'

'In the drink, thirty miles short of Great Yarmouth.'

So that was it. Now it was just a question of waiting till the juice ran out. Ian had already decided to reserve his *Window* for the return journey but it had been forgotten in the excitement. Might as well use it now — lighten the load a bit — but who could be spared to drop it? Blaney was gone, Dad half-gone, Chalky busy trying to send morse on a duff set, Napier on the tail gun, Duckworth trying to do a conjuring trick on three remaining engines. Then he remembered — he had neither *window* nor flare shute to drop it from — because it had all fallen out of the aeroplane in a snowstorm of burning aluminium together with Blaney's body when they were over the target.

Popsie was becoming increasingly sluggish. Ian sat in the pilot's seat with the wind howling round him, heaving on the control column, thinking about Imperial Airways and . . .

How long would it be before he could sail a dinghy to Dittisham and spend an afternoon picking plums? Where was Karl? What had happened to the pledge made at Becka Falls — yes, what had happened to that? *All for one, one for all, we swear it before God.* That wasn't bullshit.

Duckworth was saying something about only ten gallons left in each of four tanks once number five had run dry: thirty minutes' flying time, given luck. Through the jagged cave-mouth, moonlight had turned the sea to wrinkled carbon paper.

The outer engine on the port side faded first. The one remaining starboard engine faltered immediately after. Ian watched the

altimeter over the top of his left knee
— unwinding like hell. Duckworth was
manipulating fuel cocks in search of dregs.

Then the last engine coughed a series of
bangs — and P-Popsie was gliding. Wind
howled loud through the wreckage as Ian
began the final descent towards the sea. He
knew that the combined weight of his crew
under the rear escape-hatch would help to
keep the nose up as they hit the water, *but
would that trapdoor in the port wing-root
open after impact?* They would need to get
the dinghy out of there quicker than any shit
had ever left any shovel while Popsie decided
how quickly she was going to sink.

1,200 feet, time to turn parallel to the line
of waves. '*Ditching Stations!*'

In the last mad moment Ian was at the
controls of an Imperial Airways flying boat
— coming down for a gentle landing on a
flat-calm Sea of Galilee . . .

Popsie belly-flopped onto water that felt
like concrete. A tide crashed in. Ian undid
his straps and was hurled backwards, rolled
over and over, slammed into unseen bits of
aeroplane inside the fuselage. He was under
water, pinned against the bottom rung of the
escape ladder; then spiralling upwards in a
whirlpool of bubbles that reminded him of
that angry curtain of water at Becka Falls.

Somebody was shaking him by the shoulder. He could see a moonlit face. '*You shot out of that hatch like a Champagne cork, skipper!*'

Still choking on seawater: 'Did you manage to get the dinghy out?'

'Course we did — you're in it. We walked along the wing just like it says in the book. We all climbed in. Had to carry the Granddad, poor old bugger.

★   ★   ★

In the morning the sea was calm but Dad's eyes were dull and sunken, the empty sleeve of his jacket was dark with blood.

★   ★   ★

In Hamburg, Helga was up to her neck in stinking water. Hot smoke storming across the lake was burning her lungs as she gulped for air. The fat on her face had melted. Shrivelled ribbons of skin were hanging from her cheeks.

★   ★   ★

Karl was enjoying a black-sausage breakfast at his mother's farm.

Part Two

6

The German land had healed. On either side of the railway line, farm life was continuing as if the past years had never happened. Karl was orphaned now — that was something that happened to children but the pain was there: Mother, already a widow — killed by a bomb while weeding a flower bed. And the Gattings? All those returned letters from England — why? Every letter to that English family returned from a Plymouth Post Office — opened but re-sealed, *not known at this address*. Railways: they brought unhappy thoughts too; retrieving Helga's handkerchief on a summer's day in 1943 which now seemed a thousand years ago.

From the air Hamburg must have appeared to be no longer there — that's what Allied Reconnaissance pilots must have reported: total destruction — but things were going on underground, and that couldn't be seen from the air. *Abwehr* — German Intelligence — out of sight and busy in the immensely powerful wireless bunker on the outskirts of

81

the city. Knowledge of English — the language and the people — that's what qualified a man for the job of agent-controller: communicating with spies based in the neutral countries of Spain and Portugal by short wave from Hamburg, receiving news of Allied shipping: cargoes, destinations, routes — and the activities of enemy spies. Morse code was difficult at first but the skill came quickly enough. Then came the victor, crossing the Rhine two years later, sweeping like a tide from Osnabruk to the Elbe. May 1945: the British in Hamburg at last, unopposed by the garrison army.

Throughout the struggle to avoid starvation; talking a way out of captivity; finding a hovel made from wooden doors; carrying water; scrounging coal — through all this — two questions clung like dark shadows: *Did I kill my cousin, Andrew Gatting? Did I lead five Luftwaffe comrades to die in a British trap?* Four of the staffel's pilots had been killed, that was clear now — and the indestructible Awak had been posted as 'missing' but they might just as well have said dead.

It had been a long wait. Only now had Karl been able to organise his life, find a teaching job, have a holiday — but this was no holiday, crossing the ferry from Wilhelmshaven to Harwich to find out what he had to know.

As the train got closer to Plymouth's North Road Station, Karl began to worry about the reaction he would get from Uncle Hugh and Aunt Gerda. Eight years ago things had been different — now both countries were trying to recover from a war that had been over for five years. Would there now be a rift in the family? Five years: was that time enough for wounds to heal?

Karl had already decided that, if the unthinkable had happened — if he was about to learn that Andrew had indeed been killed in the college — he would not flinch from telling his uncle and aunt exactly how it had happened and what his own deadly part in it had been. It had to be like that. Only by making this confession would he, one day, perhaps soon, be able to live in a peaceful world with some of the guilt lifted from his back.

By the time the train started to slow on the final bend leading into Plymouth's North Road station, Karl was ready to face his uncle and aunt. He deposited his luggage in a locker. Although he had walked from the station to Glengarth on many occasions in the past, this time he was unable to recognise anything. Cemetery Road completely devoid of houses; three gutted shops were the only means of identifying the corner of Saltash Road. He walked north, then cut across a building site where men were laying bricks and pouring concrete into freshly dug foundations. Over on the far side was evidence of a residential avenue that might have been Amherst Street. The broken pavement led to the remains of the T-junction with De La Hay Avenue.

But there were no houses. Everything had been reduced to rubble or else flattened by bulldozers. Karl turned left and walked to where he was almost certain Glengarth had once stood. There was nothing there now: no trees; no big bay window; no neat garden behind a stone wall — no house.

He wandered about, looking at the uneven ground, trying to find some clue that would tell him for certain that he was in the right place. There were broken flagstones with weeds pushing up between the cracks; glass fragments; splinters of blackened wood — the staircase? Anonymous debris lay strewn beneath his feet; clumps of nettles and ground-elder. Then, amongst the rubbish . . .

He stooped to pick it up and laid it on the flat of his hand, turning it so that the swirling leaves and petals of a white daisy-type flower showed the right way up on its pale-green background: a broken tile — and the pattern on it was familiar. Against the clatter of the building site he tried to think. *The fireplace, the dining room fireplace, under a wooden mantelpiece: tiles with a pattern like this had once formed a frieze around it.* So this was the place — here was the spot where the Gattings' house had stood.

He slipped the tile-fragment into his pocket because it was all that was left of a place in which he had spent so many happy days. Even though he had only been a summer visitor, those days had seemed as if they might last forever. Plymouth had been one of the Luftwaffe's favourite targets — Karl had learned that from a colleague in *KG55 Gruppe* — but he had not realised the scale of the destruction until now.

Dejectedly he walked back to the station and picked up his luggage. A taxi took him down towards the harbour but he recognised nothing until they turned right past a badly damaged building, the Guildhall, recognisable only by its tall square tower rising precariously from the ruins. Seeing it reminded him of an afternoon long ago when Uncle Hugh had taken the Three Musketeers on a walking tour of the town — which would have been a heartening memory in any other circumstance, but now his newly acquired knowledge only served to deepen his depression.

The taxi continued its way. He recognised the solid stonework of Prysten House, more than four centuries old and completely unmarked. Then Southside Street and on past the Old Distillery to the cobbled quayside of the Barbican.

Looking across that harbour made him think of *Dapple*, a four-berth yawl, and sailing her between the narrow gap between East and West Piers with Uncle Hugh at the helm, past Deadman's Bay in a stiff breeze, out through the Breakwater into Plymouth Sound.

In a small hotel overlooking the harbour, Karl spent a troubled night worrying about what had become of the Gatting family — and wondering how he was going to get at the truth about Andrew without their help.

★ ★ ★

The train descended the wooded gradient to Kingswear Station towards the end of the following day but Karl was still uncertain why he had come to Dartmouth. How was he going to discover what he needed to know? He was still shaking from the shock of what he had discovered so far — the helpless feeling of bereavement was still there but he told himself: *I am still determined to find out the truth: somehow, somewhere I will do it. Dartmouth is a good place to start — where better than here?*

He turned his head without lifting it from the unyielding carriage upholstery at his back. Everything that he could see through the train window appeared exactly as it had during peaceful summer holidays before the war. The shipyard was still there, close to the railway line, and on the other side of the river, the Royal Naval College appeared through a gap in the trees, red brick and mullioned under its clock — just the same as it had always been.

Karl left the station and descended a familiar slope towards the wide harbour of the river Dart. As he went through the archway leading to the jetty he could see a ferry making its way towards him from the other side. A sudden squall moved across the water like cloud-shadow; two boys in a sailing dinghy reminded him of those plum-picking expeditions to Dittisham.

Once on the ferry, in midstream, he got a better view of the college — the grey slates showed no signs of damage.

He booked in to the Royal Castle Hotel. It had not changed since he had last been inside during summer holidays: the same great winding staircase was at its hub, the same mass of numbered bells on a wooden panel that might still be connected to every room by pull-wires.

He slid up the sash-window of his bedroom and looked out: anchored fishing boats tinged pink in the setting sun; half-timbered buildings with steep slate roofs — behind them, at the narrowest part of the river mouth, would be the Old Battery and Castle. Somewhere beyond, just outside the harbour mouth, the Mew Stone would still be jutting from the sea with a new generation of seagulls whirling over it.

There were subtle flavours on the breeze that reminded him again of those long-gone holidays: seaweed, tarred rope, drying nets, warm sailcloth. Something in the air was dispersing the last traces of a headache that had been throbbing incessantly between his temples ever since he had boarded the boat-train from Dusseldorf.

Three prominent towers lying in a straight line, that's how Boxhammer had described them. Karl had already seen the clock tower from the ferry; he would seek out the other two in the morning and — in the absence of any fixed plan — those three towers seemed as good a place as any to start his quest.

Karl stepped back from the window, opened his suitcase and carefully unwound a shirt from around an empty photo frame. He took a photograph from his wallet and read the faded words written on the back before sliding it behind the glass. It was of Helga, lying in long grass near the aerodrome at Charleville: the blur in her eyes wasn't tears — but caused by the badly focused Leica. Sometimes there were colours in that picture: hair like pale wheat, blue ribbons securing the plaits. Sometimes Helga's neck was a chestnut-brown above the criss-cross lacing of a bodice decorated with bright threads of embroidery. He pulled out the plywood tongue at the back of the frame and stood it up on the table by his bed so that it would be the first thing to catch his eye in the morning.

That night he dreamed of his wife and the wedding celebrations — but the dream quickly turned into an all-too-frequent nightmare in which he saw Andrew sinking into the ground under the weight of broken masonry. The vision stayed with him throughout the night — it was a familiar one. He had lived with it for a long time.

Karl woke with a thick head and deliberately avoided breakfast. He walked to the other ferry, the big one at the far end of the North Embankment, then turned away from the river to walk up Coombe Road. There was a bench facing towards the college so, in an attempt to ease the pounding in his head, he sat down and looked across at Britannia's newly gilded clockface — surprised to see that the time registered was exactly eleven thirty-six — the moment of the attack. *Had the clock stopped . . . ?* No — it had not.

The church tower had to be farther up the hill and after a short walk he recognised it: four pinnacles projecting upwards from the top — and a shuttered belfry window set into red stonework below a castellated parapet. His view of it exactly matched the photograph taken from the ground, the one that Boxhammer had produced at the briefing the day before Operation Herod. It matched, too, the indelible image that had been frozen onto his retina in a split second of terror as he flew over, trying to miss those projections. He walked up the path that led through the graveyard and found a board with lettering, yellow on black: Saint Clement's Church.

The last tower was at the top of a sloping unmade track called Pathfields Road. Karl walked towards it between houses and bungalows. The tower itself was built of chocolate-coloured stone, unlike the rest of the tile-hung building on whose south-western wall it was attached. A small panel of glazed tiles set into the wall by the garden gate identified this complex: Tower House. It must have been a school eight years ago because it was here that he had glimpsed small upturned faces scattered below like pocket handkerchiefs.

Karl turned round, leaned back against the garden wall and looked down the road. Britannia with its accurate clock was now out of sight behind the church. The trees in the churchyard would have presented another obstacle if they had been as tall as this in 1942. He stayed there for a moment, thinking about the events that had brought him to this place . . .

Adolf Hitler's *Jugend* movement had been an exciting experience for teenage boys. Karl had obtained his first *Schutz-Staffel* dagger for reciting political slogans and doing stunts on a motorcycle during early times in that organisation. Later he had been awarded a *C-Licence* at the Weil gliding school; it had been an exciting experience and it had been easy not to think about the *purpose* behind it all. Looking back now, it seemed strange that nobody had tried to discourage him from taking summer holidays in England — but perhaps it had been part of an overall plan, of which he had been ignorant at the time — a plan to improve his knowledge of the English people and their language. But he regretted now his membership of Hitler Youth and his subsequent duties in the armed forces. After the war, when he was able to return home to his mother's house, and when the terrible secrets of Nazi crimes became known, Karl had taken both his prized SS daggers from the hiding place where they had always been, and had buried them deep in the orchard without marking the spot.

The breeze was cold now. He walked away from Tower House, down Pathfields Road and paused again by the cemetery wall of St Clement's Church. He thought about the law courts at Nuremberg where, but for God's grace, he himself might well have been tried for his own war-crime. Reichsmarshall Hermann Goering: the driving force behind the *Luftwaffe*, had been condemned to die by a cold-hearted judge *for waging a war of aggression and violating the laws and customs of warfare* — so why had he not been so judged . . . ? Goering, at the last minute, had bitten into a cyanide capsule concealed in his mouth and cheated the gum-chewing American soldiers and their makeshift gallows in the prison gymnasium.

Walking down steep lanes towards the

centre of town, the thought of Goering's last despairing act was more chilling than the river breeze. What right had he, *Karl Deichman*, to be living now at the age of twenty-nine after leading a raid whose sole purpose had been the murder of hundreds of defenceless boys?

In the centre of town he noticed a sign marking the entrance to a museum. He looked the wrong way, stepped off the pavement, ignored an indignant beep from a motorist, went through a doorway and followed a cardboard arrow pointing up a flight of wooden stairs.

He had no idea what the reaction of ordinary English people would be to the confession that he was about to make, nor the probing questions he intended to ask. Perhaps such questions would seem distasteful and intrusive to those who had lived through the war in this town.

7

In the Dartmouth Museum, Barbara Carmichael fingered her steel-rimmed spectacles back onto the bridge of her nose and started turning the pages of some old copies of *Picture Post*. She wore a single string of artificial pearls and a short, buttoned cardigan; her severely pulled-back hair style might have given the impression of middle-age but in fact she was still only a month away from her twenty-first birthday.

The magazines had been donated for an exhibition: *The Fifth Anniversary of the End of the Second World War*, due to open in five days' time. It had been Barbara's own idea and it was going ahead in spite of considerable and unexpected complaints from a large number of town residents who regarded the project to be insensitive and unnecessary so soon after the event. Barbara of course held the opposing view. To her the war had been an exciting time in her life: she had lost no close relatives in the fighting and she saw it as a glorious victory worthy of celebration.

In one of the magazines she found a

photograph of a German aeroplane lying damaged in a field of corn, with a bicycle propped against it: a trouser-clipped policeman was in the foreground, writing in his notebook while a sullen German pilot, barely out of his teens, eyed a hostile group of farm workers who had gathered to watch. The caption was perfect: *Village Bobby Arrests Trespasser.*

On the same page was an advertisement apologising for the rarity of Spam, and another urging readers to keep their pre-war silk undies soldiering on to the end of the war by refreshing them regularly with Sylvan Flakes. Barbara carefully folded the page, so that the advertisements would not show, before putting it with the other exhibits.

There had been no visitors to the museum for the past two days, proving that the opposition of a few locals had indeed developed silently into a full scale boycott. Nevertheless she continued her work.

She opened a display case and took out a gas mask: exactly like the one she had carried to school every morning as a child. She put it on, remembering to put her chin in first before pulling the straps over the top of her head. As she looked out of the perspex strip and breathed in through the pig-snout filter at the front, the smell of rubber took her

95

straight back to assembly in the big schoolroom at *Tower House*. Every time she breathed out, a familiar flutter of rubber tickled her cheek — and made her wonder how it was that her friend, Thomas Bullock, had always managed to blow louder raspberries than anyone else during Miss Stobart's weekly gas practice.

Still wearing the gas mask, she continued to arrange more magazine pictures in the glass-topped display cabinet. Thinking about Thomas Bullock had reminded her of an extraordinary event that had happened on her thirteenth birthday, something that had occurred at the beginning of Miss Stobart's last term at the school — and something that had showed up a cruel side of that schoolmistress's character that none of the children had previously witnessed.

★ ★ ★

Tower House School — midday, September the 18th, 1942:

Miss Stobart mounted the dais in the Big Schoolroom. Normally when she did this the pupils automatically fell silent, but today there had been altogether far too much

96

excitement for this to happen and she had to rap her desk sharply with the blunt end of a pencil to bring the assembly to order. She waited for silence. Barbara Carmichael could tell by the look on Miss Stobart's face that there was trouble coming.

'Will the boy who wilfully damaged the glass door of number thirty Pathfields Road be good enough to come up here?'

The silence was total now — and scary.

'Come on, I want you up here now, we haven't got all day.'

There was a shuffle of feet near the back. Thomas Bullock came forward, face white and tie askew. He was looking at his shoes as he climbed three steps to the dais.

Miss Stobart surveyed him with curiosity and contempt. 'Thomas Bullock: I might have guessed it would be you. It would seem that you cannot be trusted to take your break outside without adult supervision. You are a vandal. Now turn round and be good enough to tell the whole school what a vandal is.'

'Don't know, miss.'

'Then allow me to enlighten you. Vandals were members of a Germanic race that invaded Europe and wilfully destroyed Rome in the fifth century AD. Now try again please, turn round and tell the whole school what a vandal is.'

In spite of the blush that had crept upward from his neck, Thomas lifted his chin defiantly. 'Vandals were Germans who destroyed other people's countries.'

Miss Stobart expression fell abruptly. She narrowed her eyes: '*Why do you suppose I have called you up here, Master Bullock?*'

'Don't know, miss.'

'Do you mean to tell me that after smashing the glass panel in Mrs Letts' front door, you are unable to guess why I've called you up here?'

Thomas looked her in the eye. 'Didn't mean to, miss. I was shooting at a Focke-Wulf, miss.'

It took a moment for Miss Stobart to realise that the boy was not swearing — then she remembered the aircraft recognition silhouettes hanging on public display in the town hall. '*Do you really expect me to believe that?*'

'I was trying to, miss, I mean . . . I wasn't trying to miss, miss, but I missed. The Jerry pilot's cockpit cover was all smashed up. I was aiming at his head. I might have killed him if I'd hit him on the temple.'

Spontaneous sounds of amusement burst from the children but Miss Stobart raised her voice above it. 'This is no laughing matter, do you hear? Any more of this giggling and every

98

one of you will stay in and write a hundred lines.'

She turned to Thomas again. 'Just because an enemy plane flies over the school it does not justify the reckless shying of stones.'

'Wasn't a stone, miss, it was a ball-bearing.' He delved into his trouser pocket and held up a steel ball the size of a large marble.

She opened her hand and, after a moment's hesitation, the boy gave it to her. Miss Stobart examined it closely: 'And where did you get this, may I ask?'

'My dad gave it me. He works at the shipyard.'

'I need hardly remind you, Master Bullock, that glass is almost impossible to obtain nowadays and Mrs Letts may have to wait months, perhaps years, before this damage can be put right. *Look at me when I'm speaking to you!*'

A flake of plaster, dislodged by the recent explosions, detached itself from the ceiling and spiralled down silently like a sycamore seed.

'Don't you know there's a war on?' She pointed at a bulge in his blazer pocket. 'What else have you got there?'

Thomas pulled out a crude catapult made from a forked stick and what looked like half-perished rubber from the inner tube of a

99

bicycle tyre. Miss Stobart plucked it from his hand and dropped it neatly into the waste paper basket along with the ball bearing. Then she walked purposefully to the cupboard and took both canes from their respective hooks where they had hung undisturbed since their approval by His Majesty's School Inspector halfway through last term.

She chose the heavier of the two.

'Thomas Bullock, bend over please and hold your ankles.'

'But miss . . .'

'Don't argue with me, do as I say.'

He bent over, looking nervously over his shoulder.

'Tighter please. I said hold your ankles, didn't I?'

Miss Stobart put the cane on his neck and pushed him down further. Then she lifted the tail of his blazer, folded it neatly across his back and tapped the seat of his shorts lightly, adjusting her stance like a golfer addressing the ball. 'Don't stand up until I tell you.'

Thomas made his last appeal. 'I was only trying to stop the Germanic tribes. Please miss, I didn't mean to break the glass!'

She raised the cane high and hit hard through the seat of his thin trousers. Three more strokes followed in brisk succession.

'That will do for now.'

Thomas straightened up, grimacing and clutching his behind while Miss Stobart replaced the cane.

Barbara Carmichael forgot about her birthday after that — in fact she had forgotten about it earlier, when she had heard the sound of bursting bombs and gunfire. She too had seen the German aeroplane being chased over the school roof and was worried because it was Friday, the day her mother always went to town to join the fish queue. Now the day had been further spoiled by Miss Stobart. Barbara was seething at the injustice of it. Thomas Bullock: the only boy in the school who had the guts to stand up to the enemy — the real German enemy who was trying to defeat the British Empire. Barbara had already invited four of her schoolmates to birthday tea. Now there would be five.

*   *   *

It was that episode that had made Barbara's thirteenth birthday stand out so clearly in her memory. Standing by the main display cabinet, and still wearing the gas mask, she remembered that, when she got home after school that day, her mother had shown her a small bottle of brandy which, three months later, was used to set fire to a Christmas pudding made from hoarded ingredients. The brandy had been offered to Mother by a friendly shopkeeper as an antidote for shock during the bombing but, being such a rare commodity, she had brought the precious fluid home and placed it unopened in the larder.

Barbara heard footsteps on the staircase and managed to tear off the gas mask just in time. A tall man came through the door at the top of the stairs and paid for his ticket with a ten shilling note which cleared her out of change. Predictably, he took one look at the new display and went straight through to the fossil room, which convinced Barbara that she had another *objector* on the premises.

She continued her work, unfolding a poster: *Join the Wrens and Free a Man for the Fleet*. She pinned it up next to: *Join the WAAF and Serve with the Men who Fly*.

Twenty minutes went by during which Barbara became so engrossed with what she was doing that she forgot about her visitor. When she did remember him she poked her head around the door to see if he wanted to ask questions, hoping that he wouldn't be too hostile. His back was turned towards her but his stooping posture showed that he was studying the relief map of Dartmouth, the one that had been donated to the museum by Britannia College; Barbara had put it in with the fossils because it was too big to go anywhere else.

He turned when he heard her behind him. 'Good afternoon. My name is Karl Deichman.'

She could not remember seeing him before so asked him the usual question about whether this was his first visit. He seemed to hesitate before answering. Yes, it was his first visit to the museum but he already knew the town of Dartmouth. The man had a foreign accent and Barbara began to realise that he might not be an objector after all. He told her that the last time he had visited the town was eight years ago.

Barbara did a quick subtraction — if he had visited Dartmouth in 1942 the chances were he hadn't done it for fun. She said cautiously, 'Quite a lot of people come here on business — mostly it's to do with fishing or else the Royal Navy.'

He smiled and nodded. 'You are right, my business here did have something to do with the Navy.'

He had said enough for Barbara to realise, from his accent — and the name — that he was German. Her first reaction was to worry about some of the things he might see in the display — especially the photograph of the crashed aeroplane and its glum pilot. She searched frantically for something to say: 'A lot of things seem to revolve around the navy in this town.'

'I am seeking information about an air raid on Britannia, the Royal Naval College. The raid took place on the 18th of September 1942. Do you know anything about it?'

She stared at him, still nervous but at the same time surprised because she had just been thinking about that very date — her thirteenth birthday. She told him she could remember hearing sounds of an air raid, and planes flying low over the school, but that he must be confused; it was the shipyard that had been attacked, the Noss Shipyard belonging to Philip & Son on the east side of the estuary. Some ships and a floating crane in the river had been hit too but she had never heard any mention of an attack on the college — and she told him so. It felt strange, standing in the fossil room talking to a former enemy like this. She said, 'It happened on my birthday, that's how I know it was the 18th of September.'

The visitor shook his head and Barbara could see that he was beginning to show signs of impatience. 'But surely you agree that the college was also bombed.'

Again Barbara told him that he must be referring to the shipyard. She also told him about Tommy's father being killed there on that very day: the words came out before she could check herself and a silence followed which made her feel slightly ashamed for being so tactless.

The visitor looked up from the map and passed a hand across his brow. 'Please will you show me where your school was?'

'Here, at the top of this sloping road.'

'And you are sure you were there on the 18th of September 1942?'

'Absolutely positive. Why do you ask?'

'Because I led an attack on the naval college that day. Although I was unable at the time to look back and see exactly where our bombs dropped, I believe that an important part of the building was destroyed.' He pointed to the map again. 'After dropping my bomb I flew over St Clements Church, which is just here, and over your school called Tower House. I have just taken a walk up there, that's how I know the names.'

Barbara took her time. 'Are you telling me that you were flying the Focke-Wulf that flew over our school?'

He smiled encouragingly. 'Focke-Wulf One-Nine-Zero, you know already?'

Barbara told him that in those days Tommy Bullock could recognise every different type of aircraft that flew: English and German — he even had a set of silhouette cards of his very own to prove it, so if he had said it was a Focke-Wulf 190 then it was. She also told him that the boy had shot at the German pilot with a catapult loaded with a steel ball-bearing the size of a pigeon's egg.

Then she saw him put a hand to the back of his neck and, for a moment, the man seemed to be staring straight through her. 'Please try to remember, Miss Carmichael. How many boys were killed in the college that day?'

Barbara wondered why he was being so insistent. 'I've already told you: it never happened but, if it did, surely *you* should know all about it — why are you asking me?'

He let out a long deflating sigh. 'All my fellow pilots went missing or were killed and Luftwaffe records contain no reference to the raid — possibly because it is something they were ashamed of — so I never found out. I crashed when I got back to France and was unconscious in hospital for a long time.'

Barbara, still convinced that she was right, told him finally that she had never heard of a bomb attack on the college and didn't know of anyone who had.

The German was beginning to look tired but, in spite of it, asked if there were any records that he might be allowed to look at. Barbara told him that thirty years must elapse before he, or anybody else, would be allowed to look at official documents relating to the war. She also told him that she was coming to the conclusion that the whole subject of the Second World War was fast becoming taboo in the town of Dartmouth.

Mr Karl Deichman then suggested calling at the college and asking them straight out, but Barbara told him that the Royal Navy didn't call itself the *Silent Service* for nothing and that he would be wasting his time. Then she remembered something: 'Wait a minute. Miss Stobart might be able to help you. I'm almost sure she had a sister in the Wrens who worked in the college during the war.'

'Who is Miss Stobart?'

She told him — and suggested that to put his mind at ease he should go and see her. She added, 'I'd better warn you Miss Stobart can sometimes be a bit funny — not laughing funny but *peculiar-funny*; I don't remember anyone laughing at school when Miss Stobart was around. There was this rumour going round the school that her father had been killed in the war — some said that's what made her so fierce.' Feeling more relaxed, she continued: 'I still keep in touch with Miss Stobart though lately it's only been Christmas cards. I could give her a ring if you like and see if she'll agree to meet you. She lives in Brixham — that's a small town not very far from here. You could catch a bus from Kingswear or maybe hire Mr Benson's Riley now that petrol rationing's ended. If you hang on for a minute I'll telephone Miss Stobart and see what she says.'

When Barbara came out of the office she saw her visitor get up from the bench clutching the back of his head again. 'She must be out but I'll try her later if you like. If you pop in here sometime tomorrow, I can tell you if I've managed to arrange anything.' As he thanked her and turned to leave, Barbara asked him to sign the visitors' book.

He unscrewed his fountain-pen and wrote: *9/8/50. Karl E Deichman, 23 Molenstrasse, Dusseldorf, West Germany.*

8

Anna Stobart sat on the floor. She was alone and in the dark. The luminous eyes of her cat provided the only source of light.

She had heard about Chancellor Adenauer's ridiculous plea for the rebirth of a German army on the six o'clock news and the nausea had just begun to subside when, out of somewhere — unexpectedly — *wonderfully*, one of her former pupils had telephoned.

A German pilot called Karl Deichman, claiming to have been in charge of the air raid which had killed Philippa, was over here from Dusseldorf to revisit the scene of his crime.

It was hard to believe, she was confused: did it make her happy — or sad? Angry perhaps, but fiercely elated all at the same time. There was of course a part of her that had to be sad — she was always sad whenever she thought about Philippa which was most of the time these days.

Thinking about her twin sister inevitably made her think of Dad and Geoffrey too: three brave souls — *yes, souls, they were dead weren't they?*

When Anna closed her eyes she could usually see Philippa standing somewhere close by — *that's why she was always thinking about her* — in the same room usually or, if out of doors walking close by. Either way she could nearly always hear Philippa's voice, often repeating the same single word over and over again — or, if not saying the word, urging her to . . . Philippa being alive inside her head was something that she had gradually become used to because it had been going on for so long.

But this extraordinary news! Thinking about it made her realise that *here was the opportunity* — something which she had dreamed about without daring to hope too much; the assassin had chosen to reveal himself — *and he was coming to tea.*

This German man, together with his confederates — although he didn't know it yet — had changed the course of Anna's life yes, that raid on Dartmouth — that particular one out of many on the town — *how could she have stood by and done nothing after that?* Leaving her protected occupation as a teacher to join the Women's Auxiliary Air Force had seemed *right.* And during her service in the WAAF she had been given a unique and truly wonderful chance to avenge those three deaths. Rather unluckily, however, she had only managed to kill *one* German by the time the war ended and the ever-present Philippa never stopped reminding her from beyond the grave of the brutal truth that she hadn't quite finished the job.

She got up, groped her way to the light switch and went to the corner cupboard where she poured herself a massive measure of Scotch Whisky to celebrate this new and forthcoming victory. *Opportunities like this were rare.* Barbara Carmichael had been a troublesome schoolgirl, particularly rebellious after the incident of Mrs Letts' door panel (how did she get that job in the museum?) but if this business about the German pilot turned out to be true, the girl had definitely come up with an unexpected handful of trumps. Good girl! She had even dictated the man's full address over the telephone.

Anna sat down on the sofa; the cold nose of her cat pushed up under her wrist as she remembered the sickening event that had started her quest for revenge, a quest that was far from ended. She lay back and remembered that fate-charged day in Dartmouth — the day that had changed her life and had indirectly caused wounds still suffered today.

★　★　★

Towards the end of the school day, Miss Stobart had overheard whispered comments proving that Thomas Bullock, far from feeling contrite after his punishment, had been laughing about the red stripes across his bottom and even showing them off to some of his closer friends.

But that infamous day was not quite over.

Miss Stobart hurried down Pathfields Road with her collar up against the rain. When she got to her front door she had to search her handbag for the front door key, surprised that her twin sister was not already home. In urgent need of tea, she decided not to wait so went through to the kitchen to put on the kettle. Philippa wouldn't be long; she could top up the pot when she got in. When the last of the week's ration was well infused, Anna poured herself a cup and settled back in her wing chair by the empty fireplace. She wasn't feeling very proud of herself. Perhaps she had been too hard on the boy. She tried to ease her conscience by telling herself that what had happened today had nothing to do with her own cruel streak. No, it was quite clear that young Bullock had been lying: shooting his catapult at a German aeroplane was a feeble story and the caning would have taught him a valuable lesson.

There was a knock at the door. Anna dragged herself out of her chair and looked out of the window. A man's bicycle was propped by the garden gate and behind the trunk of the wisteria she could see a bulky figure clad in a navy-blue rain cape standing in the porch. She put down her cup and opened the door. Something about the expression on the elderly policeman's face caused a sudden vacuum in her stomach.

'I'm sorry to disturb you, Miss. Is your name Anna Geraldine Stobart?'

'What is it, Constable?'

He took off his helmet and held it nervously. 'Might I have a word?'

Her knees felt weak. Trying to keep her voice steady, she said, 'Come inside, I've just made some tea.'

He stepped into the hall and smoothed his silver hair with an enormous hand. 'No tea, thank-you, must get on. It's about your sister, Philippa Louise Stobart. I'm afraid I have bad news.'

She looked straight into his unblinking eyes — and knew.

'A bomb fell on the Royal Naval College this morning. Your sister was a victim. It was all very sudden, she couldn't have felt anything. I'm afraid I'll have to ask you to call at the mortuary tomorrow to identify the body. May I say how sorry I am, miss.'

Anna thought she was going to faint. It was unreal. It was a lie. How could Philippa be dead when only this morning . . . ?

The policeman paused with his hand on the door. 'I've been authorised to tell you that the air raid was directed at the college by six enemy planes, but I must advise you that it is classified information. I am required to ask you not to talk about it. You must never mention it to anyone. Believe me it's very important — a matter of National Security.'

She watched through the window as he walked down the path towards the gate, wildly hoping that he would come back and tell her that he'd made a mistake and that it hadn't happened after all — that Philippa was still . . . but he never so much as looked back.

Anna sank onto the sofa, numb with shock, staring with unseeing eyes at the darkening sky on the other side of the window. She remained like that for several hours until the sound of the hall clock, striking midnight, made her aware of her surroundings again. She crept upstairs without supper and lay listening to the gusting rain on her bedroom window.

The following morning, still in shock, Anna

walked to the mortuary. Philippa's eyes were closed, her face unmarked. She looked as though she had fallen into a peaceful sleep and would wake if somebody were to touch her hand.

Walking up Pathfields Road on her way back to school, Anna Stobart's pace quickened and her grief began to give way to anger, a special kind of anger. By the time she had reached Tower House the anger had changed into an insatiable hunger for revenge.

★ ★ ★

Anna looked down at her cat through a lens of amber liquid. Colin was an uncomplicated animal yet somehow he seemed able to read her thoughts. She raised her glass to him. *'Here's to the downfall of Herr Deichman!'*

Colin showed claws which were long and sharp.

She knew that successful missions resulted from careful planning — it had been part of her training: the simpler the plan, the easier to carry out. The criminal was due to present himself for trial at four o'clock tomorrow afternoon. If found guilty the execution would be swift. There was work to be done.

She darted into the kitchen, rummaged for

a torch and went upstairs. After negotiating worm-eaten steps at the top of the house she opened the attic door and shone a weak beam across dust-laden joists. Treading carefully she walked across the roof space and squeezed into a tight corner behind the chimney flue. The suitcase had lain there a long time: she had to breathe out against the dust to prevent herself from choking while she extricated it.

Down in the sitting room she knelt beside the case and wiped the lid with her sleeve until the embossed initials, *CNV*, showed on the leather. The hasps snapped back easily on a lid that had remained closed since before her first short internment in King's Ash Mental Hospital — it seemed incredible to think that qualified doctors had once tried to get her certified insane.

First to catch her attention was the faintest hint of a long-forgotten perfume. She found the bottle, eagerly twisted off its ground glass stopper and inhaled a delicious fragrance of jasmine and lemon, a smell that provoked strong feelings of violence and death. The little bottle had a circular label: *Le Jade. Roger & Gallet, Paris,* and was decorated with the entwined tendrils of a climbing plant. Long ago she had secretly laced that perfume with a generous dose of cocaine and, judging by its effect on her now, it was still active.

She picked up a small cardboard box, opened it and lifted out a sharp edged Maltese Cross by its red-and-green ribbon. The central medallion was superimposed on a pair of crossed swords and bore the laurel-crowned head of a woman. Cast into the bronze were two words arranged in a circle: *REPUBLIQUE FRANCAISE*. Anna had worn her *Croix de Guerre* only once: Armistice Day 1946. It had made her feel proud but so many people had asked her awkward questions about how she had earned it that she had resolved never to wear it again.

She unfolded a pair of hand-stitched knickers that had been carefully packed between layers of tissue paper — and pictured the garlicy man who had given them to her. In separate wrappings there was a long blonde wig, and a pair of patent leather shoes with a secret compartment in one of the heels. There was a lockpick tucked into a pocket inside the suitcase, something she had made herself out of a meat skewer under the guidance of Mr Beckwith. She held it in her hand and could hear the man speaking to her: '*Heat the pointed end over a flame — bend the last inch to half a right-angle — flatten with a hammer — not too hard,* mind — re-temper by heating to a nice cherry-red and then cool quickly in water.'

Anna had spent long hours taking locks to pieces to learn how they worked. Sergeant Cox used to say that, since the war began, Mr Beckwith had spent more time in the Special Operations Finishing School at Beaulieu than he had in his cell inside Parkhurst prison.

Next to the lockpick was an envelope containing an identity card printed by a small firm in Lymington that specialised in the forgery of foreign documents for the British Secret Service. It had been important that her personal details be written in her own hand, and Anna had filled it in along the dotted lines using black ink and a rather scratchy dip-pen.

There were two inky fingerprints under the heading *Empreintes Digitales* and the photograph showed that Anna had worn her hair a lot shorter in those days.

She got up, poured herself another whisky, took a deep breath of *Le Jade* and delved into the suitcase again because she had not yet found what she was looking for. It was there, near the bottom: a small tin marked Aspirin. Anna put both capsules onto the palm of her left hand. They looked good. She put one of them into her mouth, letting it lie in the fold

CARTE D'IDENTITÉ

Nom *Viarouge*

Prénoms *Claudine Nicole*

Nationalité *Française*

Profession *domestique*

Né*e* le *23 Avril 1916*

à *Rouen*

Domicile *Rue Moulinier 34*

Le Coquet, Bretagne.

SIGNALEMENT

Taille *1m 63*   Cheveux *Noirs*

Bouche *Pleinne*   Yeux *Verts*

Visage *Ovale*   Teint *Clair*

Signes particuliers *Néantes*

of her cheek in the way she had been taught. She shifted it with her tongue then, very gently, held it between her teeth, squeezing cautiously to test the condition of the gelatine. She took it out of her mouth and dried it with a handkerchief. Yes, it was still in very good condition and its tough wall seemed to have retained all its original qualities of resilience and transparency.

The second capsule was also in perfect order.

A small neat man: clipped moustache, Brylcreem-stuck hair, materialised inside her head. '*This stuff is not compulsory. The high brass never talk about it and, if you're lucky, you'll never have to use it. There are three flavours available: Death, Death and, need I say it, Death.*'

She could see Sergeant Cox now, holding up a tiny egg-shaped capsule between finger and thumb while his audience listened intently. '*This is the L-Pill my friends: L stands for lethal. You have been trained to extend your endurance under torture for a period of forty-eight hours so that your network can disperse before you spill the beans. But if somebody were slowly squeezing your balls in a vice you might decide to co-operate with your captors a bit too early, which would be bad news for your colleagues* in the Resistance.' He saw Anna looking at him. '*You may think that Stobart here might have an unfair advantage in a situation like that but I assure you that Nazi interrogators have equally unpleasant methods for the fairer sex.*'

Nobody laughed. Cox pulled out his lower lip and dropped the capsule into the fold of his cheek. '*You can carry an L-Pill in your mouth, quite harmlessly, until you need to use it — even eat your lunch while it's in there if you're careful. Try it for yourselves some time but don't blame me if you bite it by mistake — because that's what you have to do if you want to die — bite through the gelatine coating and you will be gone in twenty-two seconds. Bite hard, gentlemen, the surrounding capsule is tough. Any questions?*'

Anna carefully repacked her weapons of undercover warfare — except for the tin of aspirins and the bottle of *Le Jade*, both of which she slipped into the patch pocket of her dress.

She sank to the floor again, propped against cushions pulled from the sofa: happier now — her only regret was that she didn't still have her Smith & Wesson .38 revolver.

★   ★   ★

On Thursday morning Anna woke early. She backed her car out of the garage and drove to the shops in search of sugar lumps. On her way back she drove to the disused mine near Sharkham Point and made three practice runs. The mouth of the main mineshaft was exactly three-quarters of a mile from her front door, a distance that took just under seven and a half minutes if she kept her driving speed down to a brisk walking-pace. The concrete slab that covered the mouth of the shaft had conveniently crumbled with age, leaving a dangerous gap, half-hidden by undergrowth.

9

Karl Deichman awoke from a bad dream and it took him a few confused moments to realise that he had not, after all, been sentenced to death at the Nuremberg trials.

Chilled by cooling sweat he got out of bed, looked at the photograph of Helga and went over to the window, diagnosing the pounding inside his head as nothing more than the chemical result of stomach-juice still at work on two pints of English beer. On the pavement there were wisps of sun-heated vapour evaporating in the morning air. He looked at the familiar shape of the skyline on the far side of the river, and reminded himself that he had work to do.

His head was throbbing again as he climbed the stairs to the museum. Barbara Carmichael looked up from her work, removed her glasses and explained that she had managed to contact Anna Stobart. 'I was expecting her to be difficult but in the end she seemed quite keen on the idea. She's invited you this afternoon for tea at four o'clock.' She handed him a piece of paper with Miss Stobart's address and the times of buses. She was being helpful, but at the same time made it clear that she remained unconvinced about Operation Herod.

Karl made his way down the steps: If the girl didn't believe his story — who would? Was this to be the reaction of these people — pretend it never happened; refuse to talk about it? She had been quite prepared to discuss the bombing of the Noss Shipyard and the sinking of ships in the river — so why had she refused to reveal what had happened to the Britannia cadets?

In his hotel bedroom Karl removed the lucky photograph from its frame and put it in his wallet, something he always did before any journey, however short, because he still nurtured a belief that the photograph of Helga had once saved his life. He looked at the street plan of Brixham that he had bought from the Harbour Bookshop and identified Yards Lane.

After crossing to Kingswear on the ferry he had to wait ten minutes for a bus which climbed away from the river up a winding road under overhanging trees. Sunlight blinked through the leaves, flashing into Karl's eyes; flashing-and-blinking, reminding him of another line of trees long ago . . .

He had not actually seen any bombs falling on the college — his own had missed the critical spot. There was now no sign of damage nor evidence of extensive repairs — even the clock was still working.

Perhaps Boxhammer had failed to score — and the other Focke-Wulfs might have been engaged by the enemy before they had had a chance to complete the job. Miss Stobart, however, whose sister might have been working in the college at the time of the attack, would be sure to know something.

Karl checked his Rolex and remembered how his friend Leo had once made an exaggerated claim about the English sacramental cup of tea: every day at exactly four o'clock — with milk. Leo's first dose — sugared and powdered — had been offered by Englishmen in black berets while travelling in a Cromwell tank to Alamein. They had buried their wireless operator in the desert and now they were allowing their German prisoner to occupy the empty seat. Was it the calming properties of English tea that had prevented those tank-men from putting a bullet through Leo's head? Would tea have an equally calming effect on Miss Anna Stobart?

Brixham: he got off the bus by the church in Drew Street, walked up Southdown Hill and was a little out of breath by the time he had taken a left turn into Yards Lane. As he approached the house he felt the first spots of rain on his face.

He rang the bell. The rain came down harder. After a long wait the door was opened by an attractive woman in her thirties: short, slim, immaculate white blouse with a high collar; but the beauty of her face was marred by an expression of undisguised hostility. As she stepped back to let him in, Karl caught a strong whiff of perfume.

She moved her head sharply to flick black strands of hair off her forehead. 'You must be Herr Deichman.' She emphasised the word *Herr* in an unfriendly way and her green eyes reflected fierce points of light from the rain-streaked window.

★ ★ ★

Anna Stobart had been watching the road from an upstairs window; and when a tall man wearing a thin linen jacket walked up to her front door she let him stand in the rain for a few minutes. *A confession — that was all she needed from this man — a simple confession and then . . .*

'You must be Herr Deichman.' She led the way into her sitting-room and turned to face him. 'I believe we have Barbara Carmichael to thank for this meeting. I expect she's

126

already told you that I once taught her French at school — it was during the war. Barbara tells me that you were in the German Air Force and that you took part in a raid on the Royal Naval College in Dartmouth — September 1942.'

'I led the squadron that dropped those bombs, yes.'

Anna could feel a cold hand closing inside her; she had to check herself to avoid shouting the verdict: **Guilty as charged . . .**

'And now you wish to ask me some questions about that bombing, am I right?' Before he had a chance to reply she continued, 'Sit down Mr Deichman while I fetch the tea.' She watched him settle himself into a chair, then she left the room, leaving the door open.

So here at last was the man. Ever since that dreadful evening in September 1942 when she had first learned of her sister's death, Anna had been trying to picture what the murderer might look like — and it was something of a surprise — now, suddenly — to know that he was quite ordinary-looking. Tall, slightly shy, a hint of kindness even, but, considering the extreme wicked-ness of the crime to which he had just confessed, an unremarkable face. She had often tried to visualise the man who had led the raid on Britannia: living his life somewhere in Germany, working, eating, sleeping, making love, free to come and go as he pleased — totally uncaring about those who mourned the results of his premeditated butchery. It was curious to think that now she would no longer have to rely on her imagination to provide the image.

She lit the gas ring and put a small jug of milk, two cups and two teaspoons on a tray. There would be no bread and butter today: no jam, cake nor biscuits. There would be sugar lumps — oh yes, she would make quite sure that Herr Deichman took a particular lump of sugar in his first and only cup of tea — the lump with the rounded-off corner.

Anna walked back with the tray. Through the open door she could see that he was no longer sitting in his chair. She entered the room soundlessly on thick carpeting. He was over by the mantelpiece with his back turned towards her. She came up behind him but he must have somehow sensed that she was there because he turned round before she had a chance to speak. She was angry: this man had one of her treasured photographs in his hand.

There was guilt in his voice . . . 'I was looking at this picture of you. When was it taken?'

She put down the tray on a low table and turned to face him. 'That is a picture of my twin sister, Philippa, murdered by the Germans in the Royal Naval College on the eighteenth of September 1942. Did Barbara Carmichael tell you that? Did she tell you that when you flew to Dartmouth that day you murdered my sister?'

A mixture of shock and embarrassment showed on Herr Deichman's face. 'I am sorry to hear that . . . Miss Carmichael never told — '

'She never told you for the simple reason that she doesn't know about it.' Anna was beginning to feel the force of her own anger. 'Miss Carmichael tells me you want to know how many casualties you caused in the Royal Naval College when you dropped your bombs, is that right?' He started to answer but she cut him off at the first word. 'How dare you come here to gloat over your victims, *how dare you?*'

'I don't understand why you think I am gloating.'

'If you can't understand plain English we will continue in German.' She switched languages and continued in a fluent tirade: '*You make me angry: why have you come all the way from Number 23 Molenstrasse in Dusseldorf to talk to me about your squalid little victory?*' She noticed, with some satisfaction, that his face registered surprise at the mention of his address.

'I was ordered to lead that attack on Britannia — we called it Operation Herod — and ever since I have been tormented with the uncertainty of not knowing what happened. My own cousin was a cadet in the college — I have come to England to find whether I killed him. Of course I regret my part in the death of your sister, but I should like to know who else was killed, and their names.'

Anna ignored this and continued coldly: 'Did you notice the other photographs on my mantelpiece?' She got up and fetched them, sat down opposite him again and held up a blurred snapshot of a young man wearing a peaked cap, smoking a pipe and leaning back on a ship's rail. Scrawled across the bottom were some barely legible words which she suspected Herr Deichman might have noticed already: *Love from Geoff, Halifax 8/8/41.*

'My late fiancé. *San Florentino* sailed in ballast from the Clyde to pick up a cargo of petrol from the other side of the Atlantic. The ship never arrived. A U-boat cut her in half 900 miles east of Newfoundland in September 1941 — exactly one year before you killed

Philippa. I heard what happened from a survivor: lifeboat barely afloat — men sitting waist-deep for ten hours. Geoffrey was picked up but died on board a Canadian destroyer called *Mayflower* four weeks before our planned wedding.'

Before Deichman had a chance to make any comment, Anna held out another framed photograph. 'Do you know who this is? This is my father, killed by the Germans near Dunkirk — they killed him *after* he had been taken prisoner.'

It was a long time since she had spoken German like this but it was coming easily; speaking the criminal's language was somehow fuelling her anger towards him. She removed the tea cosy. 'Have a cup of tea, Mr Deichman.' She picked a lump from the sugar bowl, dropped it into his tea and stirred vigorously.

Deichman took the cup from her and set it down on the table beside him. He told her about the death of his staffel-comrades, his wounds and the crash into elm trees at Maupertus.

Anna was leaning forward in the sofa, listening closely. 'What difference does it make to you? You survived, my loved ones didn't.'

'All I can say is that I shall be in torment

until I learn the extent of my crime.'

Anna was furious at such a ridiculous effort at contrition. '*Well, you can stay in torment!* I know exactly how many people were killed in Britannia College that day and, if I wanted to, I could supply you with a complete list of names. But why should I? If you are still in torment you can go on being in torment! God knows I have suffered from this business over the years, so why shouldn't you? I'm sorry, Mr Deichman, today I'm in no mood for olive branches!'

Deichman seemed undeterred. 'Like you I had a loved one who was a victim of the war.' He opened his wallet, took out the photograph of Helga and handed it to her. She allowed herself a quick glimpse before turning her head away in deliberate imitation of a child refusing cabbage. Deichman continued: 'Apart from the hair-colour and the pigtails she is not unlike your sister to look at, don't you think so?'

Sheer curiosity made Anna take the photograph from him and look at it quickly — but almost immediately her attention was deflected . . .

Herr Deichman had picked up his tea and was about to drink.

His cup paused on its way to his lips as he waited for her comment. Trying to keep steady Anna said, 'Who is this person in your photograph?'

Hell! His cup was back on the saucer.

'This is Helga — my wife: she is wearing the Bavarian dress that I bought for her the day we became engaged. Unfortunately she was in Hamburg in July 1943 when the British and Americans sent hundreds of heavy bombers to destroy the city. Forty thousand civilians were killed during that raid, Miss Stobart, *forty thousand!*'

Anna studied the picture for several seconds but, as she handed it back, it fell face down onto the carpet. She looked down quickly and managed to read some words which were scribbled on the back.

Deichman reached down to pick up the photograph but, as he did so, his brimming cup slid off its saucer and tumbled onto the carpet.

Colin darted out from under the sofa. He ran towards the fallen cup but Anna managed to grab the animal before it had a chance to get close. She left the room to fetch a cloth with the cat under her arm — and already she could feel a tide of disappointment washing the fight out of her. No time to bait another sugar lump: only one way forward now — *have to humour him a little to achieve it.* She pushed the cat out through the back door for safety, and went to find a clean cup.

Wearing rubber gloves and scrubbing at the carpet, she said to him. 'Help yourself to more tea while I clear this up. I think it is now my turn to ask you a question, don't you think?' He didn't answer so she continued: 'What made you pick that particular morning to drop your bombs on Dartmouth?'

He took a long time fiddling with the teapot. Perhaps he was reluctant to answer *her* questions.

'Come on, you can tell me that surely. I am sorry if I appeared unfriendly.'

'We picked that day because of secret information received.'

This was better than expected: 'And what was this *secret* information; who provided it?'

'It came from a spy, Miss Stobart — but why should I tell you about it if you won't tell me what *I* want to know?'

Another name? Could he be persuaded to divulge the name of somebody else directly involved in Philippa's murder? She continued to suppress her anger and even managed the outward appearance of a smile: 'All right, Herr Deichman, I'll do a deal with you. If I promise to give you details of the damage — human and material — caused by your so-called Operation Herod, will you tell me the name of your spy and exactly how he helped you?'

She watched his eyes — she had found the target. Deichman took a harmless lump of sugar from the bowl, stirred it into his tea and said, 'Before the mission our senior officer gave us a briefing: he told us that 634 teenage cadets would be gathered in the main assembly hall of Britannia — the quarterdeck — on the first day of the Christmas term. As I've already told you, that information came from a local spy.

'One year after the raid I joined our intelligence organisation on the outskirts of Hamburg's ruins and was assigned the job of Spy Controller. One of my operatives was a man by the name of Robert McGuire whom I later discovered had been our agent in Dartmouth. He is part Irish, part Portuguese, anti-British, an expert linguist, a registered conscientious objector — and reputed to believe wholeheartedly in Hitler's National Socialism. Operating undercover in Dartmouth he somehow managed to infiltrate all the Royal Naval Establishments in the area — including — '

Anna cut in: 'Why don't you ask your spy? Why don't you ask him how many people you murdered in Dartmouth — why have you come to me about it?' *As soon as she had said it she cursed herself for interrupting.*

'I have asked him on several occasions but he doesn't know. He had to leave Dartmouth just before Operation Herod because British MI5 agents were after him. He was never caught, got away from Dartmouth just in time. After that he was sent to join the Intelligence Section of the German Embassy in Lisbon — he flew out from London Airport on a scheduled flight. When I'd recovered after my crash I joined the German Intelligence Service. I used to monitor all McGuire's coded radio transmissions from Portugal, sent to our listening station in Hamburg. As a result of this I got to know Robert McGuire quite well. Part of my job was to make sure that he was kept rich enough to pay his Portuguese informers so I used to send him large sums of *escudos* via the diplomatic bag. He liked Portugal — in fact McGuire liked it so much that he made Lisbon his permanent home. He's still there. We exchange the occasional letter but to this day I've have never actually met the man.'

Anna Stobart was struggling with a confused mix of sentiments: the failure to despatch Deichman was disappointing — *but now she had identified and located another guilty man.*

Karl got up and put his empty cup on the

tray. 'Now that I have told you about the Dartmouth spy, it is your turn to tell me what I need to know.'

She went over to the mantelpiece; she replaced the photographs carefully and thoughtfully; she looked up at the ceiling, stroked her chin, turned around and spoke to him in English. 'I am rather tired, Herr Deichman — I need to think very carefully before I tell you anything.'

Deichman raised his voice. 'You must tell me now, Miss Stobart!'

She raised her chin. '*Must*, Herr Deichman, did you say *must?*'

Turning her back she strode towards the front door and held it open. 'There is nothing to be gained by discussing this matter further — not today. However, if you were to come here for tea again tomorrow afternoon, I promise — on my honour — that I will tell you everything. Shall we say four o'clock; would that be convenient?'

10

Anna sat slumped on the sofa. Ignoring the voices inside her head, she was fondling Colin's ears and making plans. She had tried the criminal, accepted his confession, found him guilty — but now his execution would have to be delayed.

The plan had been simple: drag the body out of the house — then a longer drag on a rope behind the car — put him down the mine shaft under cover of darkness, perfectly safe — but too risky to try again because the inquisitive Mr Bentall from next door was expected back from his holidays — and in any case, things were different now.

She had *two* men to deal with; a new plan to think about — Mr Deichman would have to wait his turn.

She looked at the hall clock. Yes, there was still time.

★   ★   ★

Karl Deichman sat by the open window oblivious of sweet smells in the wet Devon hedges as the bus wound its way back to

Kingswear. *This woman will tell me what I need to know. Loss of life in the college, yes — no escape from that. Anna Stobart is still grieving — like I am: Mother, Father, the Gatting family, Andrew, Ian perhaps. I am closer to the truth now. She has given me her promise. Another wait — another twenty-four hours . . .*

The thought of what he was going to hear tomorrow was not the only thing that had kept Karl awake that night. Whether to try and see a doctor before keeping his appointment with Anna Stobart was another matter on his mind. The nagging pain at the back of his head was still there and it was difficult not to think about Dr Schaffen's warning so solemnly imparted in a white-walled surgery in the summer of 1943.

On Friday morning Karl felt no better. He spent most of the day trying to read magazines downstairs in the lounge but it made his eyes hurt. The other guests in the hotel seemed reserved: unwilling to pursue a conversation beyond a casual *good morning* — he felt disinclined to broach the subject of Operation Herod with them.

He caught the earlier bus and arrived in Brixham with more than an hour to spare. He went for a walk by the harbour to pass the time, hoping that sea air might clear his head.

He watched trawlermen unloading boxes of herring on the quay under the swirling attack of sea-birds, all the time keeping a careful watch on his Rolex.

At four o'clock he walked up Yards Lane again, feeling a lot better. Nobody came when he rang the bell. He rang it again — and a third time — and kept ringing, but the only sign of life came from yesterday's black cat, watching him from the doorway of a shed in the corner of the garden.

'Are you looking for somebody?' A man was peering at him through the hedge.

'I have come to see Miss Stobart.'

'You'll be lucky. She's on holiday — left me a note to feed the cat.'

'Do you know where she has gone?'

'Never said. Where she's gone is a mystery between her and the travel agent.'

★　★　★

Service TP 573 took off from London Airport's new runway at 16.10 on Friday afternoon. Anna had had a complicated journey so far, having only just managed to catch the flight after missing her connection at Newton Abbot.

An air hostess brought a tray but she was too tense to eat. Anna pressed the button on the end of her armrest to recline her seat and from behind closed eyes refused to listen to the voice in her head. Instead she painted a mental picture of the mild-mannered Karl Deichman arriving at her house and ringing her front door bell in vain. Colin would be watching him; if old Bentall was back from his holidays by now she hoped he had found her note about feeding that uncomplicated animal.

Anna had never before flown in an aeroplane like this one: air conditioning, air hostesses. All this luxury made a striking contrast to the spartan conditions inside the Halifax bomber that had taken her to occupied France back in 1943. These soft reclining seats were quite different to that hard bench bolted to a bare metal fuselage: today there were no icy finger-tips of fear clawing at the inside her stomach, no oily smell — just the discreet whisper of a brand-new Douglas DC-4 — quite different to the noise of that bomber seven years ago . . .

★ ★ ★

RAF Station Tempsford, Bedfordshire — Thursday, July the 22nd, 1943:

The spinning propellers were invisible but for the faintest shimmer of moonlight. The din,

141

however, was colossal: a Handley-Page Halifax from 138 (Special Duties) Squadron, Transport Command, was warming for flight.

Anna Stobart got down from the truck and walked towards the big bomber with the roar of four Bristol Hercules engines drowning every sensation other than fear. The despatcher, crouched in the doorway of the aircraft and held out a welcoming hand when he saw her. Climbing the ladder wasn't easy because her parachute harness was pulled tight over canvas overalls inside which a twenty-seven year old French girl called Claudine Viarouge was about to make her vital — but unusual — contribution to the war effort. Every item of her clothing had been carefully chosen: all made in France.

The despatcher was a small, dark-haired RAF sergeant whose Welsh accent reminded Anna of somebody she knew. 'Welcome aboard the Skylark, miss.' He offered her his hand. 'Four of you tonight — I expect you know each other already. Four Special Operation agents and ten heavy containers — quite a milk-round.' He showed her where to sit. 'You will jump as soon as I've dropped the first container. Beautiful moon for it!'

The despatcher's cheerful disposition did nothing to disperse the fear of imminent danger; in spite of that, however, Anna tried to match his mood: 'It's a lovers' moon, Sergeant — but you're too young to know about things like that!'

He grinned back. 'Ignorant as a virgin but always willing to learn.'

This banter had no effect on the cramped climate of fear inside the bomber. In the glow of interior lights Anna exchanged nervous smiles with the other agents — all three of them men — who had been training with her and all bound for different destinations and individual tasks. A smile was the extent of the greeting. *Was that because of the din — or was it that nobody was in the mood for open expressions of feeling?*

As the Halifax taxied out to the runway the sergeant stood up, steadying himself by holding the static-bar. 'I am your despatcher tonight. Bear with me because I have to tell you a lot of things you already know backwards — King's Regulations and Air Council Instructions say that I have to. Our skipper is going to keep down to a height of less than one thousand feet all the way over. As soon as we cross the coastline you will hear guns shooting but it will be our air-gunners testing their weapons.'

He was standing right under the distorting light of a caged bulb which lit only one side of his face. 'Dropping altitude tonight is seven-hundred feet. Our gunners will be testing their weapons once we are over the sea. I will tell each of you when it's your turn to jump. When I do that I'd like you to stand up, check that your parachute release is correctly dog-clipped to this bar and those with separate baggage must make sure their baggage-lines are correctly attached to their leg-straps.'

The pilot manoeuvred the thirty-ton Halifax with bursts of power until it was facing the wind. Anna leaned back against an unyielding rubber pad behind her head and clenched her teeth as ear-shattering thunder from six-and-a-half thousand horsepower amplified itself inside the bare metal fuselage. The big bomber started to roll. It gathered speed over the bumps; it took an elongated hop into the air, sank back onto its fat tyres, then lifted away into the night with the vibration settling to a smooth roar.

The drop-zone was nearly two hours away. Anna leant back, closed her eyes and thought how strange it was that she had never met Major Coles until that morning . . .

★ ★ ★

Coles was a thin man. His unpressed tweeds clashed with the blue diagonals of his

144

old-Etonian tie. He had a way of peering at Anna through thick, unpolished lenses which made her feel uneasy. 'I gather from the file that you have French relations and used to spend summer hols in Brittany. You read modern languages at Oxford and enemy action resulted in the loss of some of your people. I'm sorry about that of course but I have to say that all this makes you eminently suitable for a rather tricky little operation, especially as you have expressed a desire to have a crack at Jerry yourself. *Operation Bullseye* can only be carried out by an attractive woman. If successfully completed it will be a valuable demonstration of our support for the French Resistance. We have tried various ways of removing nasty pieces from the enemy's chessboard in the past, but this is something new . . .'

Towards the end of the briefing Major Coles summed up: 'So you see, Stobart, I'm asking you to do one or two things which don't normally come within our remit. I'm confident, however, that you'll put up a good show. Sexual deviants are nothing unusual; nothing to be afraid of really, provided you stick to the plan — go to it and good luck!'

When he asked her to sign a receipt for her SOE Operations Order she had tried to do it calmly and, after memorising all the details of

145

Operation Bullseye she obeyed the final directive on the last page: **Now Destroy.**

Anna hoped that it was merely the vibration of the speeding bomber — or else the cold — that was making her shiver as she ran through the main points of the operation in her mind: the names of her contacts; the name of the night-club; the name of the VIP; the password; the sleeping arrangements; her cover-story; everything that Major Coles had emphasised during their two-hour session.

After the sudden noise of the gun-test she put her head back against the rubber and closed her eyes, remembering what she had been taught: *Close an imaginary orange door across the mind to shut out the continual force of anxiety.* She concentrated on that — fiercely — and soon she could feel herself moving on a slow current into shallow sleep.

At the end of an uncharted dream she felt herself falling; her arms had become entangled in a parachute; she was hanging in a tree like a puppet who could only be controlled by somebody else. An officer in black uniform was reaching up to her, she could feel his hand on her shoulder. 'You are under arrest. Time to go!'

'*Time to go!*'

She was suddenly awake in the oily din of the bomber.

'Time for you to go, miss, left you sleeping as long as I could.'

Barbed wire raked the inside of her stomach. She stood up precariously and clipped the static-line of her parachute to the bar. When the despatcher uncovered a large hole in the floor, wind howled like a train whistle across the gap. After the container had gone she sat on the edge with her legs in the slipstream. A rasp against her cheek, a faint smell of Brylcreem as the sergeant bent down to speak into her ear. *'Ready miss?'*

She yelled back through clenched teeth: *'Ready sergeant!'*

He squeezed her shoulder — that Welsh accent again: 'Good luck, miss. Watch for the green light; when I say go, you go — okay?'

Between her feet she could see a moonlit field on the edge of a black forest. The light changed from red to green.

'Go!'

She fell, tumbling and twisting; lungs deflating as the breath sucked from her open mouth; a grey sky toppled over so that, for a second, the ground was above her head; a whip cracked like a pistol shot as the parachute snapped open; the harness kicked into her groin. Then she was the right way up, swinging like a pendulum with cold wind in her face.

The drone of the receding Halifax was suddenly far away. There was a soft flap of silk above her head as the parachute spilled some air. *Pull on the lift-webs, check the swing, watch the ground.* She could see men scrambling out from under the trees like ants in the moonlight. The heavy canister was drifting below her, its parachute looking like a pale halo. Some of the men were running to intercept it.

Seconds later she was sprawling in mud. Before she could catch her breath there was a hand on her back. A fat man picked her up and planted a garlicy kiss. '*Je m'appelle Anton. Mes compliments, Claudine, vous êtes en France!*' He let go of her and attacked the billowing parachute . . .

At the roadside a bicycle materialised from under a hedge and Anna felt a steadying hand on her shoulder as she mounted.

★　★　★

She felt a hand on her shoulder.

'Excuse me Madam.'

Anna opened her eyes. Her ears were filled with the hushed beat of another kind of aero-engine.

'Would you mind putting your seat to the upright position and fastening your safety belt?'

This wasn't a Halifax. She was looking into the face of an air hostess. Through the little window night had fallen and immediately below she could see the dark shape of a wing drifting across countless points of light.

'Sorry, I was miles away. Are we nearly there?'

'We'll be landing in approximately ten minutes.'

★ ★ ★

Within the walls of her room at the Hotel Eduardo Septimo, Anna waited until the porter had left. There was only one entry in the whole of the Lisbon telephone directory that mattered — and there it was: *R M McGuire, Rua das Janelas Verdes, 138, 1°.*

Until this moment her mission had relied on the unreliable word of a German criminal but now, seeing the name in print — the only McGuire in the book — she knew that she would succeed. Some lucky force was turning the dice for her: this former German spy evidently found it unnecessary to hide behind an assumed name after his career of treachery.

She picked up the telephone and dialled.

A woman answered: 'Alô — quem fala?'

'May I speak to Mr McGuire please?'

'Senhor Roberto nao estar,' **e no 'ere.'** A stream of Portuguese followed from which Anna picked out the English phrase: Lisbon Players.

She replaced the receiver and opened the telephone directory again: *Lisbon Players, Rua da Estrela 10*. Again a woman's voice answered — this time speaking English in a Manchester accent: 'Box Office, Lisbon Players.'

'Don't bother him now but is Mr McGuire there please?'

'Robert's on stage, who shall I say?'

Anna gripped the receiver so hard that it nearly cracked in her hand, but she said nothing.

'Play's nearly over. When Rob comes off stage I'll give him a message if you like.'

Anna thought quickly: 'That won't be necessary. Can I buy a ticket — say tomorrow evening?'

'Let me see now, Saturday's our last night — full house I think. Just a moment.' After a long pause: 'Nothing downstairs, Terence Rattigan's ever so popular but a lot of his plays have too many men in the cast for us, but we were lucky this time. Our Robert is one of the few, bless his socks. Gets roped in for everything — should have been a professional if you ask me.' Pause again: 'I've one on its own upstairs: A27 in the gallery. What name?'

'Penny Arrowsmith.'

'Curtain up at nine-thirty, Penny. I'll hold the seat till half an hour before.'

Anna Stobart put down the receiver and dabbed at her brow with a handkerchief. It was funny to think that Robert McGuire *had* been a sort of professional actor once and these people probably didn't know anything about it.

She unpacked her things and prepared for bed. Robert McGuire was a spy and a traitor as well as a murderer so it was appropriate that he should be the first to die. She remembered another of her quotations — memorised from an embroidered inscription hanging on the wall of a French farmhouse: *Ah, la belle chose que de savoir quelque chose!* Yes, it certainly was good to know things — how appropriate — but the strange thing was that she would never have heard about the Dartmouth spy's existence if Karl Deichman hadn't spilled his tea.

McGuire: it was a common enough name but the only McGuire that Anna had ever come across in Dartmouth was a one-legged man who ran the wine merchant's shop — and had been running it for as long as she could remember.

Until now it had been an everlasting disappointment that during all her time on active service during the war she had killed only one man from the opposite side. Now she had a chance to even the score by dealing with two villains in turn, both of them directly responsible for Philippa's death. *I will not let this chance slip away.*

But in spite of the long journey, Anna was not quite ready for sleep . . .

11

Friday evening: Karl Deichman lay fully clothed on his bed in the Dartmouth hotel. His head felt as if it were about to burst. Since his conversation with the Brixham travel agent he had been trying to work out why Anna Stobart should have suddenly decided to go to Portugal. She might — *just might* — have decided to confront Robert McGuire. He had slipped that information to her innocently — not realising that she might actually decide to go over and find the man . . .

Booking a telephone to Portugal from England had been a complicated procedure and, after waiting for more than two hours, his reward was trying to make himself understood by a woman who spoke neither English nor German.

Why should Anna promise to tell about the Dartmouth casualties during a second tea party — and then suddenly go off like this? Could it be that she couldn't face him any more? Was she really the type of person who would shy away like that?

Lisbon; Robert McGuire; Anna Stobart

153

— it seemed an uneasy combination. According to the travel agent it was unlike her to go abroad at all; theatre tickets in London was her usual request. She could be dangerous — there was something about her that signalled it . . .

Dying from a disorder of the brain, accelerated by fragments of English shrapnel was, for the moment at least, something that seemed uncomfortably possible but was not yet as pressing as Robert's safety — the old wound had given no trouble for almost eight years so what he was feeling now could well be nothing more than a passing headache.

Karl missed supper and retired to bed — promising himself that he would try Robert McGuire's number again in the morning. There was probably nothing sinister about Miss Stobart's sudden impulse to go to Lisbon — he tried to persuade himself of that. Robert, however, deserved to be told about it — he was, after all, an old comrade-in-arms. If the late Oswald Deichman could somehow look down now and see his son's concern for the Irishman, he would approve — and, in the great register of right and wrong, it might serve to cancel out some of the treachery Karl had shown towards Boxhammer, Awak, Geisler, Sperrle and Weiss.

★　★　★

Kill McGuire — that was the immediate objective. Before going to sleep in Lisbon's Hotel Eduardo Septimo, Anna Stobart told herself: get close to him; control his movements; discover his weaknesses, exploit them; grab opportunities; stay alert. Tomorrow night: the theatre — she would attract him; entice him, tease, flirt, wear the dress she had brought from England — but what about the wreckage of her hair after the flight? A Lisbon hairdresser: top of the agenda for tomorrow morning.

Some of the old excitement was back. On active service again; closing in on an unsuspecting target whose final hours were already counting down to death. It was a familiar feeling — this waiting. Was it fear? No, it was more like the kick from her very first sniff of cocaine: euphoria, loss of fatigue — something akin to looking down through the Joe-hole in the floor of a Halifax just before the jump. *Operation Bullseye:* that very first mission as an SOE agent; everything carefully planned beforehand by Major Coles. It had been worth it — that experience — in spite of its horrific climax; the sight of it, and the smell — but living with the almost daily recurring memory had been tough — the occasional pinch of 'snow' had helped with that in the early days — lift the spirits a bit — never injected of course.

Operation Bullseye: she sat thinking about it . . .

★ ★ ★

France — Midnight, July the 21st/22nd, 1943:

Still not fully recovered from the shock of the parachute drop, and exhausted after the long bicycle ride, Anna climbed the stairs to a tiny attic bedroom. She ducked under the rafters and fell exhausted into a feather mattress that completely enfolded her shaking body.

The room was a haven after her violent projection onto enemy occupied soil — a chance to escape from reality and the feeling of anticipation that had been growing steadily. A fragment of something, some words, another of her quotations, Shakespeare this time — how did it go? Something about . . . yes it was coming: *O sleep! O gentle sleep! Nature's soft nurse.* She knew more — but she was gone . . .

The following day Anton came into the room and told her to keep away from the window so she spent most of the day sitting in a high-backed chair with a French novel which she read mechanically without following the story.

She was too tense to eat rabbit stew and home baked bread.

Time passed slowly.

At four in the afternoon a vehicle was moving on the path below her window. It was a small van fuelled by a tent-like bag of *gazogène* attached to its roof. Sitting amongst trays of vegetables and freshly plucked poultry she travelled into Paris. Anton was driving but he said nothing which made Anna think, for a moment at least, that she might have fallen into some kind of elaborate trap set for her by the Gestapo.

After forty minutes by her wristwatch the streets had become crowded. She was in the outskirts of Paris exactly as planned.

The house was like any of the others in the street: a tall frontage of soot-stained brick and stone, probably built a hundred years ago. The bell-push was a ceramic button in a disc of polished brass, evidently working because a stooping lady with a bun of grey hair came to open the door. No smile — just the pressure of fingers on Anna's forearm as she was pulled quickly inside.

'Welcome to Paris, Claudine. Come with me please.' Her French was cultured, Parisian but the voice was high, cracking like a boy at the brink of puberty. She led the way up a long staircase, stooping forward, heaving on the polished banister rail. On the landing she opened one of the doors and — with that bony hand now in the small of Anna's back — propelled her inside.

It was a large room: oriental rugs on polished oak; a high cool ceiling; a swan-necked chandelier of brass; an old fashioned wardrobe with an oval mirror set into its door. From a small shelf, high on the wall, an effigy of the Virgin Mary: misty smile, hand raised in blessing — looked down on an expansive double bed covered with a spotless, all-white, hand-embroidered bedspread.

'This is the room,' the old lady's voice broke into falsetto as she touched the bedhead, 'Solid iron.' She opened a wardrobe. 'All your things are ready.' From a shelf inside the wardrobe she reached down a cardboard box and took out a small bottle; on its round label, decorated with climbing tendrils of vegetation were the words: *Le Jade. Roger & Gallet, Paris.* 'This is very important, Claudine dear, did they tell you about this in England?' She removed the ground-glass stopper and held out the bottle for Anna to savour. 'This is the perfume the *Generaloberst* goes mad for. Perhaps that is why they call him *the bull*. When he smells it on a woman he can only think of . . . ' She broke off then, wistfully: 'I used this perfume to break a man's heart when I was young like you!'

Anna breathed in deeply, never guessing that this powerful fragrance — contrasting so much with the other awful smell that would come later — would remind her for ever of this particular Friday night.

'The ropes are here too, they are in this bag.' She pulled them out, four of them, for Anna to see, then knelt down painfully on the polished floorboards and produced a roll of newspaper from under the bed. 'I have been hiding this here for a week.' She unfolded the paper carefully. 'Voila!'

It wasn't right at all. Anna balanced it in her hand — no, it was quite different from Major Coles' description: too long, much thicker than expected. She said as much to the old lady who shrugged and said, 'Better too long than too short, n'est ce pas? My brother made it; I could not tell him what it was for because Louis is not one of us. God bless him, I had to accept it.' The old lady wrapped it lovingly and put it back under the bed. Long or short, thick or thin, it would have to do.

She opened a drawer. 'These little articles

will fit you: your size was coded to us from London three weeks ago, you must wear them tonight.' She put her head on one side. 'They have to be black as I am sure you already know.' She narrowed her eyes and puckered her lips, 'But never mind, black will make you look *ravissante*.'

She turned to the wardrobe again and took a black dress from the rail and her face finally cracked into a smile. 'This one is reckless enough to allow the *Generaloberst* a peep at the pleasures awaiting him.' She laid the garment lovingly on the bed and put a dressing gown alongside it. 'It is time for your bath now.'

As Anna undressed she could hear the bath running. Soon, in the adjoining bathroom, she was immersed in scalding water. Every atom of fatigue and fear began to drain from her body as the heat crept into her — but, before long, she was trembling uncontrollably in the water. *I am not doing this for Major Coles — this is for Philippa and Geoffrey and Daddy.* Strength: that is what this thought gave her — and the comfort of knowing that, if she carried out this job successfully, she could well be given further opportunities.

The sound of a bony hand, rapping on the bathroom door: 'Time to get ready,' — a hoarse command — *adrenaline flooding*

— *heart jumping.* The old lady came into the bathroom with a large towel and watched Anna get out of the bath. She rubbed her back, followed her into the bedroom and helped her to dress. The feel of a claw-like hand, fumbling with tiny hooks between Anna's shoulder blades, brought back memories of the prelude to a painful loss of virginity in her rooms at Oxford.

The old lady held out the dress while Anna pulled on black stockings. 'What a pretty picture you make, my darling, so beautiful!' Half-closed eyes: 'The Generaloberst loves to meet new talent: last week he swore to me that he could die for a girl in black lingerie and smelling of *Le Jade.*' She gave Anna's wrist a reassuring squeeze, wheezing, 'Who are we to disappoint such an important man?' Her curled-back lip showed gold amongst blackened teeth.

Anna put on the dress. The old lady turned to the cupboard again, 'There is something else we must not forget.' She waved a large square of sticking plaster under Anna's nose — and it too went under the bed. She pinched Anna's cheek affectionately. 'Try not to dirty my sheets, *mon petit chou!*'

The old lady, whose name could never be revealed, peeped cautiously through the curtains of the big window. 'Do you see it there across the street, Claudine, that doorway with the coloured lights? The Generaloberst will not be late. As you know he always comes alone; a man of his rank cannot afford the scandal. I know him well; my girls are the ones who please him most.'

She put a caressing hand behind Anna's head and gave her a quick kiss on the lips. 'Good luck, my dear. Perhaps one day you will come and work for me when this fucking war is over. Now remember: if you have any trouble you must shout for me. I shall be on the other side of that door; I know how to deal with trouble.' She glanced quickly at the Holy Virgin and made the sign of the cross.

Dressed, perfumed and ready, Claudine darted across the street. She smiled at the doorman. The brass rail slid through her cold, sweating palm. In the dimly lit basement a thin man, white tuxedo hanging in folds, stepped from behind a velvet-clad pillar. '*Good evening. Are you looking for the engineer?*'

Anna had her answer ready: '*Never mind the engineer — give me a fat Spaniard with a thick wallet!*'

He steered her into a back office. There was a desk, a heavy safe in the corner, framed photographs of draped nudes. 'Welcome to La Cave, Claudine. My name is Bobo. The bull will be here soon. I will give you this signal . . . '

Anna found a swivelling stool by the bar. The barman lit her Gauloise — which she pretended to enjoy while vultures, coyly described by Major Coles as *girls-of-a-certain-type*, eyed the newcomer from their respective perches. A relaxed man, squinting at sheet music through eyes half-closed against the reek of a bent cheroot, worked an upright piano. Men drifted in from the street. Anna prepared to repel them, praying that her victim had not been delayed. By halfway through her second cigarette, eight couples were gyrating to muted rhythms, grappling in dry semblance of sexual union on a circular dance-floor.

Bobo unfolded his handkerchief. He dabbed his brow and gave a barely perceptible nod. The man was stoutly built, tall, heavy, thick-necked — there at the foot of the stairs. Could anyone seriously expect her to deal with this brute single-handed? Impeccably turned out in a well tailored civilian suit, yes — but big in every dimension.

Anna swivelled bravely. She hitched up enough skirt to reveal inches of suspender. A waiter showed Zaunbrecher to his table, hovering with an ice bucket. Anna looked away. A cork blew.

163

The waiter hurried towards her: 'Come with me, Claudine.' At the table he pulled out a second chair, 'This is the new girl, Herr Generaloberst.'

The man licked his lips and leaned towards her. 'You are a pretty thing but it is not just good looks that will amuse me tonight.'

In spite of his smart appearance the smell of his breath was nauseating; his French was clumsy and ungrammatical. She did not answer him straight away and took her time settling next to him. Re-enacting something she had been made to practise on Major Coles, she slid a hand along his thigh under cover of the table.

His response was quick; he poked a thick finger into the top of her stocking. 'They tell me you are called Claudine: a pretty name. You may call me Sigy.' She could feel a straining fly-button against her knuckle.

Zaunbrecher waved the waiter away. They drank toasts to each other but he had little patience for conversation, other than to say that he had one thousand francs for a girl who could make him happy.

★ ★ ★

In the big bedroom across the road, Generaloberst Zaunbrecher stripped off his

164

clothes. He folded them neatly and placed them on a chair. He lay back on the bed. His considerable anatomy was already stirring.

She took the ropes out of their bag and caressed his cheek with them. Now the revolting man began to demonstrate his appreciation more clearly as Anna busied herself with knots that she had been practising for the past ten days without knowing the reason: *right-over-left, left-over-right*. It took her three minutes to secure his hands and his feet to the cornerposts.

His eyes opened wider when she unbuttoned her dress and let it fall. She leant over him, the twin points of her tightly brassiered breasts brushed his thighs. 'You must be patient, Sigy, I have a little surprise for you tonight — it is a game I like to play. First the blindfold.'

'Blindfold? What blindfold? Didn't they tell you anything? How can I see you through a blindfold?'

In spite of his disappointment Zaunbrecher was having difficulty in controlling a flow of saliva from the corner of his mouth: 'I am expecting to pay you for this, Claudine, I choose the games here! What do you want me to do — die of frustration?'

Her laugh was genuine: 'You will not die from frustration — that I can promise — but

165

for the moment you must do as I say because you are tied to a bed. Do you want me to leave you here and go looking for another gentleman — would you like me to do that? You will enjoy this — it will be a new experience for you: if you do not like it I promise we will never play this game again.'

She quickly fastened the blindfold, then reached under the bed.

Zaunbrecher moved his head from side to side in an effort to dislodge the mask but she calmed him with a kiss which started on his lips, dragged across his cheek and ended on his left ear into which she whispered softly, 'I have something in my hand which is long and hard like you.'

'What is this game, Claudine?'

Anna held the blunt end with her right hand and cradled the point in her left. She extended an index finger and nudged the vital spot under his ribs. 'Be patient. First you must tell me how much you love me.'

'What's going on here? Of course I love you, do you hear, I love you, I love you. *Damn you!*'

Anna could hear a calm voice speaking to her. *Do any of you people know what OK stands for?* It was Sergeant Cox; what was he doing inside her head at a time like this? *If there are no takers I'll have to tell you, won't I? OK stands for Offal Kebab — the quickest death in the business.*

Anna glanced up at the Holy Virgin and saw signs of encouragement in that serene face. Then she spoke her last words to Zaunbrecher: *'Would you die for me, Sigy? Do you love me enough for that?'*

Zaunbrecher opened his mouth to answer — but no sound came. The spike was already travelling, *racing*, through his body. With every ounce of her weight behind it the sharp steel accelerated through colon, pancreas, stomach, liver, spleen; cutting and perforating in one long, vicious thrust.

Zaunbrecher jolted against the ropes. A long exhaling sigh bubbled in his throat.

Anna stood over him, choking back an overpowering excess of emotion. *She had killed an evil man, her first victim, her first act of retaliation . . .*

With a foot against his body she pulled against the suction. The spike unplugged an audible gush — the smell was mephitic: stomach contents, bile, blood, squirting into her navel, soaking her knickers, dribbling warm on her thigh.

She dropped the steaming weapon. The square of plaster would not stick and a crimson flood was draining from an unexpected hole in the corpse's left armpit. She shouted for help.

The old lady swung in silently from behind the door, threw down the hammer she was carrying, reached over and shut off both flows by pinching the wound-lips together with bony fingers and thumbs. 'Fetch towels from the bathroom — what a way to treat my best mattress!'

$\star$ $\star$ $\star$

Twenty-four hours later, under moonlight that cast a gleam on the grass, Anna lay on her stomach in the bottom of a hedge. The body was tightly wound in black cloth on the grass nearby.

She remembered something that Major Coles had said: *I'm afraid clearing up the debris goes with the job, Stobart. If the Gestapo find the Generaloberst's remains there will be embarrassing reprisals on the local population — the last time we slipped up on an operation like this they put fifty civilians to death.*

Anton was crouching three yards away. Three more men were out in the field to mark the landing place with torches.

She could *feel* the reassuring throb of a Bristol Mercury engine long before she could properly hear it. A Westland Lysander, single-engined, high-winged, wheel-spats like giant feet on splayed legs, silhouetted itself like a huge insect across the moon's disc. Anton stood up and flashed the letters AV with his torch, directing the beam through a cardboard tube for safety.

The Lysander's engine quietened. Now it was like the slow *thump-thump-thump* of a motorcycle on a mud road — then a barely audible tick as the aircraft dropped into the field like a falling leaf.

A man, trilby and suitcase, climbed down from the aircraft and walked quickly towards the trees. The three Frenchmen heaved Zaunbrecher's body through the baggage door. Anton gave Anna his parting kiss. Tears were on his face, they rolled into his beard like pearls from a broken necklace as he thrust a small parcel into her hand and gave her arm a squeeze.

'From a grateful Frenchman to a brave patriot — and there is something in there from an old lady who loves you. Think of us when you use these gifts.'

She stood on tiptoe, kissed him just above the beard, tucked the parcel under her arm and grabbed the sides of the metal ladder fixed to the side of the aircraft. Her bottom, touching the rear-facing seat behind the pilot, seemed to trigger an explosion of power from the engine.

The Lysander went up like a lift. Twenty minutes later they were over the Channel with silver waves below the wheel-spats. Anna opened her parcel. There was a neat bundle of soft material wrapped around a small bottle. By the moonlight that flooded through panels of perspex above her head she read the label:

* * *

Le Jade, Roger & Gallet, Paris.

She laughed. The bottle had been wrapped in a lusty pair of knickers cut from RAF parachute silk, but her laughter soon changed to hysterical sobs that racked her throat when she tried to suppress them.

On the ground at Tangmere, the pilot spoke to her for the first time; 'Have you heard the news? Keep it under your hat because it's hush-hush gen: the city of Hamburg is burning from end to end!'

* * *

Anna opened her eyes. It was dark. The traffic had gone quiet. Somewhere out there in the city of Lisbon a man called Robert McGuire would be sleeping soundly after his performance in a play called *French Without Tears* — completely unaware of the danger he was in.

★ ★ ★

In his hotel bedroom, twelve hundred miles away in Dartmouth, Karl Deichman lay awake — not from the pain in his head — but because he was worried that, if he managed to get a call through to Lisbon tomorrow morning, Robert might not take his warning seriously.

171

12

On Saturday mornings Robert McGuire usually lay in bed until after ten o'clock. Today was no different. Although his eyes were closed he was mentally running through his part in the play. During last night's performance of *French Without Tears* he had missed a cue right at the beginning of Act Three — and he wanted to make sure that he didn't make the same mistake tonight. Robert had been appearing regularly in Lisbon's only amateur English-speaking theatre since just after the war and, as far as he could remember, had never made a mistake like that before. He went through his part, line by line, from the beginning of the play until the end — and then started again.

It was the smell of strong coffee from the kitchen that finally got him out of bed. He steered his feet into a pair of waiting slippers, hoping that no urgent translation work would interrupt his weekend. He thought too about his forthcoming visit to England, well aware of the ever present worry that one day soon his father would be forced to retire and then expect his only son to take over the business.

This presented a problem because Robert could not imagine himself serving behind the counter of an English wine shop in a small town in Devon.

He padded downstairs in his dressing-gown, picked up his *Diario de Noticias* from the doormat and, on the way up, heard movement in the kitchen. He put his head around the door. 'Bom dia, Ludovina.'

The girl turned. She was small and neat, long dark hair hanging halfway to her waist. Her smile showed an attractive hint of shyness but for those lucky enough to know her, and there had been a few, Ludovina was far from shy.

Her voice was low-pitched but child-like. 'Bom dia, Roberto, meu amor.'

Sometimes Robert wondered if it wasn't time for a change now that she had started calling him 'My Love.'

Ludovina had her own bedroom in the flat but didn't always spend the night there. She was a skilful lover — the result of some early training by a lady called Dona Fatima — but fear of a long-term commitment sometimes prevented Robert from satisfying Ludovina's hunger for sex. On Sundays she usually spent the night at her parents' house in Sacavem, but on her return to the flat on Monday mornings she had a knack of knowing if

Robert had been entertaining other women over the weekend: they were well-founded suspicions which often had the effect of making her smoulder for days like damp gunpowder.

Robert gave her a quick kiss on the cheek and poured himself a cup of coffee. He went through to the adjoining room and started to read the newspaper. There were the usual news reports about British involvement in the Korean war; some equally predictable coverage on the prosperity of Portuguese colonies in Africa so that when Ludovina placed a plate of scrambled egg in front of him, he was quite ready to abandon the news in favour of breakfast.

Last night the girl had slept in her own room and only now did she remember to tell Robert about last night's telephone calls — two of them — which had come while he had been at the theatre.

'Um senhor telefonou ontem a tarde, um senhor chamado Carlos. Uma *mulher* telefonou ontem a noite tambem . . . '

Robert was only half listening: a man called Carlos had telephoned yesterday afternoon and (oh dear) so had a woman later on in the evening . . . both callers had spoken in English . . . and the man had been phoning from England. Ludovina said she had understood very little apart from the fact that the man called Carlos had promised to ring again in the morning — *this* morning. Naturally she had very little to say about the woman.

Robert ate his breakfast thoughtfully. He knew three or four people called Carlos but he couldn't imagine any of them wanting to telephone him from England of all places. *Muito importante*, Ludo had claimed — and it must have been to warrant an expensive telephone call from abroad. No, Robert couldn't think of anything important that a man called Carlos would want to say to him. Still in his dressing gown he got up from the table and went out onto the balcony with his coffee. Ludovina never got things wrong, so who was this man?

The sun was already high above a jagged horizon of Lisbon rooftops; the air was cool. Only the distant crow of a cock and the rumble of a tram, steel-on-steel, broke the peace. On the pavement below, a man on crutches was selling lottery tickets to a group of waiting passengers, and seeing him there reminded Robert of his father again.

Dad had always claimed that if it hadn't been for the German battleship *Blucher* bombarding the Yorkshire coast on a bleak November morning in 1914, Robert — by a devious chain of events — would never have been brought up by his Portuguese grand-mother in Ireland and would never have learned the Portuguese language from her. It was this knowledge of Portuguese that had brought him here.

He looked at the ornate architecture of the Museu de Arte Antiga across an intervening jumble of roofing and felt thankful that this country was his home now; it felt natural. *It also felt safe.*

Over the sound of clattering plates coming from the open door of the kitchen, Ludovina wheedled: 'Roberto, quando vamos a praia?'

He came in from the balcony wondering why she had asked him to teach her English and now refused to practise it. Yes, it was tempting; and of course he already knew what lying with Ludo on a deserted beach was like — a day with Eve in the Garden of Eden — something like that — but these recent displays of jealousy were making him increasingly cautious about allowing the relationship to become more intense.

He was in the middle of contriving an excuse for not going to the beach when the telephone rang. He picked up the receiver and heard the operator announce a call from England, warning that the line was bad. A man's voice came through a stormy back-ground speaking in German. It was Karl

Deichman — he hadn't heard from him for more than a year.

The line crackled and buzzed: Karl Deichman was over in England for the first time since the war, trying to find out about that cousin of his, the one whom he believed had been in Britannia College at the time of the raid. Robert told him, in German of course, what he had told him several times before: nothing — he knew nothing about it.

But it soon became clear that this wasn't the reason for the call: 'I have just met a girl over here in England, her name is Anna Stobart, I had tea with her on Thursday. I tried to telephone you last night but whoever it was that answered didn't understand what I was saying.'

Robert could feel a slight tightening in the chest as Karl continued: 'This woman appears to be bitter about the fact that some of her relations were killed during the war — it seems to have given her some kind of phobia against us — Britain's former enemies I mean — I believe she could be dangerous.'

Robert let him continue, trying to guess what was coming.

'She's bought an air ticket to Lisbon and I think she may try to contact you. She knows that you were working for us in Dartmouth . . . '

'How did she discover that, Karl?'

Robert listened to his explanation with growing anger. It had been Karl's quest for knowledge about the aftermath of Operation Herod that had made him do it — agreeing some exchange of information with this Stobart woman. 'Do you mean to tell me that you told her I was the Dartmouth agent at the time of Operation Herod — and where I live now — you told her that too?'

'I told her you live in Lisbon, I didn't give her your address.'

The unfettered stupidity of the man made Robert want to explode with rage, but instead he attempted to defuse the tension by using an old technique of questioning, something learned during his espionage training: *number one rule — establish in detail what the man looked like*. It was a woman this time so it was going to be a lot more fun. Before he had completed asking the set pattern of questions, Robert was beginning to warm to the emerging picture.

He put down the receiver and sat on a low stool by the telephone dangling a slipper from his left toe. Karl Deichman of all people — the spy-master from Hamburg had blown his cover. Those five years working as a spy had taught Robert that giving away this kind of information usually meant trouble. Unsatisfactory as it was, he would just have to accept the situation and prepare himself for a confrontation with an unknown — but now easily recognised — Anna Stobart.

He remained sitting on the stool considering the situation: he was the only McGuire in Lisbon, the only resident of that name in the whole of Portugal. He could be very easily found. On the other hand, the thought of an attractive woman from England seeking him out like this, had its lighter side. He was, after all, quite used to dealing with women: angry, moody, selfish or even dangerous — it didn't matter as long as they were pretty, attractive, beautiful or better still, promiscuous and uninhibited. If this Anna Stobart was half as good as her description . . . he thought about it for a minute: yes, it had the makings of an exciting challenge, especially now that Ludovina had become so possessive. Miss Anna Stobart — hopefully she *was* still a *miss* — would dislike him at first — and that added an interesting twist to the challenge.

A glance at his watch reminded him that he had things to do: a lunch appointment with Vasco Simões and some other business on the way to the restaurant. He shaved, dressed and looked into the kitchen to say goodbye to Ludovina.

The girl turned to face him; her housecoat was unbuttoned. 'Olha! You are liking it, Roberto!'

Underneath the coat she was naked but for two diminutive scraps of cloth that Robert had bought for her in London's Shaftesbury Avenue during last year's visit to England; a persuasive male shopkeeper had managed to convince him that this was the last word in fashion swimwear for ladies, first seen on French beaches in the summer of 1947. The unusual style, according to him, had been named after one of America's atom-bomb test sites for obvious reasons.

Ludovina giggled, dropped the coat and turned round to show him the back-view. Robert's mouth went dry: *black plait crossing a thin strap under her shoulder-blades; material cleaving rounded fruit further down.* He tried to ignore his instincts at that moment because they were saying: *marry the girl; give up your ungovernable quest for sexual variety.*

She looked at him over one shoulder through half-lowered eyelashes. 'Quando vamos a praia, Roberto?'

Robert took a step back: *praia, praia, praia* — that was all this woman ever talked about.

He turned and retreated down the stairs blurting false promises about taking her there: tomorrow we'll go to the beach; some time soon I'll take you to the beach; yes, of course I'll take you to the beach; perhaps next weekend, the beach.

He slammed the front door behind him and set off along the cobbled pavement. Although it was still cool he was already sweating. He walked fast with his jacket hanging over his shoulder towards Dona Fatima's establishment, a good fifteen minute walk in the direction of the restaurant.

He was slightly out of breath by the time he had turned into Travessa da Conceição. He rang the bell of number thirty-four and waited for the familiar sound of the latch being pulled back by somebody at the top of the stairs using a long string threaded through a tortuous arrangement of brass loops.

He stepped into the stone-flagged hallway. Dona Fatima was leaning over the banisters, stretching her plump arms in welcome. 'Bem-vindo, Amigo Roberto!'

Halfway up the stairs he heard the promising sound of giggles coming from behind a closed bedroom door — but he couldn't help noticing that the paint on it was beginning to blister. Through the archway at

181

the end of the passage he saw that an expensive fall of plaster had scattered itself across one of the billiard tables.

Fatima was a big woman: over-pencilled and well past her prime, but she clasped him strongly — *hopefully? God forbid!* — to her well braced bosom, then steered him into her private sitting room where she opened the usual cupboard and picked up a decanter of clear fluid in one hand and two small glasses in the other. When she removed the stopper it was with care so as not to damage her spectacular finger-nails: 'Queres tomar um aperitivo, meu amigo?'

That perfume she wore always reminded Robert of Fatima's particular style of generosity, granted to him regularly a long time ago when he had been too busy to spend valuable time courting women — but the sweetness of her scent was soon overpowered by the reek of raw alcohol when he raised his glass.

The business that they had set up together in 1943 was alive, but not as well as it might be. After the usual lament over the gradual and persistent fall in turnover — and a quick look at the accounts — Dona Fatima unscrewed her fountain-pen, wrote a cheque — a small one — and gave it to Robert. He signed a receipt for it which she stowed in a wall-safe hidden behind a faded photograph of the statue of Eros in London's Piccadilly Circus.

Fatima spoke Portuguese in a voice that had been compromised by nicotine in early life: 'Are you still happy with Ludovina, Roberto?'

He thought for a moment, then confessed his fears about the girl's frequent displays of jealousy.

Dona Fatima winked a sticky eyelid. 'But don't you understand Roberto? Girls are jealous creatures: nature makes them so. Ludovina is in love with you, and when a girl is in love with a man she will kill to prevent another coming between. If you need a change you must let me know, but don't get rid of that girl if she still makes you happy. Forgive me, amigo Roberto, you have heard me say this many times before but it is good advice — believe me, I know about such things!'

Robert nodded: she knew about such things all right but evidently not enough to keep that door-latch clicking with the frequency that it once had.

Fatima's almost tearful smile propelled a flake of dried face-cream onto his lapel. 'It's not like it used to be, Roberto, meu amor. The few customers that come now may have money but they have no soul, no heart — no *love* any more — not like the brave lads who came here to find comfort in the old days. I have a drawerful of old letters from my boys — and photographs of their wives and children. It makes me so sad because they never write their addresses.' She made a face like a French bulldog: 'Men are so cruel! You are a man, Roberto, tell me why men are so cruel!'

★ ★ ★

By the time Robert had caught sight of the three distinctive spires of Basilica da Estrela, he was sweating again, but this time it was from the long walk. The sun was almost overhead but he still had time in hand.

Rather than wait in a stuffy restaurant for Vasco he went into the Jardim da Estrela, strolled in the shade of cool trees and sat on a bench under a weeping-willow close to where the statue of a naked woman peered thoughtfully at her own reflection in the pond.

Madame Fatima: the unsung heroine. Quietly, and without fuss, she had long ago saved the lives of several thousand sailors. Sad to think that she should be left to live out her days forgotten by a certain foreign government to whom she had provided so much valuable help in the past . . .

Robert sat there for a long time looking at the statue. Wars must have produced thousands of unlikely heroines over the centuries but probably none quite like Madame Fatima — who had never professed to be perfect but had just got on with her job of making people happy and keeping them so. The sudden thought of one of her imperfections made Robert take the cheque from his wallet to make sure she had remembered to sign it.

The cry of a peacock interrupted his thoughts: Vasco would be at the restaurant by now. He got up off the bench, dodged traffic as he crossed Rua Sao Jorge, walked beside the high wall of the British Cemetery, turned the corner into Rua Coelho da Rocha and found his friend already ordering from the menu.

★ ★ ★

Later that evening, while Robert was applying the clothes brush to a blazer lent to the Lisbon Players by the British Naval Attaché, Iris from box-office — capable, rather fat and over forty — stuck her head round the green-room door with one of her loaded smiles.

185

'Ah there you are, Rob. A young person by the name of Penny Arrowsmith was asking after you last night when she booked her ticket — she's at the bar talking to Ed.'

Robert kept his face dead-pan, just like Lieutenant Commander Rogers was supposed to do for most of the time in *French Without Tears*. 'Penny Arrowsmith? Can't say it rings a bell.'

'Well I don't know! If she doesn't ring your bell, your bell must have lost its clapper. She's a little smasher, early thirties, smashing figure, smashing smile, smashing hair and dress sense — *and I hate her already!*

It was with relief, a couple of hours later, that Robert came offstage when the curtain closed at the end of the last act. In spite of the distraction of somebody who now called herself Penny Arrowsmith somewhere out there in the audience — he had not forgotten a single line.

Ed Draper came into the green room while Robert was still removing his make up. 'You weren't half bad tonight, Robert, and I've had a field-day selling drinks in the bar. Met a fan of yours: she's read your life history in the programme and wants to meet you. I've asked her to stay behind for the cast party.'

★ ★ ★

Short, good figure, long black hair like Ludovina's, arched eyebrows, shape of mouth as expected — *calling herself Penny Arrowsmith, sipping her drink, green eyes over the rim of her gin and tonic: yes, it all fitted . . .*

Her voice too: educated, low-pitched, saying, 'I know your name already; I looked you up in the programme. Were you really a founder-member of this club in 1947?'

Flirting — *but why? Let her continue . . .*

'As you have lived over here for so long, Robert, I was wondering if I could ask you a few questions for an article I'm writing for the newspaper I work for in England.'

Christian names already . . . ?

'By the way, were you really drunk in that scene — the one when you all come back from the night club wearing fancy dress?'

Robert was looking at her lower lip: *kissable . . . How long had she been rehearsing that line?* 'You're the third person who's asked me that — talking of alcohol, have you met our producer, Vasco Simões? He's giving a barbecue lunch tomorrow for the whole cast. I'm sure he wouldn't mind if you gatecrashed. Have you ever tasted grilled sardines?' Robert offered to give her a lift there and added, 'I have to read holy scripture from Saint Paul's Epistle to the

Romans tomorrow morning at St George's Church so I'll be setting off after that.' He scribbled something in his pocket diary and tore out the page. 'Show this to a taxi driver in the morning. Infidels usually wait for me in the churchyard if they don't want to pray. Try to make it there by twelve, otherwise I'll assume you have changed your mind.'

Walking home later under the street lights of Lisbon, he knew that he would have to be careful in spite of the anticipated fun.

If Karl was right, and she really had come all this way to confront him over her war grievances, then it was just possible that Anna Stobart — alias Penny Arrowsmith — could be dangerous.

13

Karl awoke in the Royal Castle Hotel. He found it difficult to raise his head off the pillow and realised at once that he was feeling a lot worse: he still had the headache but now it was accompanied by an intermittent throbbing at the back of the head and a slight inclination to vomit. *But . . . why call the doctor — just for a touch of influenza?*

But it wasn't only that which was worrying him. Unwittingly he had placed a potential hazard in the path of Robert McGuire. He lay thinking about the warning — would Robert take it seriously? Was Anna Stobart dangerous? If so would Robert McGuire expose himself to that danger? It seemed incredible that a perfectly ordinary conversation with a woman in Brixham should lead to this: the responsibility of it weighed heavy. The line had been good enough, the message had got through but would he take it to heart? Only time would tell — but how much time would she give him?

Karl closed his eyes against the pulse in his head which had now settled to a sustained rhythm.

*   *   *

Anna arrived outside St George's Anglican church after a terrifying taxi ride across Lisbon. She walked through iron gates set in a high wall and strolled up a paved pathway under the shadow of overhanging trees where bees worked noisily amongst the flowers.

The service had already started: through the open door of the church she could hear English voices singing: *All people that on earth do dwell . . .*

She left the main path and strolled along narrower tracks where stone crosses of different sizes, some of them green with moss and no longer vertical, cropped up irregularly amongst well-kept box hedges. *Philippa was with her — talking from somewhere inside her head: Anna was glad of her company — she enjoyed sharing the sights and sounds of new places with her sister.*

She wandered amongst graves reading headstones of British people who had chosen to live out their lives in this country. One of the tombs was much bigger than any of the others: a huge marble casket set on an impressive rectangular plinth with a lengthy inscription set into stonework.

Henrici Fielding . . . Ultimam aspexit lucem.
MDCCLIV aetatis XLVII . . .

Difficult to read the metal lettering, corroded and darkening the surrounding stone; difficult to understand it all — but at least she knew enough Latin to realise that this was the tomb of Henry Fielding, died in 1754, aged forty-seven.

Quotations: she knew so many, learned in childhood. Fielding — something about death? Perhaps this . . . *It hath often been said, that it is not death, but dying, which is terrible.* It was like a prophesy — the dying of McGuire was going to be terrible.

Anna slipped in through the West door and stood behind the seated congregation. Her intended victim was at the lectern reading from the New Testament; he caught her eye as he glanced up from the page: '*For the wages of sin is death; but the gift of God is eternal life through Jesus Christ our Lord.*'

She went outside again to wait for the service to end — hoping that, before the day was done, McGuire would have received *his* wages of sin and would be experiencing the beginnings of an eternal life somewhere unbearably hot and vile. To make this happen she would have to become intimate with the man, preferably without interruption from doting theatre people at a crowded barbecue.

Anna was standing in the shadow of a tree a few yards from the door when McGuire emerged with the rest of the congregation; she could see him looking for her. 'Hello Penny, so you came after all.'

'Did you think I'd forget?'

'When I overheard Ed telling you about his yacht last night I thought you might change your mind. By the way, I meant to tell you to bring your bathing suit because Vasco has turned an irrigation pond at his farm into a swimming pool.'

All that careful packing — and then forgetting the obvious . . . but Robert was already muttering something about having to go back to the flat anyway.

His two-seater was parked in the road under the shade of a Judas tree. As they travelled through cobbled streets, lined on either side by ancient terraces, Anna thought about the plan she had worked out yesterday while sitting under the dryer at the hair salon: *suicide* . . . *the balance of his mind — upset by the burden of guilt* . . . and now, by a lucky chance, she had an opportunity to reconnoitre the flat.

Robert parked on the pavement, clear of the tram-lines; he entered a doorway and led her up a flight of stone steps. The flat: *living room; balcony leading off with high parapet; kitchen.* 'If you want to powder your nose it's through there.' Looking for the bathroom she opened the door to a bedroom: *double bed; shower cubicle leading off.*

Walking back along the corridor she saw McGuire rummaging through a chest of drawers in another room; he had changed into a pair of khaki trousers and a crumpled linen jacket. When he heard her behind him he spoke without looking up. 'It should be here somewhere, that's if . . . '

He continued to ransack drawers and cupboards, all of which appeared to be full of women's clothes. Then he turned to face her holding up a handful of red cloth. Anna disentangled the top and bottom halves of a two-piece bathing suit and held them up, one in each hand. 'Who do these belong to? I'd somehow formed the impression that you lived alone.'

'They belong to Ludovina, she won't be needing them today.'

'Who is Ludovina?'

'My housekeeper: she doesn't mind lending things because she's that sort of person. Anyway, if she wore that in public she'd be taken in for questioning by the Maritime Police. I know this is supposed to be 1950 but bare tummies, male or female, are technically illegal on Portuguese beaches.'

First complication: housekeeper. 'Does this housekeeper of yours live here all the time?'

'She does, but guaranteed never on a Sunday.'

Anna looked at the doll-sized garment and read the label: 'Marco Bellini, Milan and Paris. Your housekeeper is obviously a woman of taste but I'm not sure that I want to get myself into trouble with the Portuguese Maritime Police.'

'We'll be on Vasco's private property so you'll be okay.'

★ ★ ★

Robert put down the hood of his car and they drove to the docks. They boarded a ferry and crossed the river Tagus. Soon they were travelling fast along a winding shelf cut into a steep cliff face with endless views of rocky hills dipping steeply to the sea. Wherever the coastline made an inward curve, Anna could also see small pockets of empty sand in abandoned coves.

The lunch party . . . the friends of Vasco Simões . . . not a good idea. She had to shout. 'Don't those little beaches look heavenly — there couldn't be any maritime policemen down there surely — can't imagine how you get there though.' When he told her the only way was by boat she removed her headband and let her hair stream in the wind: 'I wish we had a boat!'

In Sesimbra they drove between rows of whitewashed cottages overlooking the harbour. Robert negotiated with a fisherman, bought prawns, salad and wine. They loaded their picnic into the boat and were soon sailing across glass-clear water towards a remote beach. They sat together in the bow while a man called Umberto steered them past a village on the south side of the Arrábida hills.

They waded, waist-deep: clothes and picnic things held above their heads while Umberto turned the boat and headed away.

They swam; lay in the sun; spread Robert's Ambre Solaire over each other to stop themselves burning. He was very thorough. As his hands negotiated around the small areas covered by Ludovina's bikini, she was trying to keep old memories of the university professor away. When she turned onto her tummy he noticed the burn-marks.

She tried to be dismissive about them: 'Nothing much — just an accident — shall I do you now?'

When she saw how easily he became

aroused Anna realised the job might be easier than she had anticipated: *but not here on the beach. Kiss, embrace, gain his confidence, stimulate his appetite, but no sex . . . not yet.* Soon she was having to deflect his attention away from it with carefully prepared questions: life in the capital city of Portugal; cost of living; the social life of the emigrant — all on the pretext of gathering material for a fictitious newspaper . . .

The sun was dropping towards the Arrábida hills when they stepped off the boat and climbed back into the car. McGuire carelessly threw the half-empty, straw-covered flagon into the space behind the seats which made Anna realise that while she had been taking frequent dips in the sea to avoid his embrace, he had been drinking heavily. The man was drunk: conveniently so; perhaps sufficiently drunk for him to have lowered his guard.

Robert negotiated the mountain road with a lot less care than he had shown on the outward journey — and he was singing a Portuguese song that Anna didn't understand.

After an erratic boarding of the ferry, McGuire slumped back in his seat and made slurred suggestions: 'Back to the flat for a shower; toy with a crisp sardine in a little place I know; drink some decent wine — unlike the piss they sell in Sesimbra. My father happens to be a wine merchant, has a shop over in England — did you know that, Penny old thing? Stuff he sells is a bloody site better . . . Where was I? Oh yes: after supper we'll come back to my flat and marvel at the etchings therein.'

Her plan was already made. Anna knew that this would be her only chance: Robert McGuire's life was as good as ended; he was about to enter his flat for the last time.

He put his arm around her as they climbed the stairs. It reminded Anna of the night she had lured Generaloberst Zaunbrecher to his death — but this time she did not expect to be awarded the Croix de Guerre. He showed her into the room with the double bed and gave her a large towel. 'You can undress in here. Give me a shout when you're ready and I'll show you how the shower works.'

She stripped — and, for the first time that day, found herself submitting to that familiar tremble of anticipation she always experienced before a big event. She fumbled in her handbag, found the bottle and kept splashing *Le Jade* onto her throat until the fumes seemed to form a cloud inside her head: *she could see a large man, tied to a bed, struggling, dying, jerking against restraining ropes . . .*

She unzipped the inner pocket of her handbag and unfolded a small square of tissue paper . . .

The shower was a gas-heated model with a head like a large watering can. She stood under it wondering how to work the taps.

Robert came up behind her, naked, pressing himself against her back and reached past . . . the gas ignited noisily. A steaming monsoon rained down alternately hot and tepid as the ancient geyser struggled to find equilibrium.

She grabbed the soap and turned to face him: moulded herself against him; lathering his chest; working down his body, relieved to find that he was ready for her.

With her arms around his neck she pulled her soapy body to his, lifting her feet from the floor. McGuire clasped his hands together under her bottom to take her weight. She bent her knees, pressed the soles of her feet to the wall either side of him, scissored him between her legs, pushed back a few inches then . . . very gently and slowly . . . lowered herself onto him, impaling herself. *Her lips were on his mouth.*

She flexed — rocked — quickened — slowed under the geyser's unreliable torrent. Teeth clenched, lips pressing; stomach slapping . . . slow — fast — pause — and then . . .

The first signals: welling from somewhere deep — building like a wave. *Tongue the capsule; move it from the fold of the cheek; be ready — wait* . . . McGuire's mouth was still tightly shut.

She continued: her body was in control; the wave was rising up, up, gathering speed, curling, breaking . . .

McGuire opened his mouth. Anna stabbed into it with her tongue, propelled the capsule into the angle of his jaw: *snatch back the hand from behind his head; a fist; a tooth-shattering upper-cut to the chin.* His jaw snapped shut with the impact. His hands parted, his arms fell slack — terror and disbelief showed as he fell back against the wall — still upright — but dying, eyeballs rolled back to the whites, gasps for air louder than the roar of the geyser . . .

Anna waited for twenty-two seconds, watching him lose his fight for life as the water rained down.

Still propped against the wall McGuire's body twisted and slid down the tiles. Half-crouching now, grotesque: emptying his lungs with a choking howl, he toppled heavily onto his side.

Anna turned off the shower. The flame gave a dying pop. She stood over him with water running off her body and splashing onto his twitching legs. She half hoped that he might still be able to hear her as she quoted aloud: '*Down, down to hell; and say I sent thee thither.*' Although the man was obviously dead, she couldn't resist another comment of her own: '*And stoke that fire for your friend Karl Deichman who will soon be joining you!*'

Anna stepped out of the shower, dried herself and dressed urgently. She was anxious to clear the flat in case *Ludo-something-or-other* should return early.

14

The air was warm and damp under the street lights. Anna breathed deeply, it helped her to keep calm.

Ludovina — that was the name *(Philippa had just reminded her of it)*. Ludovina was probably already on her way back from ... she couldn't remember. That woman (girl?) would let herself into the flat and find her employer dead in the shower. What then? Call a doctor. *Cyanide.* What would the police make of it? They would examine the body — a bruise on the chin: could it have happened when his body hit the floor? Ludovina would have an alibi backed up by her parents in ... Sacavem, *(yes, Sacavem)*. Suicide would be the favourite conclusion, even though the coroner — if they had coroners in this country — might be hard pressed to find a motive in the secret past of this man. Even after the post-mortem and the cross-examination of Ludovina, nobody would suspect a *Penny Arrowsmith* or even an *Anna Stobart*.

She turned the corner and continued up the street, thrilled to think that those who saw her now were unaware of what she had just done. The traitor would no doubt be laid to rest in the British Cemetery — somewhere near Henry Fielding perhaps — and he would need an appropriate epitaph from the repertoire: something from Hamlet might suit an actor. As she turned the corner into Avenida Don Carlos, it came to her: *I am justly killed with my own treachery*: chiselled into his headstone, it would serve as a warning to others.

After a long walk Anna pushed her way through the revolving doors of the hotel. She was in a mood to celebrate her victory. Earlier she had noticed a poster behind the receptionist's desk but hadn't bothered to read it until now: *Nuno Oliveira e os Famosos Forcados de Santarem* — illustrated by a bull's head the size of a buffalo. There was nothing else that needed to be done other than book a flight to London, but the BEA office was closed on Sundays.

The balding receptionist saw her looking at the poster: 'You would like me to get you a ticket for tonight? It is a warm evening; there are new floodlights in the Campo Pequeno.'

She asked the meaning of the word *forcados* but the receptionist politely advised her to go there and find out for herself.

By the time Anna had found her allotted

place on a long, curving, concrete step high in the crowded bowl — and had seated herself on a hired cushion — the opening parade was already leaving the ring. She had a perfect view of a wide circle of sand, now being raked smooth in preparation for the first event. All around, tightly packed rows of spectators were jammed shoulder-to-shoulder, excited and chattering.

A fanfare, an unintelligible announcement over loudspeakers and a horseman in eighteenth century costume cantered into the ring through a tunnel on the far side and stopped in front of an open-air opera box beneath a draped flag; he saluted by removing his tricorn hat. A man in a black tuxedo waved acknowledgement.

The rider turned and cantered in slow, rocking-horse motion to the side of the ring; two fearsome harpoons, brightly decorated with paper streamers, were handed up to him.

A large black bull with horns sheathed in leather, galloped into the ring — alert, head up, looking for trouble. He skidded to a halt confused by the cheers and floodlights while a colourfully dressed man, standing behind the barrier that formed an inner circle around the edge of the ring, trailed a pink cape over the stockade to attract the bull's attention.

The bull saw it. He put his head down and charged; the cape was whisked away; the bull violently butted the barrier in frustration, pawing the ground and sending sprays of sand flying back. Another cape caught his eye, held by a man who had ventured into the ring. The bull charged, the man side-stepped, the bull turned, charged again — and again . . .

The horseman had been watching, motion-less. Now he cantered in slow-motion to the centre of the ring — harpoons, one in each hand — held high. He shouted to the bull, inviting him to charge: '*Touro! Oh touro bravo! Venha, venha ca!*'

The animal spun to face the challenge; he lowered his head and scooped more sand — then charged, head down, but horse and rider were already moving swiftly away. The rider held up the vicious sticks with both hands and the apparently unguided horse cantered slowly forward. Another charge but, as the bull brushed past, the rider stabbed both prongs into his shoulder. The barbs broke away from their wooden handles leaving red ribbons and blood to mark where they were embedded while the crowd roared approval.

The bull continued to obey his instincts: charging this thing that was attacking him

— not knowing that the leather sheaths on his horns would make it impossible for him to kill his enemy.

Zaunbrecher, the bull — killed by a long prong of steel — his death had been quick. How was this bull going to die — would it be here on the sand in front of her?

Another challenge, another charge — and another dose of iron: another and another. Loss of blood was sapping the bull's energy — but now, because he was moving slower, he could check earlier and turn sooner when he felt the barbs strike. He was beginning to catch the horse more frequently — sometimes lifting its hind feet of the ground as it ran away.

The other bull had been tied to a bed — he could not move — but there was a difference — he had been guilty — this bull was innocent . . .

A fanfare sounded. The horseman proudly removed his hat and galloped round to enraptured applause. The bull stood in the centre of the ring, bleeding, panting, tongue lolling. The gates leading to the tunnel opened and the steaming, spur-raked horse carried its rider out of the arena.

Another fanfare and an announcement: 'Os forcados de Santarem.' Eight young men vaulted over the barrier. The applause confused the bull who looked around, unsure where the new challenge was coming from. At first he did not see the colourful men with their green woollen night-caps, red waistcoats and brown knee-breeches. The men walked towards the bull in a line, one behind the other; the man at the front, smaller than the others, walked with a swagger, chest out, hands on hips. He stopped close to the watching bull and jumped up and down, shouting to attract his attention: 'Touro bravo, touro bonito, lindo touro, venha ca!'

The bull took a few trotting paces towards the sound and stopped.

'Touro! Touro! Touro!'

He could see a man standing in front of him — a man who was not running away and who took another step forward, and another until he was no more than ten feet away. More scooped sand, another shout — and another pace forward . . .

The bull's half-ton body closed the gap like a locomotive. The man, who by now had advanced forward from the rest of the line, took two swift backward paces; the bull's head slammed his chest; the man grabbed the bull's horns, one in each hand; the bull ran wildly in uncontrollable, violent rage — through the line of *forcados* who tripped and fell in a tangle of knee-breeches while the bull threw his head up and down, again and again, up and down, trying to shake off the strange creature that was grimly clinging to his head. The man lost his grip, cartwheeled into the air and fell heavily on the sand.

The bull turned quickly to gore the fallen man with his impotent horns but was distracted by men scrambling to their feet all around.

The team withdrew and re-formed. The challenger was back in front, hatless and covered in sand — a river from his nose was splashing red onto his shirt but he had not lost his swagger; hands back on hips: 'Touro, mata-me!'

Kill me? But could he? Could he really kill this man who showed no sign of surrender? The bull charged again. The man took the full impact — and held on. The bull careered around the ring, unable to see where he was going, swinging his head as before, up and down and side to side — but this time he could not dislodge the man.

As the pace slowed another man grabbed the bull's tail; another clung around his neck; some linked arms across the animal's bloody back. The bull stopped — he was finished with these people.

The men stepped back, held up their arms,

bowed to the applause, vaulted over the barrier; they were safe. The bull stood exhausted with head lowered.

The gate to the tunnel opened. Eight bell-ringing cows and a herdsman carrying a long pole entered the ring. The bull, recognising his own kind at last, joined the cows and was herded out through the tunnel to await slaughter.

Anna Stobart had seen enough. It had been a cruel business, an unequal contest. All her earlier feelings of elation had abandoned her: she was depressed — she was the only one to descend the concrete steps leading to the exit. Behind her she could hear another fanfare, another roar from the crowd — like hounds catching the scent of blood.

She took a taxi back to the hotel, thinking about Zaunbrecher. This bull had fought bravely — and lost; he had wanted revenge — but had failed. What chance did he have with just his instincts and his padded horns? *The other bull had been different.*

But there was still one more man to kill before her act of revenge was complete. Anna was confident: brute strength she did not have, but guile she had — and weapons she had at her disposal: deadly weapons — and her hands were those of a trained killer, Sergeant Cox had seen to that . . .

At the hotel she took the lift to the seventh floor restaurant still busy with diners. She picked up the menu — but made a point of avoiding beef.

★ ★ ★

On Monday morning Anna woke early, anxious to arrange her flight to England. Seeing McGuire dying like that from the lightning effect of a wartime suicide pill had made her impatient. She must deal with the other victim without delay — preferably before he left Dartmouth for his home in Molenstrasse Dusseldorf. She owed it to herself *(and Philippa of course, and the other two who sometimes spoke to her)*. Get it over quickly — and get on with living . . .

Following directions from the hall porter, she walked urgently down Avenida Fontes Pereira de Melo. Again there was heat in the morning sun and Anna was wet with sweat by the time she got to the Portuguese Airways office in Avenida de Liberdade.

At the ticket office the clerk was evasive when she asked if there was space on a flight to England — but was positive enough once he had seen her passport: *there was nothing.* The clerk was polite and apologetic, but quite certain that there were no seats left on TAP

572, the only service to England that day. He suggested she try the British Airways Lockheed Constellation, due to pick up passengers at Lisbon tomorrow afternoon on its return flight from South America — and scheduled to arrive in London at 8.10 p.m. local time on Tuesday evening.

After a visit to British Airways, and with the BOAC ticket to London safely in her handbag, Anna walked at a more leisurely pace down Avenida da Liberdade to the city-centre. The Café Suisse had a dozen tables out on the pavement under a green awning. She sat there in the shade and ordered a tall orange juice.

The cold glass numbed her hand. The light breeze was cool on her body. She needed a *plan* for Deichman. Cyanide had worked well on the traitor but both her capsules were now used up. She sucked juice through a neatly trimmed wheat straw while black-and-green taxis jostled in a whirlpool around Praça Rossio. She leant back; pigeons competed for space on the head of a Portuguese king standing tall on his stone column. There were crowds on the pavement on the far side of the road, and it was something behind them that started a new train of thought.

Deichman's wife went missing in Hamburg. What was her name — Helga? Suppose Helga were *still alive.* She thought about the photograph, the one that fell onto the carpet just before he spilled his tea.

Anna abandoned the straw, drained the orange juice and spat out a pip. With the freezing sensation still in her gullet she hissed at the waiter in the Portuguese way, paid her bill and darted across the road without waiting for her change. A taxi nearly collided with her before she had reached the safety of the far pavement. She entered a shop set in an ornate frontage . . .

Out on the street again, half an hour later, Anna had her plan for the execution of Karl Deichman. If he had already gone home it wouldn't matter: there were plenty of regular flights to Germany now and the basic idea would still work even if she had to go over there and find him.

Stuck in Portugal for another day, she was determined not to let impatience spoil her enjoyment: there was nothing to worry about now; she had left no trace of evidence to link her with the death of Robert McGuire.

She boarded a yellow tram without knowing where it was going. The slatted seats were occupied so she clung to a metal ring on a strop above her head while the ancient vehicle climbed shade-dappled squares and clawed its way up steep cobbled streets, threading narrow gaps between terraces and open doorways, squeezing past a church — stopping to drop off passengers and take on others along the way. At what seemed like the highest point of the city, Anna got off.

There was a castle. She climbed a long broken stairway of stone towards it where overhanging branches cast their shadows. On the outer defences of the castle the breeze was much stronger. She looked down from the ramparts onto a multi-coloured patchwork of roofs and pastel shaded walls stretching down the hill to the heart of the city. Iron framed balconies jutted from upstairs windows. Far away to her left, halfway across the river, a ferry marked its progress with a curving wake on a moving tide of brown water. Seeing it reminded Anna of recent crossings, in both directions, less than twenty-four hours ago while sitting next to the late Robert McGuire in his pre-war MG.

Something made her think about the bull again, pitting its courage in a sad attempt to win a battle against cruel men equipped with brains and weapons.

Enjoying the leisurely pace of the day, Anna decided to walk back to the city centre. At first she allowed herself to be guided by the tramlines but soon wandered into narrow backstreets under colourful washing lines stretched between balconies. A lunchtime smell lured her into a doorway and inside she sampled sardines, smoky with charcoal, accompanied with vinegar-spiced lettuce and olive oil. In that cool cellar amongst stacks of barrels, she swallowed four small glasses of inky wine which set her teeth on edge.

The sun was still hot when she emerged. She crossed the road and walked in the cooler shadow of buildings, down the slippery pavement, feeling a pleasurable longing to handle the task that awaited her on her return home.

She had already arrived in the taxi-filled centre — when she remembered . . .

Cursing herself for not having thought of it earlier she looked at her watch and broke into an unsteady run over irregular hand-laid pavements that caught at her heels. Pedestrians in Rua da Prata stepped out of her way, turning their heads to watch her go. There might still be time if she hurried . . .

She found it — Cabeleireiro Renato — and burst in. The proprietor was vigorously towelling the head of one of his clients. Out of breath she said, 'Could you cut my hair please?'

Renato turned to look at her. His face was

smooth and leather-brown; his oily hair was sculpted into complicated waves above eyes too small for his face. 'Mees Arrosmeet, we are meeting again! Of course I cut. Sit and be waiting please.' He barked an order to a thin girl in a white coat who brought a cup of espresso coffee with an outsized packet of sugar overhanging its saucer. She sipped, watching impatiently as the hairdresser worked on the head of a talkative dark-haired girl whose eye occasionally caught Anna's in an ornate gilt-framed mirror.

Half an hour later Renato beckoned her into the chair and ran his fingers through Saturday's curls. Bending down he spoke to her reflection. 'Setting and waving again, Mees Arrosmeet — yes?'

'No thanks. Short-back-and-sides — and as quick as possible please?'

Renato was unenthusiastic. 'The back short? The sides short also?'

'Please be quick, I haven't much time.'

His face winced at the prospect. 'Why so much 'urrying, Mees Arrosmeet? We have much time for short backing and sides.'

'And I have an important parcel to collect from a shop which closes at seven!'

He cheered up immediately, chuckled, and shook his head in mock despair as he picked up an album of magazine cuttings. 'This is

Portugal, my lady, all is possible in my country. First I cut — after, the parcel — no problem. What name please?'

'Arrowsmith.'

'No, no, my lady, you tell me your name yesterday. The name of the shop with the parcel I do not know, you tell me now please.'

Feeling a little doubtful she found the receipt and showed it to Renato who glanced at it quickly. 'No problem.'

He sent the white-coated girl scurrying out onto the pavement and bent down to beam a reflected smile. 'Now we have good timings. You will see: all is possible in my country!' He leafed through pictures of girls with short hair.

Anna chose the shortest but when her hair started to hit the floor she noticed tears in the hairdresser's eye . . .

The girl's reflection again: muttering something into her boss's ear; *she was empty handed* . . .

'My parcel! What has happened to my parcel?'

Renato made a gesture of despair. 'It is delivery to your 'otel, my lady.'

'But you don't know the name of my hotel!'

'Eduardo Septimo, Mees Arrowsmeet, Eduardo the Seven. It is the name of the old

215

King of your country. Do you not remember? We talk about it on Sabado . . . no, Samedi . . . NO!' He banged his forehead with the heel of his hand until the elusive English translation fell like chocolate from a faulty machine: 'SATURDAY!'

★ ★ ★

When Anna got back to the hotel, the balding receptionist lowered his newspaper, but she was at the counter before he'd had time to get to his feet.

'Was a parcel delivered here for me?'

'An envelope, but no parcel.'

'I'm expecting a parcel.'

'A parcel, Miss Stobart — delivered *here* you say? I'm afraid you are mistaken.'

'But you *must* have it — my hairdresser told me it had been delivered here.'

The balding receptionist shrugged his shoulders. 'I am sorry but I do not think so.' He stooped and took a large brown parcel from under the counter, adjusted his glasses and read the label. 'I am sorry, no parcel.'

From where she was standing she could see that it was hers: 'There in your hand!'

He looked at her over thick horn-rims: 'This one is not for you, Miss Stobart.'

'It *is*, I know it is!'

He pushed his glasses to the bridge of his nose, re-studied the label, and looked at her again with a raised eyebrow. 'This parcel is for a Miss Arrowsmith.'

'Yes . . . *No!*'

The merest smile showed on the reception-ist's face. 'Now you will understand why we must see the passports of our foreign guests. The passport you hold belongs to *Anna Geraldine Stobart.*'

She thought quickly. 'You may not believe this but I asked them to put Arrowsmith on the parcel because it's a present for somebody of that name who lives in England.'

The eyebrow lifted doubtfully: 'One moment please.'

From an inner office Anna could hear him speaking on the telephone . . . after a long conversation he re-appeared and casually handed it over. 'We have nobody by the name of Arrowsmith in this hotel and none is booked with the agency.' He lowered his voice, speaking so quietly that Anna had to lean forward to catch what he was saying. 'This is not England, Miss Stobart. It is dangerous in my country to use a false name. You live in a free democracy: Clement Atlee and King George are not the same as our dictator, Doctor Antonio de Oliveira

Salazar.' His voice was little more than a whisper: Anna was almost lip-reading. 'Salazar demands that misdemeanours committed by foreigners be reported to PIDE.'

She was shaking: could this man know something?

She watched his lips again: 'PIDE is our Policia International for the Defence of the Estado; it defends us from the chaos and anarchy of democracy. Do not let them catch you, Miss Stobart. Many of our PIDE agents were trained by the German Gestapo during the war. Many British spies were caught and broken here in my country.' His left eyelid dropped suddenly and bounced up again like the shutter of a camera. 'You are young, *Miss Arrowsmith*: if you return here when you are old as I am now, perhaps you will see democracy and maybe even a king here — in my country!'

From a pigeon-hole he took her key — and a bulky envelope. 'Here also is the packet that was delivered for you. This one at least — *Miss Stobart* — has your correct name written clearly.'

In the bedroom Anna threw down the parcel, sat on the bed and unstuck the packet.

Her fingers touched thin material — *and grains of sand.*

It was a red bikini. She snatched up the

bottom half and read the label: *Marco Bellini, Milan and Paris*.

A miniature envelope fell from its tiny folds. She tore it open . . . something small fell out — and rolled into her lap.

It was an unbitten L-pill.

15

Robert McGuire lay very still. He was listening for the sound of the door. His right leg was bent painfully under him on the tiled floor of the shower room but he didn't want to move in case Anna Stobart came back to take a last look before leaving the flat.

There was a neutral taste of sticky gelatine in his mouth but the capsule was still intact; he had let it fall out of his mouth and it was now somewhere on the floor under his neck. He heard her footsteps on the stairs and the click of the lock as the front door closed behind her.

He sat up, spat out a fragment of tooth and picked up the capsule. Looking at it confirmed what he suspected: Cyanide — Standard British Issue. He had come to that conclusion after a quick rummage in her handbag while she was swimming in the sea. There had been a passport too, she lived in Brixham. No weapon: he knew that the moment he lifted the handbag — not enough weight. Perhaps he should have challenged her about these things there and then, but the whole situation had seemed so intriguing he hadn't wanted to break the spell. Now there was a strong element of danger and excitement in this relationship that was hard to resist . . .

He got up, put the capsule into a small white envelope and zipped it into the inside of his wallet. He was feeling a little weak. Lovers had shown their disapproval of him in a variety of ways in the past — but their passions had never run to attempted murder. He dried himself, put on a dressing gown and booked a telephone call to the Royal Castle Hotel in Dartmouth. He was going to need a clear head; secretly tipping all that wine into the sand earlier in the day had not been a waste after all . . .

A thirty minute delay: that's what the operator at the Lisbon exchange was forecasting for calls to England. He set about tidying the flat, waiting for the telephone to ring, trying to cover up all signs of Anna Stobart's visit. There was no doubt that this cold-blooded liquidation attempt had jolted him, shaken him up. The renewed contact with Karl had reminded him too that he could no longer expect the repercussions of past activities as a secret agent to grow thin and disappear like smoke now that the fire was out.

He thought about how it was in the

221

beginning — the things that had started him off in a life of secretly observing the enemy. Could it really have all begun during those summer holidays in Germany: seeing how things were done over there — comparing the German way with the rudderless drift of Britain under a bland democracy?

1938 was the year an Abwehr agent had first introduced himself so unexpectedly. Then another surprise: suddenly realising that he — Robert McGuire — was actually prepared to ... *no, it wasn't an act of treachery.* He wasn't English, not even British. How could a man who was more Irish and Portuguese than British be accused of being a traitor? Whatever the reason he had always been careful to keep it from Father who, long ago, had fought in the British Army.

A year later war did come: no more trips abroad, no more contact with Germany until that letter arrived. Quite simple at first: contact a man in London for the pick-up. It was amazing how such a powerful transceiver could be made to fit inside a small, tailor-made, innocent-looking suitcase. Obtaining permission from the British authorities to help in the shop had been the next step; Dad hadn't liked that — his own son a Registered Conscientious Objector. The thrill of that first coded request, still sharp after the years: over the airwaves; all the way from Hamburg; dashes and dots down the lightning conductor; the first directive, the first of many . . .

Ludovina's bathing suit was on the bedroom floor — still covered in sand. Robert rinsed both pieces under the tap and squeezed out as much water as he could — nearly tearing the insubstantial fabric as he did so; he did it automatically, still thinking about past times . . .

Operation Herod would never have gone ahead if it hadn't been for the *Irish Spy*. Witnessing the raid had been part of the job — the last part. Funny how the details were still so clear: everything from leaving the attic bedroom on a dull, overcast morning — until transmitting a cryptic report to Hamburg. By then of course the original wireless apparatus had been replaced by something a lot more powerful: the very latest English Type A Mark 2 — reputedly captured from a British agent in France. It had been dropped for him by parachute onto Dartmoor from a Luftwaffe Junkers 88 at a pre-arranged map-reference.

Robert stopped what he was doing and sat down on the sofa . . .

★ ★ ★

Dartmouth — Friday, September the 18th, 1942:

In his attic-bedroom, above McGuire's Wines and Spirits, Robert McGuire looked at his watch: half-past-nine, exactly two hours before the expected attack. He crept downstairs, picked up a basket and slipped out by the back so as to avoid a lengthy cross-examination from his father about where he was going — and why.

He had already reconnoitred a vantage point which afforded a good view of the college — and gathering rose-hips for the Ministry of Food was a patriotic pastime, a worthy activity for 'besieged islanders'. He walked quickly away from the centre of town with the basket under his arm, up steep and narrow lanes, across College Way — making for a certain hedgerow at the edge of a particular field.

He picked enough fruit to cover the bottom of the basket then sat on the grass with his back to the hedge. The college clock showed eleven-fifteen over the complex sprawl of buildings below him in the middle distance, brick and stone, dull under the overcast . . .

Shortly after half-past-eleven — a little later than scheduled — something that sounded like distant thunder gradually changed to the surging throb of German aero-engines. Although they appeared as little more than black specks to begin with, Robert already knew that he was looking at six Focke-Wulf 190s, each loaded with a standard SC500 Spreng Cylindrische high explosive bomb.

He watched the leading two break off and fly across the river to come in low towards the clock. Artillery batteries in the grounds of the college put up a screen of protective anti-aircraft fire. Just as the leaders were about to release their bombs — suddenly, out of cloud — twelve Spitfires dived amongst them — *but they were too late to save the college.*

The first bomb appeared to explode harmlessly against the wall of B-Block. The second toppled through the slated roof of the quarterdeck. The ear-bursting shockwave came four seconds later. The eruption was like a volcano: fire, smoke, rubble high and higher in the air; a brown cloud raining lumps of masonry; rafters sailing up end-over-end — up and up. No human sounds came: no screams, no shouts above the crash of masonry and the gunfire.

The first Focke-Wulf was heading directly towards the spot where Robert crouched. He threw himself flat, pressing his face to the grass. A screaming engine blotted out every other sound; a gale of hot exhaust ruffled his hair; the rose-hip hedge disintegrated behind him in a splintering crash.

Raising his head, Robert saw the second Focke-Wulf curving away to the right gushing smoke; its wing hit the turf; it spun like a catherine-wheel — breaking up in a shower of burning fragments.

The bomb-dust thinned. A debris-filled crater showed where the college quarterdeck had been; a fierce air-battle was overhead.

Robert picked up his basket and started to run. He could hear gunfire and bombs bursting on the far side of the river as he hurried on down the hill towards the town. When he reached the shop he ran across the back yard but, halfway up the stairs . . .

'Robert, is that you — Holy Mary where have you been?'

'Picking rose-hips, Dad.'

'Rose-hips — *rose-hips* did you say — don't you know there's a war on, son?'

'They are for the war, Dad, the Ministry of Food has a collecting point in the town hall, remember? *Vitamin C from the Hedgerows of Britain.*'

'Well never mind about that now: fetch the ladder and reach me down one of those quarter-bottles, Mrs Carmichael's come in to take shelter so she has: a woman in powerful need of Hennesey's swift sensation if ever I saw one!'

Then he was running up the stairs again, levering up the floorboard under his bed. His message to Hamburg would be nearly ten minutes late. He took out the transceiver, plugged in the morse-key and tapped out his personal call-sign . . .

Almost immediately a static-free signal from Hamburg pulsed down the lightning conductor: the pass-phrase.

Robert transmitted: *'One hundred and thirteen for seven; middle stump; match declared — I repeat: match declared.'*

They would know what it meant: Direct hit. Quarterdeck destroyed 11.37. Initial observations reveal no survivors. Repeat, no survivors.

★ ★ ★

While Robert was hanging Ludovina's swimming costume on the window shutter to dry, the telephone rang — it was his booked call to Dartmouth.

As before he spoke in German. *'Is that you, Karl? Robert McGuire here, I'm sorry to ring so late.'*

Before Robert could continue, Karl was

interrupting: something to do with having a headache, feeling unwell but not wanting to call a doctor . . . Then the line began to fail . . .

Robert shouted against a roar of interference: 'Listen Karl, it's about Anna Stobart.' Robert kept talking; hoping that he could still be heard from twelve hundred miles away. 'Anna Stobart arrived over here, just like you said. She tried to kill me and she thinks she has succeeded. Listen carefully: Miss Stobart will soon be back in England. When she gets there she will be looking for you. She intends to kill you and she will succeed if you are not on your guard. I now know what this woman is capable of. Take care of yourself — you warned me about her, now I am warning you. *For God's sake be careful!*'

Karl's reply was barely audible. 'I can't hear . . . Robert. *Robert?*'

The line went dead. The operator declared a fault that could only be put right on Monday. Robert replaced the receiver, sat down on the stool and tried to work out what to do next. He knew from experience that repairs to international lines sometimes took more than a week. If Deichman was ill he was even more vulnerable.

Anna Stobart's intentions were clear as far as Karl was concerned. What was it she had said while he was lying on the floor under the shower — what was it? *Stoke up the fires of hell*, something like that — melodramatic but she meant it — and now there was no way of telling whether Karl had heard the warning. So much for the Anglo Portuguese Telephone Company. Now there was only one right course of action . . .

But in spite of the danger and the urgency and the deception and the treachery, Robert was still unable to prevent himself from thinking about the *other* side to Anna Stobart. Long ago there had been another attempt on Robert's life during his undercover career, but not from a lover: it had put him in hospital for two weeks — painful, frightening. But Anna Stobart's attack on him had been altogether thrilling and exciting. That body . . . the abandoned giving . . .

He could picture her lying next to him on that isolated beach beyond Portinho da Arrábida: smooth skin under his hands, erect nipples under the thin material of Ludovina's swimsuit — *but what had caused those burn marks on her back?* Yes, Anna was beautiful — too enticing to be resisted, in spite of masquerading under an assumed name; her possession of an L-pill; her hatred of the enemy. In spite of all that her attitude would change once he had told her the whole truth

— and rather conveniently Brixham was in Devon, not very far from Dartmouth.

No, he wasn't prepared to let her go — at least, not yet.

★ ★ ★

On Monday morning Robert woke early. Booking the flight had been easy but he didn't want to miss it. He had hated disturbing his friend Manuel Saramago — especially on a Sunday night — and getting him to agree to prevent a woman (Anna Stobart according to her passport) from travelling on Flight TP 572 on Monday morning had taken quite a lot of persuasion even though that man received an unofficial *Christmas Cake* from the British Embassy every year for helping to make things happen. Sometimes Robert wished the embassy could do the same for him: he would be a lot keener if the occasional *cake* were to come his way — and it wouldn't matter if the silver salver underneath wasn't quite as thick as the one they invariably chose for Saramago.

While shaving he could hear Ludovina busying herself around the flat, singing one of her songs. In many ways she was still a child . . .

Todos os patinhos sabem bem nadar,
Cabeça para abaixo rabinho pelo . . .

Robert was translating to himself as she sang, altering the meaning a little to preserve the rhyme . . .

All the little ducklings never seem to care,
Head beneath the water, bottoms in the . . .

The song stopped abruptly. There followed what seemed like at least a minute of complete silence. Then she was working again but now he could hear her angrily muttering to herself, banging shutters, clattering saucepans . . .

She came in and shoved a plate down on the table in front of him without exchanging a word. Her face was like a storm over one of her beaches — but not quite ready to break . . .

'*Did you have a nice time on Sunday, Roberto?*'

'Just a quiet day — and you?'

And then it started: 'My girlfriend asked me to go to Carcavelos beach . . . no fun at all . . . I came here to collect my bathing suit and . . . '

Now there was a distinct smell of damp gunpowder; *such an elementary mistake, the bathing suit of all things.* Stay cool and friendly: 'Perhaps it's just as well you couldn't find it. You know you shouldn't wear a two-piece on a public beach. Where did you last see it?'

'You mean where did *YOU* last see it. *On whom* did you see it . . . ?

Avoid the question . . . 'You were wearing it in the kitchen on Saturday morning, don't you remember? I'm sure it will turn up — it's probably still in your room — have you tried all the drawers?'

'If it is in my drawer . . . ' *Now the anger:* 'If it is supposed to be in my drawer, why is it hanging on the window shutter with sand in the pants? There is sand in my pants and sand on the floor and sand in the shower and you never take me to the beach and you . . . you . . . ' He put his arms around her but she snatched herself away. 'Why did you give it to me, Roberto? Was it really just for me? Why do you never take *me* to the beach instead of some . . . some . . . woman who is . . . not even . . . will never be . . . *in love with you!*'

Ludovina lifted her apron to her face and caught the full force of the bursting flood — and continued to cry for several minutes, silently — except for irregular and rending inhalations of breath that shook her whole body with spasms of what could only have been genuine grief.

Robert was beginning to hate himself. 'I'm sorry, Ludo — it was important. I can't explain now. I'll bring you something nice from England. I must be quick now or I will miss my flight.'

She looked up sharply, choking back sobs: 'You are going to England — *today* — just like that — without telling me?'

'I have to take my holiday a week early.'

The challenge was back: '*Who are you going with?*'

'I'm going alone. My father has been taken ill.'

The effect was immediate. 'Senhor Alec? Aiee! Nossa Senhora!' Her hand was half across her mouth. 'If Senhor Alec is ill you must go to him at once!'

The ruse had worked. Ever since Ludovina had helped the one-legged Alec McGuire climb the stairs to the flat after he had flown out to Lisbon in the Aquila flying boat for a short holiday last year, she had treated the old man like one of her greatest friends. After he had gone back to Dartmouth she had sent him an elaborate home-made card for his sixty-eighth birthday — and one of her embroidered napkins for Christmas.

The lie was reinforced with further detail:

'Senhor Alec has had a mild heart attack. He has to rest. I must find somebody to cope with the wine shop . . .'

Ludovina carried on clearing the table, busying herself in the kitchen, quieter now. Intermittently she would stop to ask for more details and even helped to pack Robert's suitcase.

He kissed her goodbye and started down the stairs — but Ludovina's final act was to hurl the precious garment after him, retreat to her bedroom and slam the door. Without looking back, Robert shoved the bathing suit into his blazer pocket and let himself out onto the street, vowing to dump both pieces of troublesome cloth into a litter bin at the very first opportunity.

On his way to the airport, when the taxi was halfway up Avenida Fontes Pereira de Melo, Robert saw Anna Stobart leaving Hotel Eduardo Septimo. She was on foot. Seeing her gave him an idea. He asked the taxi driver to stop outside a stationery shop where he bought a large brown envelope.

16

Anna Stobart sat on her bed in the Hotel Eduardo Septimo with both pieces of Ludovina's bikini scrunched to a tight ball inside her left fist. Her heart was pounding; she felt as if she had been running uphill.

She had seen Robert McGuire actually dying — the man had fallen over, gasped for breath — his eyes had rolled back, knees buckling — *and he had died* — exactly twenty-two seconds after ingesting cyanide — as expected and in the manner so exactly described by Sergeant Cox.

Robert McGuire was an actor, it was true; she had seen him performing on the stage of the Lisbon Players — but was he *that* good? If Robert McGuire was alive, where was he now? Had he gone to the police, the Portuguese police, the Gestapo-trained PIDE who might even now be on their way? What was his game?

She sat there staring at the little crumpled garment in her hand. No note. Nothing to say why. Nothing to say *who* had sent these things to her. What was going on?

Then, gradually, a feeling of overwhelming

disappointment made her ignore the possibility that Robert McGuire might shop her to the police. She had failed — it was depressing — for the second time she had failed.

★   ★   ★

The sun was already showing Wednesday morning's first light over Sharkham Point when Anna let herself into her house in Yards Lane.

Throughout the flight, bolstered by alcohol and heavy breaths of *Le Jade* — and during the subsequent train journey to Brixham — she had been running through her plan for Karl Deichman. She had not, of course, forgotten about Mr Robert McGuire — certainly not. Although it seemed certain that he was still alive, and now over a thousand miles away, that spy — if he was wise — would never again be able to relax or consider himself safe. She knew where to find him and she had already sworn to the ever-present Philippa that she would seek him out again and deal with him when Deichman was dead.

She picked up the telephone. 'Dartmouth 378 please . . . hello, is that the Royal Castle Hotel . . . ?'

While she spoke on the telephone Colin rubbed against her legs. He was hungry, he had been miaowing for food from the moment Anna had crossed the threshold so she fed him before running the bath.

Lying back she could remember the nervous anticipation she had felt on the night she had murdered Generaloberst Zaunbrecher with an outsized metal spike. *Hot water* — nothing like it for making a person think (but it would take more than hot water to stop Philippa butting in from time to time — even as a child she had been like that). According to the hotel receptionist, Herr Deichman was ill: confined to bed by a doctor but there was no way of knowing for how long. If old Dr Hoskins had been attending him the assassin would have been told to rest until well after Christmas. Helga's rather intimate message — five little words of it — had been clearly written on the back of that photo, the one that had fallen to the floor and prevented Deichman from drinking his tea. And Helga's appearance: long plaits; laced bodice — *Bavarian* . . .

A wave of warm, relaxing water rippled over her stomach. *French Without Tears*: a wonderful play and an enthusiastic audience. Anna remembered A27: from that narrow balcony seat it was not only Lieutenant Commander Rogers, played by Robert McGuire, who had caught her attention.

There had been somebody else — a young female playing the part of Jacqueline Maingot, daughter of the proprietor of a French language school. Halfway through the second act Jacqueline had been preparing to go to a party in fancy dress . . . and somebody called Diana had commented about that dress: *It isn't quite Bavarian . . .*

The dress in the window in Lisbon had been almost identical to the one in Deichman's photo — and an exact replica of Jacqueline's fancy dress in the play. Somebody from the Lisbon Players had probably been to that very shop. Anna's Portuguese peasant's dress had needed some adjustments: an inch off the hem, a tuck in the back of the embroidered bodice to make it fit across the shoulders — the criss-cross lacing at the front was adjustable. The outfit wasn't Bavarian but it was close enough.

Now for the plan: *Enter the Royal Castle Hotel wearing the disguise; carry a coat; enter his bedroom; surprise him for a few seconds by saying those five intimate words; kill him, take off the wig, put on the coat, leave the room unseen — walk away . . .*'

Good old Sergeant Cox: that man had made his students stab a dummy — *sideways into the bread-basket* — with such monotony and frequency that after a while there was a hole in the sacking so big that half the straw had fallen out. The forthcoming murder of Karl Deichman, simple though the plan was, perhaps would one day rank with the more notorious of Scotland Yard's unsolved crimes: *a woman of German appearance was seen to enter the hotel just before the murder — unfortunately nobody saw her leave.* Anna hooked her big toe around the old fashioned tap at the end of her bath and added more hot. Although several days had elapsed since she had stooped to pick up that snapshot of Deichman's widow from her sitting room floor, every detail of it was still clear: face, hair, clothes . . .

The rasp of a threadbare carpet scuffed her heels as she walked naked along the landing to her bedroom. She knelt down and pulled out Claudine's suitcase from under the bed and took out the wig.

Sitting on the edge of the bed Anna started to plait her wig into two long pigtails. When she had finished she put it on in front of her dressing table mirror, adjusting it carefully to cover her own black hair — easy enough now that it had been cut so short — but her eyebrows were the wrong colour. She plucked them carefully and lightened them with make-up. Then she opened the parcel — the one that had caused so much trouble in a

Portuguese hotel — and put on the dress.

When Anna was ready she opened her wardrobe door and looked critically at herself in the full-length mirror. She had only been able to study the photo of Deichman's widow during a few short seconds but she knew that the disguise was good enough to confuse her victim for the few vital seconds necessary to get close — that was all it needed: a few seconds and no witnesses — and so much safer now that he was confined to his room . . .

Most important of all was the fact that she no longer looked anything like Anna Stobart or even Penny Arrowsmith — a notion confirmed by Colin who, when he came into the room and saw her standing there, arched his back and ran away, hackles up and hissing like a snake.

Anna splashed *Le Jade* generously to the underside of her chin and breathed in deeply. She knew that her old instructor would approve of her fighting on like this, even after the cease-fire.

She put her raincoat over her arm and opened the front door a crack. In the garden next door there was no sign of Mr Bentall; if he was indoors he would be unable to see her opening the garage so she tip-toed confidently along the path and reached for the bolt. It was jammed. She rocked the door backwards and forwards, pulling on the bolt at the same time until it slid down . . .

'*What the devil d'you think you're doing!*'

She spun round. Mr Bentall was stepping over the low part of the hedge.

'You're on private property! What's your name?'

She could feel her face going hot. 'Hello, Mr Bentall, it's me, Anna Stobart.'

He strode towards her across the grass. '*The hell you are!*'

'I got back last night.'

Mr Bentall stopped, put his head on one side and somehow managed to check a look of utter disgust before it had fully developed. 'I didn't recognise you, Miss Stobart, straight I didn't — not with you all dolled up like that. You've had your hair dyed — pigtails too!'

'Do you like it?'

'I thought you was a teenager trying to pinch something out of the garage. Sorry if I spoke out of turn I'm sure.' He scratched the back of his neck and changed the subject to cover his embarrassment. 'Colin's been off his grub, fed up with that foreign chap who's been knocking on your door more than likely.'

'Really? A foreigner calling at my house?

What did you tell him?'

'Told him to try Jackson's Travel when he asked where you was — what else could I say? I found your note about feeding Colin but you never said where you was nor how long you'd be gone.'

Anna backed her Morris out onto the road and was about to drive off when Mr Bentall came running out of his gate.

'One of these days I'll forget my own head, straight I will. This telegram came for you yesterday, you wasn't here so I signed for it.' He handed a small yellow envelope through the car window.

As Anna drove towards Dartmouth she became curious. She pulled into the side of the road and unstuck the flap . . .

AM IN DARTMOUTH STOP HOPE WE CAN MEET STOP THERE IS SOMETHING YOU MUST KNOW ABOUT ME STOP WILL CONTACT YOU STOP ROBERT

17

As she got nearer to Dartmouth, Anna began to realise that McGuire must have been able to hear what she had said to his 'dying' body. Philippa of course, had the exact words: *Stoke that fire for your friend Karl Deichman who will soon be joining you!*

If McGuire had heard that — and if he was in England which was now certain — he might well be trying to protect his 'friend'. Anna became so distracted by this possibility, something which she had not allowed for in her plan, that she almost collided with an ambulance that rushed out of a turning right in front of her. It was sounding its bell.

When she got to the Royal Castle Hotel she saw the ambulance again, stopped outside the main door. Anna parked her car. She had wrapped the knife in brown paper so that it would not damage the pocket of the raincoat she was carrying over her arm. She entered the hotel and walked towards the desk: *practise the words, German accent, look the receptionist in the eye, stay cool.* A few paces from the desk she heard movement on the stairs: two ambulance-men descending the lower flight carrying a stretcher. *Could it be . . . ?* The person on the stretcher was heavily wrapped in blankets. Closer now, as the procession pushed past, she saw the patient's face: death-white, eyes closed. It was Karl Deichman.

Anna had barely recovered from the shock of seeing her victim escaping like that when a man, walking beside the stretcher, looked straight at her for frozen seconds. *Robert McGuire*: but he showed no sign that he had recognised a foreign-looking woman with blonde pigtails and a raincoat hanging over her left arm.

She followed the stretcher onto the street. Philippa, from inside her head, was trying to say things like — *keep a discreet distance from the crowd* — but Anna was, for the moment, too dazed to listen. Under a kind of numb hypnosis she watched her intended victim loaded into the ambulance and found herself walking to her car. When the ambulance moved, she followed, alert again, driving fast, covering the first five miles to Halwell and Moreleigh in as many minutes, trying to keep the ambulance in sight, matching its wild pace towards Plymouth.

While driving, Anna tried to tell herself that the plan to kill Deichman was still a possibility: *follow him, look for another*

244

opportunity to get in close. She forced herself to remain optimistic, not yet ready to give up.

The ambulance turned into the emergency gate of Plymouth General Hospital. Anna pulled her car into the side of the road, waited for twenty minutes, then, carrying her raincoat as before, entered the building by the public entrance.

Remembering to keep up the planned illusion, she used her German accent on the woman at the reception desk. 'I am Frau Deichman. I have come from Germany to see my husband.'

The woman at the desk gave a sympathetic smile, her voice was caring but practical. 'Ah, Mrs Deichman. I'm afraid you can't see your husband yet, he is under sedation, the surgeon wishes to operate without delay. If you come with me I'll show you where you can wait. I'm about to go off duty myself but I'll make sure that somebody calls you as soon as the surgeon says it's all right. That will be after the operation so I'm afraid you are in for a long wait.' She led the way to a small waiting room with chairs against the walls and magazines on a low table. 'Make yourself comfortable, I expect you are tired after your journey.'

She sat down wondering how long it would be before they would allow her to be alone with Deichman. His condition must be serious — but if he were to die from whatever it was that was making him so ill, it would give her little satisfaction because, if that happened, there would be no act of revenge to satisfy the demands coming from inside her head.

She opened a magazine and stared blankly at the page. There was no reason why her plan should not work equally well in this place — a hospital was bigger, more impersonal than a hotel and if she could be alone with Deichman — a few seconds would suffice — she could deal with him as planned then remove the wig and put on the raincoat — and, as before — if nobody were to see her actually leaving his room there would be nobody to link her with the woman who called herself Frau Deichman.

Her optimism was building: this hospital may well prove to be the best place. If Deichman was on some kind of life-sustaining apparatus it might even be possible to kill him without using the knife . . .

The magazines were uninteresting.

After a week during which her emotions had been repeatedly raised and plunged, and having slept badly throughout, Anna was in need of rest in spite of the tension she still felt. No amount of adrenaline, however, was going to ward off sleep in that tiny, airless room. Over in the corner there was an upholstered armchair. She moved across to it, sat down and leaned back. There was nothing she could do now but wait.

Anna drifted to sleep almost at once. She entered a lucid dream: a review of past incidents in her life, minimally distorted. She could see herself in calamitous need of medical treatment for injuries indirectly caused by a traitor not unlike Robert McGuire who had infiltrated her section of the French Resistance shortly after her second parachute drop into occupied France. It was like watching an erratic film jumping backwards to a point where she herself — Lucrèce this time — could see members of her circuit rounded up and manhandled into a big van — but Lucrèce was later trapped in the attic of a farmhouse: *gunfire, death, a Gestapo interrogation, torture*. Lying on the floor of a cell in Amiens Jail. Shivering — *was it cold or fear?* Would she survive the next 'interview'?

Half-awake now, she remembered that Robert McGuire had asked her about those scars while massaging her back with suntan oil on a Portuguese beach, clearly ignorant of what a red hot poker can do to human skin. Luck had played a big part in her escape from

Amiens — luck and a handful of highly trained aircrew — had they been brave or reckless? *Operation Jericho*: if it hadn't been for that squadron of low-flying RAF Mosquito aircraft sent from England to breach the walls of the jail with their carefully placed bombs, the woman called Lucrèce would have died in that place — probably from cyanide before the Gestapo had extracted what they were so keen to hear. The L-pill again: hidden in the fold of the cheek, funny how that useful chemical kept cropping up in her life. *Sudden thunder: aircraft flying up the main street of the town, bombs bursting against the walls of the prison, dust, smoke, screams, piles of rubble . . . daylight!* Many inmates had been killed — mostly Resistance people waiting to be forced by interrogators — but, during the breaching of Amiens jail she had been one of those able to scramble out and, in her case, make the starving walk to Paris away from roads, across fields, dragged by snowdrifts to a house opposite a night-club called La Cave — where an old lady she already knew took her in. It didn't take long for those burns on her back to heal once she had been seen by a French doctor who secretly treated her in his cellar. As for the old lady: there was only one way that Anna could pay her for all that kindness

248

— thank goodness not every man who went to La Cave was like Zaunbrecher . . .

Then she remembered another doctor who, when she arrived back in England in 1946, diagnosed a condition that was really shell-shock. He had called it Hebephrenic Schizophrenia but, whatever it was, he must have considered it serious because he tried very hard — without success, thank God — to get her certified insane.

Anna opened her eyes. She was fully awake now, shifting in her chair. At first she thought she must be still in the grip of that confused dream because there was an ugly woman sitting bolt upright on one of the chairs set against the opposite wall, looking at her through asymmetrical eyes set in red-blotched skin that had a hard sheen to it like crumpled greaseproof paper. Her hair was thin in places — and showed sharply defined patches of grey. The lips were stretched and distorted, unable to close properly.

As Anna watched, the terrible features warped into what might have been a smile, and a voice came from between those lips which, strangely, showed little sign of movement. '*You have been sleeping much time.*'

Anna blinked and sat up, for the moment her plans forgotten. The woman continued: 'I do not — like this . . . ' She seemed to be searching for a word, 'I do not like in — the hospitals.'

This woman was probably Austrian. In spite of a kind of stuttering impediment, probably caused by her disfigured mouth, Anna was fairly sure that her accent resembled that of an Austrian language teacher she had once known. She answered cautiously in German without taking her eyes off the grotesque face.

'Have you come here for treatment, or are you just visiting?'

The woman brightened immediately and replied fluently in her own language. 'No treatment for me, thank God, I've come here to visit somebody. I have had enough of the inside of hospitals I can tell you. I suppose you can guess that just by looking at me.'

Anna felt a crawling sensation on her own skin and tried hard to resist taking off the wig to scratch an itch that was developing on her scalp. 'Excuse me for asking but what happened to you?'

The hideous woman shrugged her shoulders. 'It is nothing. I got caught up in something. It's several years ago now. I got off lightly compared with most.'

Anna couldn't help her curiosity. 'Do you want to tell me about it?'

'There is not much to tell. I was staying in a big town. During the night I woke up and found that the house I was in had caught fire. I ran outside and everything else was on fire too. I ran through what looked like a long tunnel in the flames and my hair caught fire. The whole town — it was a city really — much bigger than an ordinary town — the whole city was blazing — everything — every house, every building. I kept slapping my head, trying to put out the flames — look at this.'

She held up misshapen fingers — *that shiny skin again.*

'A terrible whirlwind was dragging a spray of burning tar into the air, fire engines ablaze, splintering, roaring, flames everywhere — high as rooftops. I kept on running, my feet were slithering and sucking down into the flaming tar. Children I remember: two of them, crouching, hugged together, screaming — stuck like insects onto fly-paper; they were burning, their faces were melting. And the wind, like a hurricane it was. I saw trees whirling over my head like aeroplanes on fire. I kept on running, falling, twisting, turning, jumping over pitiful shapeless heaps of charred human flesh.

'The screaming — I shall never forget it, so loud it was — even against the roar;

thousands of tortured people running, trying to escape the flames, all on fire, clothes falling off their bodies. I had never been to this city before but, earlier that day, my aunt had shown me a big lake where children were happily swimming and paddling near the edge to keep themselves cool under the summer sun. Old men had been sailing their model boats in that lake too. But where was the lake now? That is what I was trying to remember but now, in the fire, everything was different. The air in my mouth was burning my throat as I breathed. My lips would not close. I was choking on ash and smoke. Flaps of roasted skin were hanging over my eyes . . .

'I kept on running. I ran across Gannse Market. I saw the roof of the railway station, then past the Alster-Hof Hotel spouting fire from every window. Still running I recognised the Fockwall Road and the Operahaus; my aunt had pointed out all these things to me while we strolled around the city the previous afternoon. Then, suddenly . . . '

For a moment the woman's stammering halted abruptly — she was choking with emotion . . .

'Suddenly I found the lake, waded till my chin touched the water. Then something soft: my toe touched it — a man's body thrust up to the surface next to me; his hair was wet but

I couldn't believe what I was seeing: his hair burst into flames. There were thousands of people around me; some were screaming, some were silent, some kept ducking under the water again and again trying to put out the flames because they were covered in something that had dropped onto them from the sky that clung to the skin and the hair and the clothing and *would* not stop burning . . .

'I stood there, up to my neck, dousing my face in the stinking water. The flames made a high wall all around the edge of the lake and a terrible scorching wind drove floating corpses against me. I could barely stand, but I stayed there — it was a good place, the safest place to be that night.

'When morning came I felt myself slipping down into the water and at last I felt something soothing on my face — something smooth and healing for my burns. It was then that I noticed, in the morning light, a thick, dark-orange scum across the lake: *a tide of human fat.*'

The ugly woman had become so engrossed in recounting her experience that neither she nor Anna heard the door. They did, however, hear a woman's voice asking: 'Excuse me, which of you is Mrs Deichman?'

Anna opened her mouth to reply but the ugly woman was already on her feet.

'Come this way please, Mrs Deichman, you can see your husband now.'

Anna walked quickly out of the hospital without saying goodbye.

★ ★ ★

Karl Deichman tried to open his eyes but something tight, wound around his head, prevented him from doing so. He was lying in a bed. The pain had gone but he was unable to move. In spite of the bandages he could hear people talking nearby.

A woman was standing close to him. Just by the way she breathed he knew who it was. Her hand was stroking his hair. Her cheek was brushing his. Her skin against his own skin just below the bandage felt familiar: wet with tears but rough and hard like parchment.

When she spoke it was in Bavarian German — a voice that he knew well after ten years of marriage. *'You're a fine one, frightening me like this! I've been up all night waiting for you to come round. I let you out of my sight for a week, Deichy, and look what happens! Too much English beer, that's what the surgeon said. Why else would you pass out like that in a hotel bedroom? The things you get up to when you go on holiday without me!'*

He could picture her leaning over him; he imagined her tears making shiny twisting rivers on her fire-scarred cheeks.

'After they telephoned me from England I caught the very first aeroplane — and it cost me enough I can tell you. Do you remember those bits of metal that Dr Schaffen warned us about? They've gone now, Deichy, and the surgeon here says you'll get better if I keep kissing you. It might be just his silly English sense of humour but I'll keep on kissing you just in case he means it . . . '

Karl wanted to tell her that he loved her but his voice wouldn't work. He wanted to apologise for leaving her alone in Dusseldorf — but it would have to wait. Perhaps it didn't matter that he couldn't say these things because she would already know what he was thinking — she usually did.

Helga moved farther away and he could hear her trying to speak English again.

'Doctor, my husband, he is . . . he is not hearing — yes?'

'It's early days, but you could try holding his hand and telling him to squeeze if he can hear you.'

She came back to the bed and as soon as she put her hand in his, Karl gave it a squeeze that nearly cracked her knuckles.

'So you *can* hear me, Deichy,' she crooned, 'you could hear us talking right across the room! These doctors say it is a miracle that you are alive, but I told them. I told them you were a tough old dog, I told them that it would take more than two little scraps of English steel to kill my Deichy!'

He could picture hairpins dropping out of the coiling hairstyle she had adopted after Hamburg — perhaps a lock of silver hair, breaking free and tumbling across her face to expose the naked patch of scalp.

He wanted to lie to her, and tell her that she was prettier now than she had ever been, prettier even than on the day he took that photograph but, for the moment, he would have to be content with squeezing her hand.

The hospital atmosphere that surrounded him now made Karl remember a heart-stopping wait for news after Hamburg — and the overwhelming tide of relief when he heard she was alive. When he finally found her in that remote country hospital, far away from the ruins of Hamburg, she was bandaged like he was now . . .

He smiled to himself — Helga was off again: '*Not even a postcard, Deichy, I'd have expected a postcard by now — eight days is plenty of time for post to arrive from England. If I didn't know you better . . .*'

He wouldn't have minded if she had gone on scolding him for the rest of his life: he was alive — and so was she — and that was all that mattered.

Hours later Karl woke up. He could remember something that Dr Schaffen had said to him during that final visit to the surgery: never give up hope, he had said. Medical science was moving forward at a tremendous pace; the war had given German doctors a wonderful opportunity to carry out all sorts of medical experiments on human subjects; the trials would continue once the war was over. Schaffen had claimed that one day soon German doctors would be able to spread their knowledge throughout the conquered world, lead the way in the field of human medicine, invade the inner recesses of the human brain without killing their patients. *There are already some remarkable results . . .*

In the morning Karl squeezed Helga's hand again and it didn't matter that he couldn't see her. This was his Helga and the strange thing was that, even though they had been parted for less than two weeks, it seemed like a lifetime.

Long ago, Helga had written some lucky words on the back of a photograph, and now he could feel her scarred lips scratching the bandage covering his left ear as she whispered them to him:

'*Bed me tonight, Deichy darling!*'

Typical Helga: always the optimist.

★ ★ ★

Anna Stobart sat on the floor in her house in Brixham. She was stroking Colin and speaking to that insistent person who dwelt inside her head . . .

'Be patient, Philippa. Those two murderers may think they are safe — *but they are not and never will be . . .* '

Part Three

18

Karl Deichman picked up his *Allgemeine Zeitung* from the doormat and went into the kitchen. He lit gas under a newly invented kettle, looked at the headlines, waited for the whistle and poured boiling water over thirty grams of Kenyan coffee grains. He put the pot on a tray alongside two cups, carried it upstairs and climbed back into bed. Helga poured — then raided the newspaper for the middle section. It was their morning routine, adopted during school holidays when there was no need for history teachers to scramble out of the house without coffee or breakfast.

Karl considered a long article about anti-US demonstrations in East Berlin: it was worrying but he knew it wouldn't hold his attention for very long . . .

He leaned back against a pile of pillows behind his head and closed his eyes. His own problem was still there, unresolved: far more important than anything in the newspaper. He knew what *he* wanted to do during the summer holidays this year but he didn't want to leave Helga on her own again — she deserved better than that — but would she agree to another trip to England?

He looked at his wife. Something in the paper had obviously caught her attention and when he put his question she answered without looking up. 'Don't forget what the doctor said, Deichy, peace, quiet and rest is what he recommends: Baden Baden would be nice don't you think — all those healthy brine baths and massage and gentle walks in the Black Forest. Haven't you had enough of England after what happened last year? Apart from those doctors and a nice lady I met in the hospital waiting room, the whole thing was a complete nightmare.'

Still half-reading, she turned over a page. 'I suppose if we did go it would give me a chance to put my English to the test after all those classes; I never realised what a difficult language it was until now.' She thought for a moment then looked up. 'Come to think of it there *is* something that I'd rather like to do in England . . . '

★ ★ ★

Service BE 483 took off from Dusseldorf's Lohausen airport on the morning of Friday the 17th of August. Helga looked down on the partly rebuilt city and spoke to her husband without turning her head . . .

'When you were still in a coma following your crash, Dr Schaffen advised me that once you were conscious again I should never discuss Operation Herod with you. Now here we are raking over it again. He told me you would want to forget the whole episode because all the pilots who went with you were your friends — it seems he was wrong — about wanting to discuss it I mean.'

Karl folded his newspaper and tucked it into the pocket on the back of the seat in front of him. 'They weren't all killed you know: Boxhammer, Sperrle, Geisler and Weiss were killed, that's certain now, but Awak was posted *missing*. I thought you already knew that.'

Helga was looking at the winding thread of the river Maas catching a glint of sun as it wriggled across the border from Belgium into Holland. 'Dear old Awak — I loved that boy: I believe that I might have married him if I hadn't been lucky enough to meet you first, but like so many of our friends he never came back. Killed, missing, what's the difference if it means we never see him again?'

The bus and railway connections from London worked as planned and the train

263

pulled into Kingswear station on Friday evening under electric lamps. There was a sailing-breeze on the river. Karl could see lights in the college windows. Would that building *ever* give up its secret? There must be people in this town aware of the full extent of the tragedy but so far — and for some reason — the mystery remained intact.

It was strange that Robert McGuire had never mentioned Anna Stobart when he visited the Plymouth hospital last year. He had once stated — rather unclearly on a bad telephone from Portugal — that she was dangerous, but McGuire had a love for the melodramatic — he was, after all, an actor.

In the Royal Castle Hotel, Karl made a telephone call to Lisbon on a much improved line. Yes, Robert McGuire was still there in Portugal and, as predicted, was about to make his annual visit to Dartmouth on Monday: he would be staying with his father at the wine shop and they promised to meet.

On Saturday morning, anxious to get started, Karl took Helga to the Dartmouth museum. Barbara Carmichael was rearranging her display cases: *Devon Smugglers of the Seventeenth & Eighteenth Centuries* was the theme, already successful with both visitors and locals. In spite of what she had claimed was a boycott on war memories, there were two posters still pinned up for all to see:

Join the Wrens and Free a Man for the Fleet
Join the WAAF and Serve with the Men who Fly

Barbara said that she had been wondering about the outcome of Karl's meeting with Anna Stobart last year and was shocked to hear of his sudden illness. After a quick tour of the exhibits she took off her glasses and polished them with a lace-edged handkerchief.

'I'm glad you've come now because a man came in here last autumn who might interest you. He was searching for something too: trying to trace a girl he met during the war. He's married to her now. They pop in here from time to time for a chat but hardly ever look at the exhibits so I don't like to charge them.' She picked up her visitors' book and leafed over some pages. 'Here's his first entry. I've got the phone number somewhere if you want to give him a ring.'

Karl read the entry: *Squadron Leader Ivo Kauky DFC, Sycamore Cottage, Dittisham.* 'But why should this man interest me?'

'Oh, didn't I tell you?' She took back her

book and closed it with a snap. 'He was a member of one of the Czech squadrons of Fighter Command. I thought you might be interested because Ivo Kauky was flying one of the Spitfires that attacked your Focke-Wulfs over Dartmouth on the 18th of September 1942.'

★　★　★

Helga poured tea. She had been reading in a magazine about twelve hectares of bomb-site having been cleared in the middle of London for an exhibition centred around a great big dome called *Discovery*. The whole thing was due to be cleared away at the end of September to make room for permanent rebuilding. 'I'm just reminding you about it, Deichy, because it's the only reason I agreed to come to England. It must be worth seeing if British Airways are advertising two flights every day from Dusseldorf — *two flights* — can you imagine that?'

Karl wasn't listening — he was searching through the contents of his wallet for the third time . . .

Helga continued: 'Did you know that, every day, fifty-one toy gas balloons — one for each year of the century — are released and each one carries two tickets. If we are lucky, we might get in free.'

Karl was still rummaging. 'What are you talking about?'

'The Festival of Britain of course. Once we've penetrated the so-called English cloak of reserve that my language teacher keeps talking about — and put Operation Herod to bed for good — we can go to London and enjoy ourselves.' She picked up a small jug of milk. 'Are we supposed to pour this into our tea or what?'

'I don't think you've been listening to me, Sweetheart.'

'I am listening, Deichy and I'm *also* trying to think what we've done with the Squadron Leader's telephone number. I distinctly remember that girl in the museum writing it on a piece of paper and giving it to you.'

He shook his head. 'If the museum wasn't closed I'd go back there and ask again, I shan't rest until I've discovered if that man is able to tell me how many cadets were killed.'

Helga passed him a cup of tea. 'You be careful: the British are one thing but the Czechs are something else.'

Karl took a sip of tea. 'Perhaps you too should be a teacher, then you could explain to a lot of puzzled people, including some of my students, what really started the war and why we all tried to kill each other for six years.'

Helga said, 'If it's so important — that telephone number I mean — perhaps we can find it in the directory: there can't be many people in England with a name like Kauky.'

A waiter brought the directory and Karl found the page. He ran his finger down the names: *Karn, Karslake, Kass, Kastrian, Kauffmann* — yes, there it was — *Kauky*. He tried the number but got no reply — and continued to try at intervals throughout the evening but without success.

*   *   *

Lying in bed that night Karl reflected that if Squadron Leader Kauky was a Czech he might not be burdened with the English reserve that Helga had been talking about, but there was still no guarantee that he would know who, or how many, had been killed during Operation Herod. It was possible, of course, that he might refuse to talk to a former enemy. There were however questions that he *would* be able to answer: did the RAF have prior knowledge of a planned attack on Britannia *and if so how did they know?* Had those twelve Spitfires been deliberately positioned over Dartmouth to await six

Focke-Wulfs from Maupertus? Could it have been because somebody found a message hidden in a cartridge case?

He thought about Helga; how she had coped so bravely with her dreadful disfigurement for the past seven years, never shy about it. He was always aware of that initial half-hidden look of horror on people's faces that Helga seemed oblivious to. People had been staring at Helga since their first meeting: first because she was such a pretty girl — and now . . .

Karl lay still, staring at the ceiling. Light through half-drawn curtains showed the walls of the bedroom slightly off vertical. Was that how they built houses in 1639? Was it true that this hotel was built as long ago as that? His eye traced down the far corner of the bedroom to a small table. There was a copy of the directory on that table: seeing it there made him think about a list of names beginning with the letter K . . .

Taking care not to wake Helga he eased out of bed, crept across the room, picked up the book and took it into the bathroom. He closed the door quietly behind him, switched on the light, sat on the edge of the bath and found the place: *Karn, Karslake, Kass, Kastrian, Kauffmann, Kauky* . . .

His eye flicked back: *KAUFFMANN A W*

A, *Kauffmann* — double F, double N. AWAK! He stared at the name, then carefully folded the page to mark the place. *AWAK:* the missing man, flying third in line behind Boxhammer during the attack on Dartmouth: missing, assumed dead . . . Could it really be him — *here in England?* How many Kauffmanns there could be in the world? Probably thousands of A Kauffmanns and possibly a few hundred A W Kauffmanns. But *A W A Kauffmann?* Memories of Charleville, 1940: abandoned livestock, cows bellowing to be milked, the staffel grounded in that endless month of bad weather and Awak, the farmer's son, spending hours every day milking those cows — sitting on a three-legged stool in the rain: butter and cream in the officers' mess. Karl remembered another episode: Awak turning up at Maupertus, wet but safe, with his lucky rabbit peeping trouser-button eyes from the open zip of his chest-pocket.

Even if there were ten million Kauffmanns in this world, there could only be one, rather simple, agricultural, extremely indestructible, ever-smiling Awak. Karl looked at the book again: *Hilldown Farm.* It was him . . . *it had to be.*

Karl was so engrossed that he never heard the bathroom door. Helga was there, blinking

270

in the light. He stood up. 'Tomorrow we will hire a car and visit an old friend of ours, somebody we haven't seen for nine years.'

She put a hand on his shoulder. 'Come to bed, Sweetheart. Sometimes I think the English surgeon must have left one of his spanners inside that head of yours.'

★   ★   ★

It was a wild expanse: gently sloping hills, wild ponies, strange pillars formed from piles of rock, lonely farmhouses, a pair of buzzards making circles in the sky.

Helga was trying to follow their progress on the map. When they reached the turning that she had marked, Karl swung Mr Benson's Riley off the road and bounced up a track between large boulders. Helga folded the map and put it back in the glove compartment. 'The farm should be about five kilometres ahead of us, but I still think we should have telephoned him first and anyway, how can we be sure that this Mr Kauffmann is really Awak?'

Karl needed no convincing: 'He's going to get the surprise of his life when he sees us. He used to adore you, Helga. Just you wait till he sees you getting out of the car.'

'Suppose he doesn't recognise me — and

what is he going to think when he sees my burnt face and what's left of my hair?'

'Don't be silly, you're a pretty girl: only your hairdresser knows about the bald patch.'

'Liar!' She looked away, searching her handbag for a handkerchief: 'Awak will have changed too, don't forget that — and what makes you so sure that he will want to see us?'

The farm was a clump of isolated buildings, slate roofs grey against a green hill that rose to trees on the skyline. Karl drove slowly over the final distance, steering around potholes, trying hard not to break the springs of Mr Benson's car — and quietly hoping. At the end of the track the farmyard gate stood open and, as they stopped the car, a woman appeared in the doorway of the house and walked towards them.

Karl said, 'Could you tell me if Albrecht Wilhelm Andreas Kauffmann lives here?'

The woman said simply, 'You've just missed him. Was it something important?'

Numbness: that was all that Karl could feel — a numb feeling of relief and surprise — and a simple thought: the indestructible nine-lives-Awak had done it yet again. *How could I have ever believed otherwise?*

19

Mrs Kauffmann explained to Karl and Helga that her husband had taken both daughters to spend the day with friends at a neighbouring farm — when he had dropped them off he would probably come straight back.

Karl had to duck his head as they went through into the sitting room. Late morning sun from the window traced a latticed pattern on the flagstone floor. There was a glass-fronted cabinet in the corner of the room with a display of two-handled silver cups; more cups on the mantelpiece and, on the walls, framed photographs of cows wearing rosettes, some of which included an unmistakable Awak dressed in a white coat.

They talked together for a long time. Karl and Helga explained how they had come to know Awak and how they had found out he was living in England. Mrs Kauffmann listened intently and appeared not to notice Helga's disfigurement.

Helga said, 'How did you meet your husband, Mrs Kauffmann?'

'That's a long story. The funny thing is I didn't realise he was German when I first met him — he still teases me about it — I thought he was a Welshman from Cardiff, can you imagine? Why don't I make some coffee and tell you about it. I tell this story to everyone — I suppose because it's so unusual. By the way, please call me Pauline; I feel I've known you both for ages.'

Pauline brought in the tray. As she poured coffee she said something about how easily the whole course of one's life could be changed by the events of a single day, the day the owner of the farm had left her in charge in September 1942. To illustrate the point she told them what had happened to her on the day of Operation Herod . . .

★   ★   ★

Hilldown Farm, Dartmoor — Friday, September the 18th, 1942:

Before Mrs Beresford left, she wound down the window on the passenger side of Beryl's lorry, leant out and said to Pauline: 'If the impossible does happen and Film Star starts to calve before I get back, just keep an eye on her — you won't need to do a thing. Two little hooves will appear, then whoosh! If the calf gets stuck just grab its feet and pull

— preferably at the same moment that Film Star decides to push — and by the way, make sure she is bedded down in plenty of clean straw. Whatever you do don't go pestering the vet, that man has far more important things to use his petrol coupons on than a simple act of parturition. I'll be back in a fortnight. Look after everything while I'm gone.'

Watching the milk-lorry until it was out of sight made Pauline realise how alone she was. She walked across the yard, opened the top half of the loose-box door and looked at a big South Devon cow lying in a generous bed of clean straw. The animal was chewing contentedly.

Pauline went up to the paddock and continued with the fencing. She unwound precious reels of pre-war wire along a line of new posts which she had been hammering into the ground over the past week. She attached the ends of the wires by winding them neatly around the straining-post which was an old railway sleeper set into concrete in the corner of the field.

Walking towards the other end, with the Patent Australian Wire Tensioner over her shoulder, the sound of aeroplanes from somewhere high in the clouds was enough to break her concentration . . . She took her Ingersoll from the back pocket of her dungarees: it was already after eleven: time for morning break. She sat on the grass, filled the cap of her thermos and took a gulp of tea. The aircraft sounded directly overhead now — probably a massed formation on its way to Europe with another load of salt for Adolf's tail.

Sitting there, at the top of the hill, with the farm lying in the valley below, the war seemed a long way off — too far away to alter the quiet routine of Hilldown Farm. Being in charge was a new experience. She had never been left to cope on her own; neither had she in the Hammersmith Bookshop, where she had learnt very little apart from what it felt like to be buried alive in rubble after the building had taken a direct hit.

She wore the standard green sweater of the Women's Land Army but had long ago abandoned the corduroy riding breeches for a more practical boiler suit. A red ribbon in her auburn hair was her only adornment: this wasn't London and on the farm she never met anybody. The nearest farm belonged to Mr Kimber, three miles away, and Mrs Beresford had already warned her about old Kimber and his habit of borrowing things — never coming himself but preferring to send one of his workers on foot. Rather disappointingly this had never happened since Pauline had come here to work.

Yes, a farm might be a safe place to live during a war but it was lonely. *Safe but lonely* — somebody should write a song about it. She thought back to her first encounter with the Land Army recruiting officer, a lady not unlike her games mistress at school: *We are fighting a war, Miss Richards*. Then something about not being expected to kill German soldiers — not yet anyway — *but the food we produce is vital for our nation's survival. Unskilled farm staff have been called up long ago: it's up to us now.* Then she had likened it all to answering a bugle call to arms; *chin up and never complain.*

Pauline had signed the contract without reading it — now she knew most of it by heart: *You are now a member of the Women's Land Army . . . pledged to hold yourself available for service on the land . . . you have made the home fields your battlefield. Your country relies on your loyalty and welcomes your help.*

Suddenly it sounded as if that battlefield wasn't very far away: aeroplanes again but much lower now — and some distant explosions . . .

She tipped the dregs of her tea onto the grass and stood up, thinking about what was written on Mrs Beresford's home-made calendar to mark Friday the 2nd of October 1942. Neat handwriting predicted the forth-coming event and a red arrow emphasised its importance: *FILM STAR DUE.* Pauline knew nothing about midwifery and Dartmoor wasn't like London where there were neighbours to help in a crisis. Beryl who drove the milk lorry was the only regular visitor and the Mr Kimber, the nearest neighbour, lived more than three miles away. More thumps and bangs came from the direction of Torbay or Dartmouth and now the crackle and chatter of guns were making a contribution.

Pauline used her fingers to count: the 2nd of October was still fourteen days away and, although Film Star was already bedded down in her loose-box to await the event, there were as yet no signs of *imminent parturition*, as Mrs Beresford would say.

By five o'clock the sky had turned black. Pauline called in the cows, loudly because they had wandered over the hill and were out of sight. In the beginning, when she had first started this job, she had felt stupid; talking to cows made her feel slightly awkward but it was, after all, the only way to bring them down off that hill. *Come on! Come on! Come down from there* — something like that. As the first cow showed itself in the distance

Pauline felt the first spots of rain on her face.

After milking she let the cows make their own way up to the hill again where they would spend the night. Back in the yard she opened Film Star's door. This time something was happening. The cow was standing up, breathing in a series of grunts. Pauline went inside and ran her hand along the animal's back, it was damp with sweat. It was then that she noticed something she had been dreading: sticking out from under the raised tail there was a small, wet hoof. *Oh my God! Can't you wait till Mrs B gets back?*

In her head she began trying to sort out Mrs Beresford's advice: *clean straw; don't phone the vet; you won't need to do a thing; two little hooves; whoosh!*

She was forcing herself to keep calm but Mrs B had said *two* hooves; Film Star had produced only one. She ran to fetch more straw, then stood ankle deep in it, watching helplessly, listening to rain drumming on the tin roof. The cow was straining at regular intervals — but the single hoof made no further progress.

An hour passed. Nothing changed. *Grab hold of the little feet and pull*; that was Mrs Beresford's other piece of casual advice shouted from the cab of Beryl's lorry — but there were no *feet* — just a foot.

Pauline grabbed hold of the hoof; it was soft and slippery, and she couldn't get a proper grip. Using a handkerchief she tried again but, when she let go, it jumped back as if attached to elastic. She was close to panic as she ran to the house, splashing through puddles, telling herself that the vet may not have much petrol but at least he could give advice over the telephone. Pinned up all over the office wall were little bits of paper, visiting cards, snippets from the Chronicle: blacksmiths, plumbers, an agricultural contractor, animal feed merchants, an insurance company. She scanned them frantically — there was a pessimistic card from the knacker: *fallen stock removed at short notice* — but no vet. She read through all the scribbled notes on the back of the calendar and rummaged through the desk — no stray vet's bills, nothing. Then she remembered that the telephone was out of order because the line was still down after the gale.

A genuine but bad tempered prayer escaped through her clenched teeth: '*Help me God, for Christ's sake.*'

She turned to run across the yard but stopped abruptly . . .

There was a man standing in the porch.

She lost her balance and would have fallen if he had not caught her. With a hand over her mouth she said, 'Sorry, I didn't see you!'

He was young — and smiling: about the same age as Pauline, who quickly freed herself from his grasp, realising at once that he must have come from the Kimbers' farm.

A narrow beam of hope: the Kimbers had a much larger herd of cows than Mrs B. If this man was allowed to be a farm worker in wartime it meant that he had special skills. Perhaps God had heard that prayer after all. 'Film Star is trying to have a baby. She seems to have got stuck — been straining for ages. Can you help?'

For a moment the man looked completely mystified. The smile was still there but he said nothing. Pauline, now desperate, took his sleeve and literally towed him across the yard. Leaning over the bottom half of the door she said, 'I swear that animal will die if we don't do something quickly!'

The man watched the cow for a full minute, then turned to her again. 'Where is the film star?'

'*That's* Film Star — that cow with a hoof sticking out of its bottom!' She unbolted the door and pushed him inside. The cow staggered sideways against the wall, mouth open, tongue lolling; breath continuing in short, painful gasps.

The man peered at the tiny hoof. He

scratched his head, stroked the animal's sweating flank and muttered something unintelligible. The cow cocked back an ear to listen. Raising his voice he said, 'Hot water and soap I must have.'

Pauline sprinted across the yard to fill a bucket from the kitchen tap. It was heavy, it slopped into the top of her gumboot as she staggered back. The last block of Sunlight was jammed into her back pocket on top of her watch, and the towel over her shoulder was soaking up rain. She pulled back the door and put down the bucket — alarmed to see that the man had stripped to boots and underpants. It was worse than a nightmare: he was talking to the cow in some unintelligible language.

He dipped his hands into the water and soaped himself to the armpits. He splashed copious amounts of soapy water onto the little hoof and all over the back end of the cow; then, instead of pulling the hoof, Pauline was dismayed to see him *pushing it back in*.

'*What on earth are you doing?*'

Without replying, he caught the cow's swishing tail with his left hand. Pauline was speechless as she watched him slide his right arm into . . . *Oh my God*. Stomach-numbing nausea welled inside her at the sight of it. The man's body was covered in muck, his arm was up to the hilt. *Please God, don't let him kill Mrs B's best cow.*

He was leaning forward now, eyes closed in concentration, cheek pressed against the cow's side. He looked over his shoulder. 'Light, I need light.'

Pauline ran back to the house in the gathering darkness. The torch didn't work — no battery. She grabbed a candle and matches from the top of the dresser, ran back, lit a match, melted the bottom of the candle and stuck it to the bottom of the upturned bucket.

Film Star took two unsteady paces forward. The man, arm completely buried, was forced to follow.

'Eine Halfter — please?'

'A halter?' She fetched one, fitted it over Film Star's head and held the rope. The man let go of the tail; Pauline caught it one handed but not before it had lashed her painfully across the face. She could see sweat channelled in the furrow of his spine as he began to withdraw his steaming arm. He was pulling on something. The hoof re-emerged into the light; she looked again. *Now there were two.*

The man said, 'You must be talking to the film star. The film star like to hear your voice. She no longer has fear if you speak to her.'

Pauline gave the man a strange look, then glared into the cow's bulging eye. *What was one supposed to say?* She managed: 'Come on old girl, do your bit for England. Don't you know there's a war on?'

The cow grunted, and the man laughed. 'Your cow speak very good English. If the film star fight the war, will she be a sailor or an airman or a soldier? Which side she take?'

'Ours, of course!' *Stupid man.*

As if in response, the animal produced powerful contractions — a nose appeared between the hooves — another grunt — a deafening moo — more heaves — a head — a neck — and suddenly a large steaming mass slithered into the man's arms. As the calf made its first high pitched complaint, the umbilical cord deflated like a pricked inner tube and snapped off close to the navel.

'The cow can be free now.'

She let go of the rope. Film Star swung round and put a sharp hoof on Pauline's gumbooted foot. She yelled, staggered back and fell over the bucket supporting the candle. In seconds the straw was alight. Pauline hopped towards the open door. The cow ran into the yard with afterbirth hanging out of her like wet bedclothes. Pauline grabbed the calf and heaved it outside; the man flailed at the flames with his overalls.

Pauline picked up the cowshed hose and turned on the tap. Three frantic minutes later the flames were out. They emerged into the yard gasping for air. Film Star was calm, standing in the rain licking her calf.

After they had settled cow and calf into clean quarters for the night, Pauline led the stranger into the house. 'Look at you: nearly nothing on, soaking, filthy, no clothes to change into! You must have a bath. The water should be hot enough — at least for a five-incher, and somewhere in this house there are clothes that belonged to the late Major Beresford; I never met him, so I haven't the foggiest if they'll fit.'

'The five-incher — what is this?'

'Oh, you know — for the war effort!' Pauline made a passable imitation of the Minister of Fuel and Power's wireless voice: *'Filling your bath to a depth of no more than five inches, saves fuel and helps defeat the Hun* — in your case I think the said minister might be prepared to turn a blind eye — especially as you have just made a contribution to the nation's milk supply. I don't mind telling you, that cow would have died if you hadn't come along: if I were Minister of Food you'd jolly well get an MC.'

'MC?'

'Midwife's Cross — don't you country folk

know *anything?* By the way, my name is Pauline, I don't think we introduced ourselves.'

He bowed his head and shook her hand rather formally, but did not say his name.

When he was halfway up the stairs she had a sudden thought — and followed him up. 'What was it you wanted to borrow?'

'Borrow?'

'Mrs Beresford says that whenever she sees somebody from the Kimbers' it's because they want to borrow something!' She pulled a towel from the airing-cupboard and shoved it at him. 'Sorry, perhaps I shouldn't have said that!'

His expression was blank as he tried to repeat the word: 'Kimbers?'

'From Quarry Farm. Aren't you from there?'

'No.'

Pauline frowned. 'If you're not from Quarry Farm where *have* you sprung from? You can't have just dropped out of the sky — what brought you here?'

'I walk. My friends expect me . . . ' He broke off abruptly.

Pauline went into the bathroom and turned on the hot tap. 'I'm afraid you won't be able to contact your friends because the telephone doesn't work.'

He seemed resigned. 'Now I cannot return.'

She thought it best to stop asking questions and let him get on with his bath. At least one thing was clear: this rather simple but skilful man would be staying the night at Hilldown Farm.

'I'll make up the bed in the spare room and find you some clothes. Come down when you're ready and we'll have supper.'

Downstairs she put more peat on the kitchen range, and opened the damper a notch to compensate for what sounded like an extremely deep bath running upstairs. The sound of rain dashing against the window was muffled by the blackout curtains but there was a cold draught coming in under the back door which made her decide to light the open fire as well.

Pauline crumpled last week's paper into the grate, realising how lucky she was to have had this unexpected help. Where had the man come from if he wasn't from Quarry Farm? He hadn't given her a straight answer about that, in fact he had seemed rather evasive. But thank goodness he had come! Perhaps he was a cowman from some other farm and had left after a row. Anyway, he had been jolly useful — and nice too. After a dubious beginning he had turned out to be the capable and silent type with a smile thrown in free of charge.

She dug into the log basket looking for apple twigs. She crumpled newspaper into the grate. *The Asburton Chronicle* had arrived by milk lorry only yesterday; even though Pauline hadn't finished reading it the fire would take priority — in any case there were no old copies in the house because Beryl had just taken away all the waste paper for the salvage collection. When Pauline had finished laying the fire she put a match to it and watched the flames take hold.

Then she remembered something she had read in this week's edition which was now well alight: *The Cardiff Rapist*, that's what they called him. *The Cardiff rapist — escaped from a Dartmoor working-party. Do not approach this man!*

The stranger upstairs had said very little, but enough to show that he had a most unusual accent; he had a strange way of saying things too: he couldn't be a local man. Was he Welsh — from Cardiff? What was it he had said? Something about his friends expecting him?

Pauline was already regretting that she had offered him supper and a bed. *A rapist — here at Hilldown — God help me.* Run three miles to the Kimbers' place? No, keep calm. Behave normally. Get through the night

288

unharmed, try to slip a message to Beryl when she comes for the morning milk.

Keep calm — yes, keep calm — that was the way — give him the supper. Be prepared for trouble — and be aware that whatever this man wants it will be something very different from the amorous fumblings of an elderly man called Mr Drake in the musty seclusion of the Victorian Romance department at the back of a bookshop in Hammersmith.

Pauline took a carving-knife from the kitchen drawer and slid it under the blackout curtain where she could reach it quickly.

'That evil man over there, and his cluster of confederates, are not sure of themselves — what is this?'

An egg slipped from her hand and broke over the top of her shoe. The man was wearing the Major's dressing gown and reading from Mrs Beresford's calendar. *Keep friendly — not too friendly.* 'Mrs Beresford wrote that, it's her patriotic quotation of the month, something Mr Churchill said about Adolf's lot — rather good, don't you think?' She added, 'Mrs Beresford who owns this place once told me that if a Jerry parachutist were to knock on that door she would kick him hard.' *Say something else quickly:* 'Supper will be ready soon. Was there enough hot water?'

The man said nothing. He sat at the table and was silent for so long that Pauline was forced to turn her back on him while she prepared the meal. There was no conversation — just a stifling silence.

When she finally turned to lay the table, the man was asleep — still sitting there, but body slumped, head resting on outflung arms. She crept upstairs to fetch a blanket and laid it across his shoulders — gently so as not to wake him. Standing at the draining board she ate a double helping of omelette and leaving the washing-up undone went upstairs with broken eggshell stuck to her shoe — and the kitchen knife in her hand.

In the early morning Pauline crept downstairs and opened the blackout curtains. The man was still in the kitchen. He had moved; now lying on the floor by the fireplace. He had pulled the blanket over him so that only his head was showing and his snoring was loud enough to drown the squeal of the backdoor hinge.

Cold air filled her lungs. Calling the cows down from the hill for milking, loudly as she always did, helped to shake away the uncertainties of the night. While milking Pauline tried to think how best to get him off the premises. Wash his clothes, somehow get them dry — then — hopefully, *goodbye*. The man had eaten nothing since his arrival so he would need breakfast.

Pauline closed the gate behind the last cow and watched the animals make their way past the half completed fence at the top of the paddock and up onto the hill to graze the last of the autumn grass. When she got back to the kitchen the man was no longer there. She could hear him moving about upstairs.

Mercifully there was a fresh drying breeze. She washed his shirt and underclothes and hung them on the line. She picked up the overalls: an unusual design, much too elaborate for prison issue, a lot of zips, each with a sensible leather tag for easy grip: one on each sleeve running from wrist to elbow and zips down the outside of either leg. There was something lumpy in the chest pocket; she drew the zip across and put her hand inside: something woollen, knitted, too small for a sweater. *A rabbit:* long ears, trouser-button eyes and horsehair whiskers — *a child's toy*. There was something in the knee-pocket too: a thick wad of cloth-backed paper which she placed next to the rabbit on the end of the draining board.

In a state of growing confusion Pauline finished washing the overalls and hung them on the line next to his other clothes.

291

Back in the scullery she picked up his belt: leather — the fastening was a square aluminium slot with a design stamped into it. By the window, where the light was better, she made out the clear outline of a laurel wreath and a flying eagle.

Then in one paralysing second she saw it: *clutched in the bird's talons was Hitler's symbol of death.*

She dropped the belt, dashed back to the draining board, snatched up the cloth-backed paper: *Karte von Grossbritannien* — a map of England.

A scuff of slippers: 'What are you doing, Pauline?'

She turned to face him, holding out the map, defiantly, unable to say anything because her throat wouldn't open.

He was smiling again — like a schoolboy caught with stolen apples. 'You are right, Pauline, I drop — from the sky, I drop down. You must not be afraid of me — or kick me like Mrs Beresford.'

He walked towards the back door. 'The film star is good today? The baby is good also?'

He waited for her answer but none came. Calmly he put on his boots, tucked in the legs of the pyjamas, and walked across the yard in the direction of Film Star's shed with his hands in the pockets of Major Beresford's dressing gown.

★ ★ ★

Pauline got up from her chair. 'You asked for it, now you know!' She went over to the window and looked out across the yard. 'That must be him now, I can hear the car.'

A battered Austin Seven came to a stop. As the driver got out Karl, who had stepped into the yard, shouted across to him. 'Können Sie mir sagen, wo Awak ist?'

Albrecht Kauffmann parted his lips, cocked his head slightly, and narrowed his eyes; he was saying something but neither Karl nor Helga could hear what it was.

He walked towards them. '*Deichy?*' He took Karl's hand between both of his. '*Karl Deichman?* Is this a dream? How did you get here? I thought you were . . . '

He turned to Helga and said in English, 'You will have to excuse me, I knew this man many years ago; now, seeing him like this — alive . . . I . . . '

Karl clapped his hand on Awak's shoulder. 'It's Helga, for goodness sake, don't you recognise her?'

'*Helga?* Your wife, Helga? It can't be!'

She smiled. 'Hello, Awak.'

293

Awak put his arms around her. 'But . . . '

She cut in quickly. 'On the outside I've changed, I know that — but I'm still Helga inside — and you are the same old Awak, you haven't changed.'

He looked from one to the other. 'Of course none of us has changed but *how in Heaven's name did you two find me?*'

Karl pointed into the distance. 'We were motoring along that road and Helga thought she could smell cows — it made her think of you!'

Awak threw a playful punch. '*Same old Deichy!*' He turned to Pauline and spoke to her in English. 'I last saw these friends on the morning of the day we met — the day Film Star gave birth to Ginger.'

Karl added, 'We thought Albert, as you call him, was dead — it's a surprise for us too.'

Awak countered. 'It is Deichy who should be dead from what I saw.'

Helga joined in. 'Karl once thought that I died in a big fire but I am alive also.'

Pauline pretended total confusion. 'Would those who are still in the land of the living fancy some corned beef and salad for lunch?'

20

The two former Luftwaffe pilots strolled across the yard, wandered up the long sloping paddock, went through the open gate at the top and out onto the hill beyond. Brown cows dotted the slope.

As they walked past the edge of a wood, Karl turned to the subject of Operation Herod. 'Could you see Boxhammer from where you were? Did his bomb fall through the quarterdeck roof?'

Awak was looking into the distance in the direction of the cows. 'Boxhammer scored a direct hit, the roof fell in just like he said it would.'

'Do you know what happened to the boys inside, Awak, do you know anything about that?'

He glanced quickly at Karl, then turned away. 'There was a war on, Deichy, don't you remember? In a war soldiers kill the enemy because if they don't, the enemy kills them — and don't you forget it.'

'But they weren't soldiers, were they? The cadets in Britannia were boys, unarmed teenagers — some of them were only thirteen years old.'

Awak gave Karl another playful thump. 'Come on, Deichy! Why are we discussing ancient history? It's time we forgot all about it — this is 1951, more than halfway through the century. Worry about the future but spare me your guilt about the past!'

Did it matter — temporarily upsetting an old friend like this if it meant taking another step towards the truth? 'Of course I'm interested in the future: that's why I talk about these things.'

Awak said, 'You're not making any sense, Deichy. Let's forget it, let's go back and have a drink with the girls . . . '

'I can't forget it. I've never told you this before — but you might as well know now. I believe that one of the cadets in that college was my cousin — a childhood friend — close, like a brother. *Did we kill him?* That is what I am trying to find out.'

'Your cousin — in the Royal Navy?'

'My aunt married an Englishman, he was their son.'

'You never told us that, Deichy. We knew you'd spent holidays in Dartmouth during peacetime but I never realised you had relations in this country. I'm afraid to say that if your cousin — or anybody else for that matter — was in the quarterdeck at 11.30 on that day, I don't see how he could have survived.'

Was this the proof, was this enough? Did this make him guilty — finally? Andrew Gatting killed at the hands of his German cousin? All for one. One for all until death. We swear it before God! 'You say that none could have survived but you don't *know* that for certain, do you Awak?'

'Neither of us will ever know for certain.' Awak looked down at the cluster of farm buildings below. 'That Dartmouth business brought Pauline and me together so now I prefer to regard it as something good, something that changed my life for the better. I try not to think about all those dead boys — if I did I would have to live my life believing I had done something wrong by fighting for my country. The war is finished, Deichy. It's over, done with and finished. That means the wounds are healing. The fighting men have shaken hands. As for those boys — yes, there was a time when I thought about them every day, *every bloody day*, but I'm over that now — it's in the past.'

They continued walking. It was calm. The trees were silent, they could almost hear the grass crushing under their feet.

Karl, subdued now: 'I didn't see what happened to you because I was in front. I also had a Spitfire behind me and was too busy trying to see where I was going.'

Awak looked into the distance. 'I was behind Boxhammer, third in line. When we made landfall I could see him relaying your hand-signals back to me. You led us to the wrong place, Deichy: Torbay I've since discovered. We followed you along the coast until you found that landmark — what was it called — the Mew Stone? It's funny but there are some things in life one never forgets. I thought I'd forgotten about those naval cadets until you reminded me. Yes, it's all still there: everything that happened to me on the day of Operation Herod. Do you want to hear about it . . . ?'

Karl nodded. It might help to dispel the uncomfortable atmosphere that seemed to have come between them.

'When I saw the Mew Stone I closed up behind Boxhammer, entered the harbour and flew over the railway station . . . *three towers in a straight line*, remember? I began my first shallow turn of the waiting-circuit and saw you and Boxhammer on the bombing run. Your bomb missed the main building and it looked as though Boxhammer was going to crash into the clock — but somehow he managed to put his high explosive right through the slates. It blew up leaving a big hole. The Spitfires seemed to come from everywhere: Mark Fives, dropping out of the clouds, trying like hell not to hit the ground or fall into the river. They were travelling very fast. I remember thinking they couldn't possibly be the lame machines that Boxhammer was so keen on ridiculing. One of them was on your tail.'

Karl nodded. 'I flew right through a hedge trying to get away from him.'

Awak continued. 'Boxhammer seemed to lose control: his wing-tip hit the ground and the whole aircraft disintegrated. I came out of my waiting-pattern. There were two vessels and a floating crane clustered together in the river below me. As I released my bomb there must have been a Tommy behind me because I saw tracer hosing forward over my right wing. I remembered one of Boxhammer's sayings — you remember the one: *always try to wrong-foot the enemy by turning* **towards** a narrow miss — flip into the opposite turn while he's still trying to correct his aim. But by now fragments of propeller were breaking off and slamming into my windscreen. The engine was vibrating as I tried to make height. There was rising ground ahead sloping up into cloud and I wasn't getting any pull from the damaged prop.

'I was completely blind inside that cloud — and I was sinking towards enemy land, engine banging like hell and too low to jump.

I went hurtling down through the fog and remembered Boxhammer again: *pick an unobstructed line . . . don't lower your wheels for a forced landing unless you want to dig into unseen holes and finish arse-upwards . . .*

'Unobstructed line — that was a joke. I went through the crash-drill: *harness tight and locked; flaps down twenty; speed 155; throttle closed; switches off* — remember that? I glided — no I didn't, I was more like a meteorite. I could see rocks and bushes and stunted trees dashing towards me and disappearing under the cowling. I remember noticing that my speed was ninety-five kph when I hit. In spite of the din I distinctly heard the tyre on the tail-wheel exploding. A wing sheared off, the engine broke away, small trees were knocked flat. *Werk-Nummer 0130314* — I can still remember that — was scything a path leaving a trail of scrap. There I was: tightly held by straps; stretching out my legs to protect my body; arms in front of my face; still ploughing along — then silence. I remember wondering if death was silent until I smelt fumes of evaporating fuel.

'As soon as I stepped down onto enemy grass I felt myself sinking. I was in a kind of quicksand. I was waist deep but found something solid under my right foot and managed to struggle out. Once I got myself out of that hole I hid under a bush and slept for an hour — then I walked to the farm. When Pauline asked me to look after a pregnant film star I thought I was still dreaming. Now you tell me something, Deichy. Boxhammer was killed but what happened to the others?'

'They were killed too.'

'I was afraid of that. Do you remember meeting Geisler's mother and father? Do you remember how proud they were of him that time they came to Maupertus for his nineteenth birthday? I can't imagine what the news of Operation Herod must have done to them.'

At the top of the hill they turned to look across the valley again. Awak said quietly, 'Life in the Luftwaffe is a long way behind us now, thank God. If we are the only survivors of Operation Herod it makes our lives seem more valuable, don't you think? Pauline and I come up here sometimes; we look around and remind ourselves how lucky we are. This is the most beautiful place on earth, bet you didn't know that, Deichy? When I think of some of the things that happened to me in the German Airforce I say to myself *why me?* Why was I chosen to survive all that Tommy opposition over Dartmouth; cheat death in a lot of other places and come here and enjoy all this with my English wife? Was it *really* because an obliging beefeater kicked my arse at the crucial moment — or did the big man in the sky have a hand in it?'

They started back towards the farm but after a few paces Awak stopped. 'Why do you suppose those Tommies were there, Deichy? You know what I mean: time and place, all just right. Do you think they could have known we were coming?'

Karl looked away — he wanted to know the answer to that too but he wasn't prepared to discuss it with Awak. 'How should I know? I always assumed those Spitfires were there by chance, can't we leave it like that?'

'I'm not so sure that we can. Talking about it like this makes me think that perhaps they *did* know something. Think about it: the Tommies must have been already in position; they must have been ready and waiting for us while we were still out over the sea. It was a whole Tommy squadron, Deichy, I counted twelve. They outnumbered us two to one; they had the advantage of height and consequently the diving speed to catch us; they were screened by cloud but they knew exactly when and where to attack even though we had crossed the Channel *under* the enemy's radar screen. Can't you see,

Deichy? If they knew we were coming it means we were betrayed — somebody warned them. Who could it have been?'

'I thought you told me the war was over and it was time to forget and shake hands?'

'Treachery amongst our own people is something completely different. Even killing unarmed British teenagers seems unimportant when you compare it to having a traitor in your midst — trying to kill us all and jolly nearly succeeding. I know all this brought Pauline and me together but if I ever find out who betrayed us I'd kill him — I don't mind who he is. Somebody like that is a hundred times worse than a straightforward enemy airman trying to obey orders and doing the best he can for his country.'

Karl was silent while Awak continued with his story . . .

'There's a prison near here called Dartmoor, they took me there after I had given myself up: not pleasant from the inside I can assure you. After Dartmoor I was taken to a camp called Cockfosters near London where I filled in a Red Cross card to tell my parents I was still alive. They never replied because by the time my card reached Germany they were both dead. I was moved to an interrogation camp where an army major kept asking me why I'd been wearing a vest made by an

English firm called Morley with the name H G Beresford marked inside the neck in indelible ink. I told them I'd looted it from a crashed Lancaster bomber in Germany but they told me that the only H G Beresford to join the RAF had been killed by Wahabi tribesmen near the borders of Iraq in 1928. I was convinced they were going to shoot me for being a spy until I told them I was responsible for the heap of scrap aluminium near the quicksands.

'Once I was settled into a camp at Featherstone in Northumberland I spent a long time trying to improve my English by reading books and attending classes: I wanted to escape and find my way back to Pauline but before I could do that I was sent to Canada. On the way over we were terrified that one of our own U-boats might sink us in mid-Atlantic.

'In 1945 I came back to England and joined the workforce here. At that time there was a shortage of men in this country as you can imagine, so when I heard that some single men were being allowed to stay here I volunteered to go before the examination board to declare that I had no sympathy with the Nazi movement and would, in due course, take British nationality. My application was accepted.

'That's enough about me.' Awak picked up a piece of baler-wire lying in the paddock. 'If a cow swallows this stuff I have to get the vet to her; he diagnoses the problem with a mine-detector, knocks her out with chloroform and cuts a big hole. Come on, I'll show you my favourite cow, born on the day of the world famous Operation Herod.'

★ ★ ★

In the farmhouse kitchen the women had been talking too. Pauline explained that she had fallen in love with Awak while he was still hiding on the farm. 'Albert told me that his mother and father had a farm in Westphalia where they ran a herd of over two hundred: the old cowman who worked there taught him all he knew.

'Soon after she had gone off to Eastbourne, Mrs Beresford sent a card saying she had to go to London to look after an aunt who'd had a stroke — so Albert decided to stay here for a bit. He lived here for six whole weeks and helped me finish the fence. He milked the cows, trimmed a few overgrown hooves and taught me how to play chess. By the time Mrs Beresford got back here Albert had already given himself up but, to protect me, he never told anybody where he had been living. Then towards the end of the war Mrs B was in London again: a German V2 rocket killed her in February 1945. I got a letter from her solicitor saying she had changed her will and the farm was mine — no family you see. It feels funny never having been able to thank her for it.'

There were things she didn't tell Helga: the hunger she had felt for Albert when she saw a candlelit river of sweat running down the channel of his spine. Their last night together before he walked to Two Bridges to give himself up: the full-moon in a ring of haze; the tug of adrenaline in her stomach as she entered his bedroom; her hair on his face, his hands on her back. She wouldn't have been able to describe the rip-tide that swept repeatedly through her as they made love . . .

'By the time we got married we had a ready-made, four-year-old daughter. We have two girls now; they'll be sorry to have missed you. Did I tell you they are spending the day with our neighbours' children?' She took off her apron and hung it on the back of the kitchen door. 'Let's see where those men have got to.'

Pauline and Helga went out into the yard. Awak turned when he heard them coming and said in English, 'I was just telling Karl that Ginger here is due to calve next week.'

Helga looked over the loose-box door. 'Is she called Ginger because she is brown?'

'No, her real name is Ginger Rogers: she's the daughter of Film Star.'

Helga laughed. 'Pauline has already told us about Film Star and the calf that didn't want to be born.'

Awak pointed to the hill beyond the paddock. 'Film Star is up there with the others, she's the one with the crooked horn but you can't see that from here: twelve years old now, that's a lot for a cow. In the summer and early autumn — like now for instance — the cows have the run of the hill and wander away until they are out of sight. They must have good ears because they always come when I call them for milking.'

Pauline laughed. 'He calls to them in German — our cows don't understand English any more!'

Aware of Awak's suspicions about some-body having compromised Operation Herod, Karl wasn't sure that what he was about to suggest was wise — but decided to risk it anyway. 'We've discovered the name of one of the Spitfire pilots who gave us such a hard time during Operation Herod; he's a Czech — lives over here now, but we haven't met him yet. If I manage to make contact, would you two like to meet him?'

Awak laughed. 'Those Czech guys killed four of us but the war's over now, so why not?'

Pauline looked doubtful. 'I'd be interested to meet him too but our problem is that Ginger is due to calve — one of us will have to stay behind.'

Awak was quick to extinguish that idea. 'I'll ask Ben Kimber to come over and keep an eye on things, he won't mind.'

'If you say so, darling — but we are always asking favours and borrowing things from the Kimbers — don't you think it's getting a bit one-sided?'

21

Even though his appointment was not until eleven-thirty, Karl left Helga sleeping in the hotel. After breakfast he went for a walk by himself along the South Embankment where he bought a *Times* newspaper. He paused to look at an old cannon about which Uncle Hugh had once explained: *Crimean War — a joint effort by Britain and France nearly a hundred years ago, Charge of the Light Brigade, seventeen thousand British soldiers killed by disease, Florence Nightingale.* Uncle Hugh was now dead but his voice and the things he said still seemed alive.

After finding the agreed meeting place Karl carried on past the ferry landing-stage. From the cobbled walkway of Bayards Cove he got a good view of Dartmouth Castle in the distance. He entered the ruins of the other ancient castle, the smaller one called Bearscove which, one week before Operation Herod, had produced an accurate challenge from modern weapons hidden inside it during the reconnaissance flight over Dartmouth. He walked back to the appointed place and found a bench on the embankment close to a flight of stone steps leading down to the water. Sitting there in the sun he tested his knowledge of English on the *Times'* crossword puzzle to keep his mind off what would probably turn out to be yet another disappointment but he quickly discovered that the puzzle was too difficult so he watched the river instead . . .

He watched a trawler entering the crowded harbour: seagulls wheeling over it like torn paper in a gale — hungry, like the birds in Brixham on the day of Anna Stobart's tea party.

Eleven-thirty brought the sound of a slow, puttering motor and the shape of a white boat-hull showing clearly as it cruised past a grey trawler taking coal from a floating bunker.

Ivo Kauky brought his boat alongside and stepped ashore — precariously. He tied up to a metal ring at the foot of the steps with some difficulty because he was stooping, crippled in some way: body bent forward, rounded shoulders. His thinning white hair seemed to emphasise his disability but he was dressed smartly enough: ironed shirt, tie, new-looking blazer with a crest — probably RAF.

They sat together on the bench. Kauky pulled a cigarette from a crumpled packet of Senior Service, straightened it carefully and lit up with what appeared to be a gold plated

Ronson. He blew a long breath of smoke into the lightly moving air and spoke in German: friendly, relaxed — the conversation that followed came easily which made Karl deliberately refrain from asking his questions too early.

Ivo Kauky explained what had made him return to England: love for an English girl, he claimed — someone he had met while stationed at RAF Exeter during the war. He said something about love for a woman being the best reason for going anywhere. 'People sometimes ask me if I miss my home country — but I don't — not any more — not now that I've found my girl and married her. I had quite a job tracking her down when I got here last year. You see, Janet was going to join me in Czechoslovakia after the war but things never work out the way you plan.'

Karl wondered if it was wise to reinforce this truth by recounting some of his own experiences but, for the moment at least, he let the other man do the talking.

'It's wonderful to be here,' Ivo continued. 'This is a free country: one of the few nations that fought for freedom and managed to hold on to it — but sometimes I think that it is not a very *happy* country. When I got back here around this time last year I was surprised to find how depressed and downcast everybody was — not a bit like wartime. I know things are still bad: five ounces of meat per week; whisky nearly six pounds a bottle — but these people are *free* and certainly a lot better off than most folk in my country. The schoolmaster who taught me English — a man called Hugo Brejcha — used to say: *What stands if freedom fall?* I don't suppose you've heard that quotation before. Somehow I can't imagine the sayings of Rudyard Kipling being high on the agenda of German schools.'

Fortunately Ivo Kauky was showing no signs of hostility but this irrelevant conversation was beginning to make him impatient. Karl heard himself say — rather suddenly — 'As you know already, I was flying one of the Focke-Wulfs which were attacked by your Spitfires over this town in September 1942 . . . '

'That's right, you told me that over the telephone. It's perfectly all right by me, I won't bite.'

Karl told the Czech how the raid had been timed to coincide with the start of term, and asked — quite bluntly — if the RAF had been pre-warned.

Ivo drew in a lungful of smoke and exhaled as he spoke. 'I certainly knew nothing about it beforehand. As for anyone else knowing, I've never given it a thought. After your telephone call I looked up that day in my diary: it was a day much like any other except for something rather lucky that happened.'

Karl said, 'It certainly *was* lucky — for you that is. Who would have thought that so many Focke-Wulfs could be shot down by Mark Five Spitfires?'

At last there was the merest suggestion of hostility in the Czech's voice as he replied: 'That wasn't luck. We had the height and the speed — but I wasn't referring to that. Something else happened *after* the battle which really *did* depend on luck.' He put a hand on the back of the bench and levered himself up painfully. 'It's nearly twelve. If you want me talk about the war I'd rather do it over a glass or two of English beer.'

They walked a little way along the South Embankment. Kauky's conspicuous limp slowed their progress. In the Quay Hotel they bought drinks at the bar and sat at a table by the window . . .

★ ★ ★

RAF Station, Exeter: dawn, Friday, September the 18th, 1942:

Flying Officer Ivo Kauky had been sleeping soundly until a vicious alarm clock close to

313

his left ear thrust him into another day. He groped blindly to silence the din, switched on the light, took his diary from the bedside cupboard and read yesterday's entry. Diaries were against King's Regulations but Ivo felt no loyalty or obedience towards the British king. He hoped, however, that today, unlike yesterday, would bring him an opportunity to push Adolf Hitler another inch towards his downfall. Every day, bit by bit, inch by English inch — that was how it was done. Each day another step towards freedom; not for Britain who was free already but freedom for a much smaller country that lay twelve hundred kilometres to the east, a country that had been treated like sacrificial meat by France and Britain in a vain attempt to prevent this war.

He got off his bed, switched out the light, opened the blackout curtain and looked out in the direction of the English Channel. A tinge of red coloured the unbroken cloud cover. No fog. *Thank-you, God.*

He held onto the waistband of his pyjama trousers as he walked along the corridor, without slippers the linoleum was cold on his feet. He put his head round Borovec's door and spoke to him in Czech. 'Are you awake, Emil?'

Guttural expletives came out of the

darkness followed by: 'I know, five-fifteen: *Shagbat Duty*, you don't have to remind me!'

Ivo retreated to the ablutions and looked at himself in the mirror. His body was strong and upright but in the thick black stand of hair that added inches to his height he noticed for the first time some scattered flecks of grey. While shaving he asked himself: *How much more of this can the enemy take? How much longer before I can go home?*

At half-past-six Ivo and Emil took off from Exeter in the two long-range Mark Five Spitfires of No 310 (Czech) Squadron's Green section. Ivo led his wingman in a long climbing-turn over the sea, levelled out just under the cloud and saw the sun coming out of the ground like a fiery balloon and rise towards the clag. Over the leading edge of his port wing he could see the straits of Exmouth and a long finger of wake marking the place where an Air Sea Rescue amphibian struggled to get airborne. He hummed an English song, recently learned.

A Shagbat one day flying over the sea,
Found Sweet Fanny Adams but didn't
find me.
It found a fat mermaid and King Neptune's
daughter,

But left me down here all alone in the water.

The Supermarine Walrus Amphibian — half boat, half aeroplane, unarmed, designed to splash down in mine-infested seas to rescue ditched aircrew — did not always know where to find what it was looking for. That was the situation this morning: Boston bomber missing, assumed ditched; crew still adrift in a rubber dinghy after four days and still alive — *might be*. No wireless transmissions. No position-fixes. Today's duty was something the squadron commander usually referred to as *going through the motions*. Hopeless: probably all dead by now. Ivo had a radio-channel already tuned to Air Sea Rescue but he wasn't expecting to use it because, although the English Channel might look small on the map, it was really rather big.

The Shagbat had been climbing steadily, and was now close enough for its pilot to see Ivo's wave of acknowledgement as the two Spitfires adopted their usual square-search positions to protect the Walrus from the enemy above and help search the sea below: a familiar routine, slightly complicated by the low cruising speed of the amphibian. Today the conditions were bad for searching: the light was poor and — because all three pilots were forced to fly under the cloudbase — they were too low to get an extended view of the sea.

Ivo throttled back, weakened his petrol mixture and trimmed for level flight. Down there — anywhere — somewhere — maybe not there at all — in six-thousand square miles of life-sapping sea . . . The enemy might be out there too — sharp-eyed under the cloud and looking for opportunities.

Although alert to the search, his mind began to wander: he thought about his mother and father, and his brother and sister. *Is the family bakery still prospering under Nazi rule? Does Uncle Viktor still work in the Skoda factory? How long will it be before my family is reunited? What am I doing fighting this war — will it bring freedom to my country?* He thought about these things while his eyes worked on the sea and the horizon and the ceiling of cloud under which he was flying — it helped kill the monotony . . .

Shortly after eight o'clock, a glance at the fuel-gauge reminded Ivo that it would soon be time for breakfast. The two Spitfires of Black section were already in position so now it was time for the Greens to break off, head for home, and leave the Shagbat to continue with a fresh escort.

Although Cocholin's mouth was full of bacon, he was putting out theories: this time it was something to do with the squadron commander's proposed flying lesson later that morning. Somebody contributed: 'Won't be satisfied till we are able to fly close enough for mid-air copulation — like dragonflies.'

Ivo warmed his hands on a mug of coffee, trying to shake off the fatigue. 'I thought Yellow and Red were on convoys this morning.'

'They're to be back on the ground and refuelled by eleven — no excuses accepted.'

The debate continued — a mixture of Czech, English and RAF slang. Formation practice? Waste of juice — waste of time — waste of British ships that need our protection. Why now? What about Prague and the Homeland — how are *we* to benefit from this? Borovec was indignant too: in his best English he imitated an elderly civilian they sometimes met in The Anchor. 'Haven't these blighters realised yet? Does a bomb have to burst up their backsides before they notice there's a war going on?'

The legs of the crew room table bent under the weight of Squadron Leader Dolezal. His bulk half-obscured the sad photograph of

Valousek's upended aircraft and its caption: *The Spitfire has Good Brakes — Misuse of them will put You on your Nose*. He blew two immaculate smoke rings and addressed his pilots in their own language. 'Tactics are changing. The entire squadron will be working as a single unit more frequently from now on. It has nothing to do with arithmetic: the thinkers at Group tell us that a formation of twelve Spits carries *more* than six times the punch of an isolated pair. Fighter pilots will therefore no longer rely so much on single combat. The whole squadron must learn to fly very close together right up to the moment we engage the enemy.'

As if to illustrate the point, Dolezal blew another smoke ring and puffed two smaller ones through its rolling circle in quick succession. 'Take off at eleven-fifteen. It's a non-operational squadron practice but as always we'll be fully armed. At eight thousand feet we'll close into a tight formation so that we can see each other's hand-signals. We will, of course, observe radio silence throughout. We will practise turns for thirty minutes and then dive in line-astern for a simulated attack. *If at any time I break away, or if you hear my voice over the R/T, it means that ground control are vectoring us towards a real attack.* Any questions?'

The squadron's twelve long-range Mark Fives took off in pairs. They penetrated a thick blanket of cloud and formed up in tight formation in the clear air above. Dolezal led the squadron in a southerly direction. Ivo was flying close enough to see an old bullet-furrow under the paintwork of his leader's wing.

Halfway through the first manoeuvre — just as Kimlicka was passing underneath the squadron to take up his position on the inside of the first turn — Dolezal showed his duck-egg-blue underside and pulled down towards the white cloud-tops. Eleven pilots followed closely like beads on a string.

They dived blindly through cloud: no sensation of speed, just a violent buffeting as Ivo's airspeed needle swung past 450 mph. His altimeter was unwinding fast: five-thousand feet . . . four-thousand . . . *three . . . praying now.*

Dolezal in the headphones: '*Tally-ho. Six bandits at nought feet. Attack on sight. Cloud base 1800 feet.*'

Ivo burst into the clear: *water . . . the mast of a ship pointed up like a finger.* His vision was blacked momentarily with g-force as he pulled out — but he was aware of a dark shape passing over the top of his cockpit. He tipped into a turn, vision clearing, airframe

shuddering, wings flexing under the strain
— *turn the safety-ring to FIRE.*

From over his right shoulder a Focke-Wulf 190 flew towards the clock tower of a large building. The speeding shape of another enemy aircraft cut into the circles of his gunsight but a barrage of ground artillery made it swerve to one side before he could fire. A bomb detached and toppled end-over-end to burst somewhere behind the main building . . .

Stay close. his target clipped the brow of a hill and smashed a hedge in its effort to get away. *Over the hedge: target centred . . . two-second burst . . .* A large piece of cockpit came whirling back, slamming into the leading edge of Ivo's port wing.

Out of sight again: the FW had dropped behind a church trailing a mist of oil. Ivo cleared the church. Now he could see the Focke-Wulf, flying low between bungalows and houses bordering a narrow road. He dived, thumb on the firing-button; but never pressed it because now he could see the upturned faces of children on the ground below, circled in the rings of his gunsight. *Over the corn-stacks at full-throttle; across the cliff-face; south over the sea.*

Halfway across the Channel, with barely fifteen gallons of petrol left, Ivo broke off the chase, turned for home and set his engine controls to eke the last of his petrol . . .

If he had looked at his dials for half a second longer he would have missed it — as it was he only caught a glimpse: a smudge of yellow between wave-crests on a dark sea. Turning steeply to starboard, he craned his neck for a second look. Yes, a waving arm — in a dinghy drifting at least thirty miles outside the Shagbat's search pattern.

Ivo selected a channel and pushed over the switch of his microphone. 'Hello Seagull, Hello Seagull, Dogfox calling, do you read me? Over.'

The voice of the Shagbat captain, half-drowned by the slog of his Bristol Pegasus engine, came over the ether from somewhere far away. 'Go ahead Dogfox — receiving you strength three — over.'

'Dinghy below me, four survivors. Stand by for a fix — over.'

The crackling voice again: 'You clever little man.'

Ivo dropped his right hand to the console and switched to another frequency: 'Dogfox to Bolt Head, Dogfox to Bolt Head. Dinghy with four survivors below me. Give me a fix please. How do you read? Over.'

A girl's voice answered. 'Hello Dogfox, hello Dogfox. This is Bolt Head receiving you loud and clear. Transmit for thirty seconds. Over.'

Ivo was so low that he could see men lying motionless on the rubber floor of the dinghy — and the frenzied arm still waved as he skimmed over. Thirty seconds the girl had said — *thirty more seconds of precious fuel.* Nobody knew how it was done but they were getting better at these radio-fixes all the time.

Ivo swivelling his head, searching for the enemy: *'Hello Bolt Head. Hello Bolt Head. Dogfox calling. I think I have found the crew of the ditched Boston. I am low on fuel — repeat — low on fuel. Give me vector for emergency landing before I fall into the drink — talking of drink — beer, whisky, gin, sherry. I love Amanda, Beatrice, Carla, Enid but I have low oil pressure. Repeat, low oil pressure.* **Is that thirty seconds?** Over.'

'Hello Dogfox, hello Dogfox. You are twenty-two miles from us. Vector three-five-five for Bolt Head landfall. Leave the rescue to us now, over.'

'Thank-you Bolt Head. Have you got the wind, Sweetheart? Over.' He didn't expect her to laugh.

'Two-five-zero — fifteen — gusting thirty. Good luck. Out.'

But Bolt Head: a pig to put down on at the best of times. When the tiny patch of clifftop grass finally appeared, Ivo swore that he would never complain about having to land there again — even in gusts of thirty miles per hour. The needle on his radiator gauge had pushed well past the end of its dial: oil pressure dead now — and all three petrol tanks showed empty as he approached the cliff. *Touch wheels: bump across grass at eighty mph; propeller immobile — seized engine. Pray the whole bloody thing doesn't blow up with the heat.* But in spite of that possibility, Ivo put his head back and remained sitting in his cockpit after the Spitfire had come to rest: *Terra Firma* at last: the more firmer the less terror.

He telephoned base from the control-tower: *engine seized, prop won't move.* Yes, a lift to Exeter by car would make a pleasant change.

★ ★ ★

Ivo lit another cigarette. 'I married the driver who came to fetch me. Puncturing a tyre on the way back to Exeter helped break the ice: some muscle-bound airman had done up the wheel-nuts so tight that I had to help her get them off. *Wheel of Fortune* — that's Janet's name for a flat tyre now.'

Karl said, 'You haven't yet told me if your

squadron commander knew about our planned raid on the college.'

Ivo shrugged. 'Can't be sure about that. It's possible that Dolezal knew something — but I certainly didn't. I didn't even know that the building was a college. At that time most of us had been stationed in Exeter barely a month. The only thing that mattered to us — if you'll excuse me for saying so — was killing the enemy: as many as possible and as quickly as possible. It was only after talking to Barbara Carmichael that I realised that I'd been here before. To the pilots of 310 Squadron it was just another interception: we just happened to attack six enemy aircraft raiding an anonymous town that day and I ended up chasing one of them across the Channel. He was faster than me even though he was damaged. I lost him.'

Karl said, 'Out of the six who took part in that raid, only two remain: the other survivor came down in the middle of Dartmoor — so the one you chased across the Channel was me.'

Ivo smiled, drew on his cigarette and looked at Karl. 'If it hadn't been for you I wouldn't have found that dinghy. You saved the lives of four allied airmen that day. Not a bad day's work for a Luftwaffe pilot.'

While drinking his third pint of beer Karl

asked his final question, even though he knew that it must now be a waste of time. 'Do you know how many people were killed in the college during the attack? It's something I've been wanting to know for a long time.'

Ivo shrugged. 'Nobody ever told me that and frankly I wasn't interested. Why is it so important to you after all these years?'

Karl told him and it took a moment for Ivo to think of something to say. 'I'm sorry to hear that. If I could help in any way, believe me I would. What you need is the casualty list.'

'I know that — but I'm beginning to think that I'm never going to see it.'

Ivo finished his beer and thoughtfully wiped his mouth with the back of his hand. 'You told me that the 18th of September was the first day of the college term — how did you know that?'

'We had an agent working for us in Dartmouth, the information came from him.'

'An agent? Do you mean a spy — right here under our noses?'

Karl nodded.

Ivo turned to look out of the window. After a long pause he said, 'Has it ever occurred to you that it might have been your spy who told the RAF about the German plan to attack Dartmouth — an awful lot of your agents were forced to change sides you know.'

Karl, in an injured tone: 'Our own man? That's impossible. He was one hundred per cent loyal. A year later I worked closely with him, I trusted him, he was reliable. He would never have betrayed us. He would have given us a full report *and* a list of casualties if he'd been given the chance but he told me he had to leave Dartmouth *before* the raid to avoid arrest. If you don't believe me you can ask him yourself — he's arriving in Dartmouth this evening to spend a few days with his father who runs the wine shop.'

'Wine shop? — there's only one in this town. Do you mean to tell me that this man is the son of old Alec who runs McGuire's Wines and Spirits?'

Karl nodded.

'But I'm one of his customers!'

'Then perhaps you'd like to meet his son, Robert.'

'I might want to strangle him, but yes, I most certainly would!'

'And there is somebody else you might like to meet.'

'Somebody else?'

'Yes, the other surviving pilot from our staffel. His name is Albrecht Kauffmann. He's a farmer now and lives on Dartmoor. Yesterday, when I told him I was planning to meet you, he said he would like to meet you too — so would his wife.'

Ivo said, 'I'd very much like to meet these people. Let's all have lunch at Taylor's Restaurant on Wednesday.'

22

The proprietor of *McGuire's Wines and Spirits*, small, elderly, one-legged, got up from his chair behind the counter. He introduced himself and mopped sweat from his bald scalp with a spotted handkerchief. 'If it's Robert you're after he'll be back presently.' He shifted both crutches, splayed them to make a tripod and dragged another chair from behind the counter. 'He's somewhere around the town — best take the weight off you feet while you wait.' The man's neck was invisible between hunched shoulders. 'Will you be taking Hennesy's swift sensation?'

Karl's hesitation was just long enough to cause Alec McGuire to turn and push through a door behind the counter, body swinging like a pendulum between his crutches. He returned with a bottle and stooped behind the counter again. 'So you're a friend of Robert's.' He put two small glasses on the counter and poured generously. 'Everybody likes our Robert, he would have been a famous film star by now if the war hadn't put a stop to it. His mother was in the

Music Halls: he gets it from her.'

He pushed a brimming glass along the counter. 'Robert was born in November 1914. He was barely two weeks old when his mother was killed — killed by a German battleship — can you believe that? Steaming along the coast, large as life, loosing off its big guns at the town of Scarborough: the bed landed in the garden, I was still in it with Robert's mother next to me but she never lived to see the morning.'

Karl drank most of his brandy in one impatient gulp as the man continued . . .

'Robert liked it over in Dublin; my parents spoiled him there. Like all Portuguese ladies my mother adored little children. I was out of a job so I joined the British Army and lost my leg in Belgium — that limb would have had a Christian burial if the rats hadn't got to it first. My Robert was never a soldier; he helped me in the shop before he went to Portugal. It was hard after he'd gone. Busy times they were: all those contracts with local service establishments. You'd be surprised how much alcohol our shore-based sailors need to fight a war.'

Karl glanced at his Rolex.

Alec McGuire rattled on for another twenty minutes. He told Karl how Robert had been to summer camps in Germany as a boy scout before the war — and later had attended the Olympic Games in 1936 and given Adolf Hitler a Kraut salute — all these trips paid for by his Irish grandfather. Karl watched the door, trying not to listen, mentally phrasing and re-phrasing the question that he had been preparing for Robert, and declining a second glass of brandy.

Alec McGuire banged back the cork with the flat of his hand: 'I've just remembered something, Robert's taken his new wife to the hairdresser's for a permanent, he'll be waiting for her in the George and Dragon like as not.'

★   ★   ★

In the smoke-filled pub, Karl and Robert sat opposite each other at a small table. As always their conversation was in German . . .

After explaining that he had fully recovered from last year's operation on his head, Karl took a sip of beer and set his glass down carefully. 'I have a question for you Robert.'

'Really? What sort of question?'

'*Did you leak information about Operation Herod to the Allies?*'

Robert's mouth fell open. Then he quickly adopted a mood of wounded indignation. '*What put that idea into your head?*'

'Did you or didn't you?'

Robert finished his beer in long, nervous swallows. 'I'm going to need another of these before we go any further. Drink up and I'll put another half in the top of that one.' Karl refused and watched Robert walk thoughtfully to the bar to replenish his glass. *Yes — it was clear now:* this man had been hiding something.

Back at the table Robert said, 'Before I answer your question there is something I think you should know.'

Don't interrupt — let him do the talking . . .

'During the war, when you were in Hamburg and I was in Lisbon, I sent you reports on Allied shipping movements, do you remember that?'

'Of course, I was your controller, wasn't I?'

Robert smiled. 'Do you remember where most of that information came from?'

'Tarts, expensive ones, working the dock area of Lisbon — that's what you told me. I had to send you impressive sums of money via the German Embassy's diplomatic bag.'

'Oh yes, *the money* — that's another story, but let's not talk about that now, do you mind?' Robert shifted his glass awkwardly and leaned forward, 'Did it ever occur to you that during . . . ' He broke off suddenly and looked away.

Give the man time, he'll tell me . . . ' Go on Robert, I'm listening.'

'Nearly all those messages from Portugal were based on false information.'

A traitor? Is it possible? Was Ivo Kauky right? But the casualties — what about the casualties? Let him continue . . . There was a pause while both men eyed each other across the table.

Robert again: 'I'm not supposed to divulge any of this because I signed The Official Secrets Act. It means I have to keep my mouth shut until death — rather melodramatic don't you think?' He drank some more beer. 'But I've kept it back for far too long — high time you knew. Old comrades in arms: no secrets, friends for ever?' Robert reached across and clinked his glass against Karl's undrunk pint, 'I don't like deceiving old comrades.'

Karl mentally blotted out a twinge of pain somewhere near the base of his skull. *Here it comes . . . give him enough rope.*

'You're not going to like me after this . . . ' *Slurred now, slightly drunk, defences down . . .* 'All my transmissions: ship-names, cargoes, destinations, tonnages, timings, movements, cargoes in and out of the river Tagus and all that other information about the activities of Allied spies: everything was secretly vetted by the British

333

Embassy before transmission — and most of it was fiction.'

'You can't expect me to believe that.'

Robert leaned forward. 'As for those ladies-of-the-night — I was the one who interviewed them because I was the only member of the German Embassy staff who knew how to speak Portuguese. Do you remember me warning you that my sources of information were drying up — do you remember that?'

'You said Salazar had ordered the Portuguese police to clean up . . .'

'I'm sorry, but all that stuff about the police trying to enforce morality wasn't true. You might as well know it now while I'm still in the mood: immediately after Dartmouth I took the train to London and flew to Lisbon — at the time there was a scheduled service still running to Portugal as I'm sure you remember. I was met by somebody from the British Embassy who asked me to set up a kind of home-from-home for British seamen, right there in Lisbon. I had to be discreet about it because I had to carry out my duties in the German Embassy at the same time. The British wanted something that would keep their boys off the streets and out of the clutches of information-seeking dockside harlots in the pay of the Germans. I agreed, of course, and a Portuguese lady called Dona Fatima helped me do it. You'd be surprised how difficult it was to persuade the British Embassy's Shipping Department to use tax payers' money to set up a brothel. Unfortunately the consul happened to be a colonel in the Salvation Army. Once over that hurdle War Office funds were allocated and I set to work.

'With Fatima's help I created a haven for Allied seamen which was unbelievable value for money: dancing, sex, table-tennis, billiards, an extensive library of English books, canteen and bar. I recruited the staff and Fatima trained them — top security all the way — no questions asked — no questions answered: no ship-names, no cargoes, destinations, tonnages; never where the ships were going to nor where they had come from.' Robert finished his beer, put down the glass and wiped his mouth. 'I'd like you to know that *Fatima's Family* was officially recommended to all English speaking crewmen who were lucky enough to disembark in Lisbon. Between us, that Portuguese woman and I stiffened morale and shortened the war. We protected those boys from the deadly SS, *syphilis and submarines*. That's how it was — that is how we kept British sailors away from those VD-ridden whores in the pay of the Nazis. Fatima's Family is still open for business even today: no more British subsidies of course but still going strong. Standards have slipped but only slightly. Fatima is still there, she likes to remember those brave old days when she was making a unique contribution to the Allied war effort. You have to remember, Karl, that in October 1943, Winston Churchill reminded the British House of Commons that the Portuguese nation had, and still do have, a treaty with England that has been going on since 1373 — so it's easy to see why, deep down, they were so sympathetic to the Allied cause.

'There you have it, Karl. Right from the beginning I was working for the other side — not through any sense of loyalty you understand, but because I always believed that America would sooner or later come into the war like they did last time — and I didn't want to be caught on the wrong side when the tide turned.'

Karl's silent anger had turned to dumb surprise. He pushed back his chair and straightened his legs. 'Now I know why those Spitfires were waiting for us!'

Robert hardly paused. 'I was coming to that. The *Dartmouth Conspiracy*, as I like to call it, started at this table — this very one where we now sit. I remember the date because the British were mourning the death of Prince George at the time — he was the Duke of Kent, the King's youngest brother. I used to meet a man called Mr Carter at this table; we used to drink together. Carter was small and thin: defiance and patriotism in a pin-striped suit. Instead of the normal 'hello' or 'good-afternoon', his greeting was invariably: 'Have you got anything for me?'

'If you can spare the time I might as well tell you about that while we're at it — I've got nothing to lose.'

★ ★ ★

Dartmouth — Tuesday, August the 25th, 1942:

Carter put down his glass of Tizer — carefully, on the mat provided — and said very quietly: 'Have you got anything for me?'

A tiny nod was all that he expected. After that, and like everybody around them, they talked about the tragic flying-boat accident that had killed Prince George on his way to Iceland. Carter, who always seemed to know everything, said, 'Twenty-four years ago Prince George was a cadet at the college here in Dartmouth, missed the last lot by a whisker and went out to China in 1925. He joined one of our Insect Class gunboats patrolling a thousand miles of Yangtse river to protect British concessions out there, quelling riots. My brother was one of his shipmates.'

After the usual decent interval McGuire and Carter left the pub together and once they were in Coronation Park, Robert began to unload: 'Funny you should mention the college, Mr Carter, because that's what I have for you today. Do you remember, back in May, we were asked for a ground-plan of RNC Britannia?'

Carter cocked his head like a beagle: 'Yes, we arranged for someone to deliver a copy of the original architect's drawings to the German Embassy in Lisbon within three weeks of their asking — nice of us, wasn't it?'

Shortening his step to match Mr Carter's, Robert continued: 'I was beginning to think Jerry's interest in the RNC had gone off the boil — but last night they brought up the subject again.'

'What do they want this time?'

'They are keen to know exactly whereabouts in college the cadets assemble on the first day of term — also the date and the time.'

Carter swore quietly. 'If you ask me it's only a matter of time before they'll be asking us to send them the crown jewels!' He picked a speck of something from his sleeve and flicked it onto the grass. 'I suppose these people realise that Britannia is on leave at the moment?'

'Correct, but they want the dates confirmed: somehow they've discovered that Britannia's terms always start on a Friday. They told me that last year the Christmas Term started on Friday the 19th of September and the year before — meaning 1940 — it was on Friday the 20th. For 1942 they are assuming Friday the 18th — but would we kindly confirm?'

Mr Carter stopped walking, fumbled for his pocket diary, put on a pair of half-moons and flicked over some pages. 'The buggers are right: the 18th does fall on a Friday. I'll have to check with the Navy if term starts then but if the Krauts say so I'll bet you half-a-bloody-crown it does. What did you tell them?'

'Usual ploy — said I didn't know but would find out pronto.'

Carter closed his diary with a well-manicured hand. 'Keep walking and look natural for God's sake. This is bloody serious: the blighters are up to something unsavoury, judging by the smell. You'll have to stall them till *you-know-who* decides what should be done. Whatever happens we can't afford to blow your cover so you'll have to keep them waiting till we have a decision. Luckily we've still got the best part of three weeks to come up with something.'

As if to release the tension Mr Carter suddenly smiled and rubbed his hands together like an obliging peacetime grocer: 'Is there anything else we can we do for Jeremiah this week: half a kilogram of *Hammelfleisch* — a little *Sauerkraut* perhaps?'

Robert had been waiting for the opportunity: 'There are a couple of other things as it happens: they want to know what type of vessel is being built by Philip and Son in the Noss Shipyard.'

Carter shook his head in despair. 'All this curiosity is getting damned unhealthy for Britain if you ask me. What did you tell them?'

'I told them about the Air-Sea-Rescue launches being built for the RAF which I suspect they know already — but that isn't all. My controller asked me to find out the exact location of Longford House.'

Carter's tone changed abruptly. 'Now that *is* serious! The buggers must have spotted those Froggie torpedo-boats from the air; they mustn't have the answer to that one; if they succeed in bumping off Philippe all hell will break loose — you'll have to give them duff gen. You know, I'm beginning to think that having General de Gaulle's son based here in Dartmouth amongst his fellow officers in the Free French could turn out to be a bit of a liability in the long run.' Carter squared his pin-striped shoulders. 'Sometimes I wonder what the Brylcreem Brigade do all day, honestly I do, allowing Jerry's reconnaissance chappies to fly up our river whenever they feel like it, bold as bloody brass as if they owned the place!'

A squall of rain sent them sprinting for the bus shelter where Carter continued in riddles because there was an old woman with a hearing-aid already sheltering there.

'But they're *not* on their home pitch, old chap — not yet anyway. Keep the visiting team guessing at all times, that's my strategy. The wicket may have been taking a heck of a lot of spin lately but I happen to be rather good at spotting a googlie — and usually well before it's left the bowler's hand.'

When Mr Carter appeared in the George and Dragon three days later, his mood had changed. They avoided the park and walked together along Sandquay Road. Carter spoke so softly that Robert had to stoop to hear what he was saying: '*You're to tell them the truth about Friday the 18th of September. The cadets and staff will be gathered in the*

341

quarterdeck at 11.30 in the morning.'

Robert stared in disbelief. 'But if I tell them that, it's going to cause hundreds of deaths!'

Carter avoided his eyes. 'We have to tell the truth on this one. Your role is far too valuable to be compromised. I'm not prepared to discuss the ethics so you will just have to do what I say and let others worry about the consequences. I know it's hard but it's for the best, believe you me.'

★ ★ ★

The George and Dragon was filling up with holiday-makers. Karl's glass stood almost untouched on the table in front of him. The truth was coming out — *pouring out* at last but it was depressing, chilling to hear.

But Robert had not quite finished: 'On the morning of Operation Herod I sat at the top of a slope and saw it all happen, then I hurried home to tell Hamburg that the roof of the quarterdeck had fallen in exactly as planned. At the time I believed that there had been a huge loss of life.'

Karl sensed a flicker of hope: '*Tell me about the casualties!* You know about them, you *must* know!'

Robert inspected the fingernails of his right hand for so long that Karl had a strong desire to lean forward and shake him violently. Then he looked up and stared, unfocused, avoiding Karl's eyes. 'As a matter of fact I do know. It was all extremely unfortunate because a woman was killed . . . '

'A woman? . . . *One woman?* Karl's sigh of relief sounded like escaping steam.

'Yes, Anna's sister. It should never have happened. She was a wonderful person, I feel really bad about it — so does Anna of course, in fact sometimes I think she'll never get over it. Anna still talks about getting her revenge which I find extremely worrying — especially as I know from personal experience how determined she can be on the subject.'

'Do you mean to tell me that there were no cadets in the quarterdeck during Operation Herod?'

Robert nodded. 'The college was practically empty. Cadets and staff were on leave, Carter told me about it afterwards: one week before the term was due to start a letter was sent to all personnel due to rejoin Britannia. It contained a directive along these lines: *The beginning of term has been deferred by one week which is necessary every year in six — in order to phase correctly the Christmas leave.* This adjustment to the college calendar was the best idea they could come up with at such short notice without compromising my position as a double-agent. All the cadets and staff accepted it as perfectly reasonable and gladly accepted an extra week's leave. The Spitfires came from Exeter: their commander was a man called Squadron Leader Dolezal who was the only pilot entrusted with the secret. The college suffered extensive damage to the quarterdeck, a lot of classrooms and laboratories were destroyed. D-block lost all its windows on the south side.'

Karl felt weak with relief. 'So the cadets were completely unaffected.'

'They were. The seniors returned to a rather draughty Britannia on Friday the 25th, and the junior cadets were temporarily billeted in Muller's Orphanage in Bristol. Soon afterwards the college re-joined at Eaton Hall, a stately home near Chester belonging to a duke and naval training continued, there on the banks of the River Dee, until 1946.'

Karl started to say something but . . .

Anna Stobart had come into the pub.

She looked around, spotted them and made her way over to the table. Without looking at Karl she said, 'Am I interrupting something, darling?'

Robert got up and pulled out a chair. 'Karl, this is Anna, my wife. I believe you two already know each other.'

23

On Thursday the 23rd of August the 8.35 a.m. train from Kingswear hauled its seven coaches away from Dartmouth on an upward slope along the edge of the river estuary. Karl had the window seat. He still had Monday's *Times* newspaper but had long ago abandoned the crossword.

Instead of reading the newspaper he looked across the river to where the tower of Britannia caught shadows from a bank of fast moving cloud but the track was far too low for Karl to see the other two towers lying in a straight line behind the clock. The engine panted in low gear as it tackled the gradient. Down below, through a gap in the trees, he caught sight of the Noss Shipyard from a new angle and noticed a plaque attached to the end of one of the sheds: *Philip and Son, established 1858.*

Even after the train had threaded itself into a long dark tunnel, Karl continued to stare out of the window, too busy with his thoughts to worry about choking coal smoke from the engine coming in through the open window — and he was still thinking about things that

Ivo Kauky had said to him during the lunch party at Taylor's Restaurant when the train emerged into the light with the smoke sucking back and the train gathering speed on the flat.

Ivo had seemed keen to unburden his worst experiences. The Czech had talked freely telling how, when he and his fellow pilots flew their Spitfires back to Prague to form the nucleus of a new Czech Air Force, they met an aggressive Russian Air Force on full alert — that is how they were welcomed back to their homeland. Although the Americans had liberated Western Czechoslovakia in April 1945 they had allowed Russian forces to enter Prague a few days later. According to Ivo that had marked the start of a period of tyranny, enslavement, persecution, hardship and injustice in a wicked and oppressive regime.

It had felt strange talking so openly about it with somebody who had fought on the other side. The Czech was probably more bitter than he was prepared to show. He had said that imprisonment gives time for a man to think and by all accounts he'd had plenty of time for that. Britain had betrayed his country: Britain, France and Italy — the three of them together. Would Ivo ever be able to forgive them for that treacherous

346

alliance of September 1938 when a large part of his homeland was lost to the Nazi blackmailers? Yes, blackmailers they had been: Karl had long ago reached that conclusion. *This is the last territorial claim I have to make in Europe*: imagine the British believing that! Thirty pieces of silver in exchange for peace.

Karl turned to Helga who was sitting beside him. 'I had a long conversation with Ivo Kauky. He could remember what it was like in the flying school he attended when Hitler moved in: at first everything carried on as usual, most students believing they could still make a career in civil aviation but, after the school was disbanded, the trainee pilots were forced to join our army, but Ivo successfully applied to do 'essential' war work as a civilian.'

Helga said, 'So how did he end up in the Royal Air Force?'

'He went to the Skoda works in Pilsen and shared a flat with his Uncle Viktor who was a draughtsman. At first the idea of working in an arms factory seemed like treason to Ivo but he soon discovered that, even in a Nazi-controlled industry, there were patriots ready to serve their country. When Ivo first saw the complete technical specification of a tank that was being built there — and the engineering drawings — spread out on his uncle's bed late one night, it seemed impossible that so much paper could be concealed on one human body. The British had offered a reward: the job of smuggling those plans to England was considered vital and by the time Ivo arrived in Pilsen all arrangements had been made except for the choice of courier. Ivo wanted to leave the country, join an air force and fight for the Allies so he was the obvious choice.

'He said that the bicycle route to Poland nearly killed him. Eight days, and he sweated all the way, so much that he was afraid the plans would fall to pieces under his shirt. He completed his journey on foot to avoid border posts and a British agent organised his passage to Tilbury.

'He got to London in January 1940. Everybody seemed more concerned about the fact that the River Thames was frozen bank to bank for the first time since 1888 than they were with the war. Ivo was made to strip, officials helped unpeel him and in due course he signed a receipt for one thousand gold sovereigns — the money to be deposited in an underground bank vault.'

Helga said, 'I suppose that's how he managed to set up a furniture workshop and buy a house — and that boat. He also insisted on paying for our lunch.' She smiled, 'I like rich men — so do you by all accounts — you seem to have got on really well with Ivo.'

'You know how it is when I start talking to aviators. He told me about the Hawker Hurricane: built by women at the rate of 200 per month. He flew one in the Battle of Britain but Ivo told me he he wasn't fighting for Britain but for himself — and to save a certain bank in London. His last mission was in August 1945: a patrol over the Channel Islands to protect the liberating forces. Although Winston Churchill had leaned over a balcony somewhere in London to say, *Long live the cause of freedom* — it wasn't anything of the kind for Czechoslovakia.'

Helga said, 'But why is he all hunched up like that? — he can't have been like that when he was flying.'

'Chained arms and legs — a punishment for his first escape attempt. He was like that for so long that it crippled him permanently. The authorities were fearful of anyone who had fought with the Allies. 'Westernised' Czechs were only allowed menial jobs at starvation wages and it was prison for anyone who objected. Ivo said that one of the warders allowed him an exercise session, unshackled him in a rare moment of mercy, left him unguarded and he escaped. He must have been extremely determined. How could a man in that condition make a run for freedom?'

'And what about Janet — did you find out how they met?'

Karl explained how Ivo had landed his Spitfire on a clifftop on the day of Operation Herod, and how Janet was sent to fetch him. 'Ivo said that she looked far too young to drive a car — not that he was qualified to judge, having never driven a car himself. Their last evening together was in Exeter; Janet showed me a heart-shaped locket they had won by singing a duet together in a crooning competition.'

Helga said, 'I'm really surprised you and Ivo got on so well together; you'd think he'd had enough of Germans.'

'But he likes Germans. He shared a cell with a former German officer in a Panzer regiment and became his greatest friend — the cell mate had also been classed as a Western Troublemaker and was most surprised at Ivo's detailed knowledge of the P38(t) tank.'

'It must have been hard on Janet over here in England during all that time with just a heart-shaped locket to keep her company.'

'Her letters never reached him. He was hoping to find a house and a job, then come back for Janet — but they put him in jail instead. It's lucky he left all that money in England.'

'What happened to Uncle Viktor, did he tell you that?'

'Shortly after Ivo's bicycle ride Viktor was betrayed by a fellow worker and never seen again.'

The train slowed to negotiate a series of curves. They moved across to the other side of the carriage to look at the sea. Steep cliffs reached down to a solitary man, collar up against the wind, throwing a stick for his dog. There were seagulls diving on a fishing boat . . .

Karl said, 'Did you notice anything strange about Anna Stobart yesterday?'

'You mean Anna *McGuire*. I can't say I noticed anything strange but I had a long talk with her — all about her new life with Robert in Portugal.'

Karl thought about it: for Helga it was different; she hadn't been to tea with that woman in Brixham last year, hadn't seen her blowing off steam. He had noticed Anna being friendly towards Awak too, interested in his flight to Dartmouth; crashing on Dartmoor; his long walk to the farm — and Anna had found it *amusing*. All that business about Film Star trying to give birth to a calf and

Awak dropping out of the sky to give a hand. Awak of course had been behaving normally: flirting like he had in the old days with blushing girls from the dressing station. Anna Stobart, however — or *McGuire*, as she now claimed to be, had *not* been behaving normally.

'I can't understand that woman: she was acting out of character. I can understand her making peace with Robert because in the end — and I can still hardly believe it — it turns out that he was working for the British all along. She was friendly towards Ivo and Janet too which is quite natural. What I can't work out is why she should want to make friends with Awak? Of all people why him? Last year that woman was so bitter about her wartime grievances that she was incapable of forgiving anyone who had fought on our side, yet there she was making friends with Awak — a man who took part in the killing of her twin sister.'

Helga, as always, had a simple answer: 'Awak is an attractive man. Women adore him. If you were a woman, Deichy — God forbid — you would realise that. Remember Charleville — all those nurses? And, from what you say, Anna has changed too. When you told me about the trouble she caused last year I said all she needed was a good man in her life — do you remember that? Now she has Robert: it has changed her. What's so extraordinary about that, and what's so extraordinary about Anna showing an interest in Awak's favourite subject?'

Karl was not convinced: 'I wish I could inspire my students like that but unfortunately none of them have yet demonstrated the slightest enthusiasm for cows.'

The train rumbled on. People behaving out of character usually meant they were trying to hide something — the Abwehr had taught him that one.

Helga added: 'As far as I'm concerned, the only strange thing about Anna was that I kept thinking I'd met her somewhere before, either that or she reminded me of somebody — I'm not sure which. Apart from that I found her quite charming: when I told her we were going to the Festival of Britain she insisted that we spend an extra day in London to see the sights. She wrote down a list of places, wasn't that nice of her? But I don't know whether we'll have time to get through it all.'

Karl settled back, trying to ignore the persistent feeling of foreboding that was dominating his mood. He opened his newspaper in an attempt to divert his attention onto something else — and noticed a headline:

GERMAN TRADE RECOVERING INFLUENCE ON INTERNATIONAL TRADE

German exports have all but doubled during the past twelve months. By comparison, Britain is suffering runaway inflation and weakening exports.

It seemed impossible; how could the victor be worse off than the vanquished? Karl folded his paper. From the train window he could see an oil tanker regularly disappearing behind moving hills of water; smoke from its funnel was blowing forward in the gale. What do world markets matter when your own country has been split up by post-war politics?

'Talking about Communism makes me think about the dangers that still exist at home. What do you think will happen in Berlin, now that the city is divided into two politically opposed halves that may never be reconciled. Nobody wants to live in a restrictive regime so what's to stop everybody crowding into the free half of the city?'

Helga gave her husband a gentle dig with her elbow. 'You're sounding like a school teacher again. Don't be so serious, Deichy, you're supposed to be on holiday. I expect the mayor of Berlin or somebody equally important will put up a big fence right across the city, or better still a wall, so that the people on the Russian side won't know what they are missing.'

'*A wall?* That wouldn't last long! It's not a joke, Helga, we're talking about *people* now — not Awak's cows!'

'I know it's not a joke. If we had won the war our country would be properly united now. But there is one thing in our favour, food. Every item of food in Britain is still rationed — even at the restaurant there was a legal limit on how much Ivo was allowed to spend.'

'Sugar is still rationed in our country and I don't think you would find a super-abundance of things to eat in the Russian sector. In any case, I don't look at it as winning or losing any more — unlike some of my history students who think that wars are like football matches. Sometimes I try to explain how wars start by using a simple illustration from my own childhood.'

'What do you mean?'

'I tell them that my aunt married an Englishman, and during a summer holiday over here, I made a pact with my two cousins: a formal alliance between three separate participants — but I knowingly dishonoured the arrangement and tried to kill one of the members.'

'What do they say to that?'

'Some want to know more, others aren't interested. I try to show that treachery means war — something like that. Then again, if there had been a bit more treachery in Hitler's camp I suppose we might have been saved from a vain attempt to dominate the world.'

The sound was different now: a rapid metallic beat as the train sped towards Newton Abbot. Karl picked up his paper again and turned to the foreign news.

GERMANS SENTENCED TO DEATH IN PRAGUE

The trial of five former German officers accused of war crimes ended on Saturday. They were all sentenced to death. Major-General Max Rosztock, allegedly responsible for the razing of Lidice, was also accused of murdering men and boys who lived in the village and removing women and children to concentration camps. Major-General Schmidt, whilst commanding the 254th Infantry Division in Slovakia, was accused of ordering the destruction of

Svatz Mikulas, another village, in February 1945. Again, all women and children were imprisoned, men and boys were shot to death. Ernst Hitzegrad, head of a Gestapo department in Jicin (Moravia), was found guilty of murder and extorting information by torture.

Karl felt suddenly weak. He read the column through again, swallowing against rising nausea. *Lidice* — he almost said it aloud. Wasn't that where Ivo had once lived? *The murder of men and boys, the removal of women and children?* It was a disgrace, impossible to believe — yet there it was. During all that long conversation Ivo had kept this part of the story to himself; he had said that his family were all killed during the war — that was all . . . Now this — and it appeared that Lidice was not an isolated case.

Karl decided not to tell Helga about it — and hoped she wouldn't notice the headline should she decide to look at the newspaper; he put it on the seat beside him, out of sight. During a short wait at Newton Abbot while the Kingswear coaches were attached to the 9.26, Karl fetched coffee from the station buffet and, at the same time, dumped the newspaper into a bin on the platform.

When the train began to move again Karl said, 'I'm determined to see those Gatting boys again. 1938 is a long time ago; a lot can happen in thirteen years. I want to find out where Andrew is and satisfy myself that he really is alive — and Ian too. Those two were not just members of my family, they were my friends. That childish treaty still means a great deal to me. The Gattings' house in Plymouth has been destroyed by bombs and we have moved to Dusseldorf. I don't want to lose touch.'

'That will be our project for *next* summer, Deichy: find the survivors of the Gatting family come what may. Now, if you don't mind, it's my turn. The Festival of Britain, remember? It's the only reason I agreed to come to England with you. I've had enough of searching into the past — the future is what should concern us now. I read somewhere that the last British event along the lines of this Festival was the Great Exhibition of 1851 — so if we miss this we might have to wait a hundred years.'

'I don't know. They might organise something to celebrate the year twenty-hundred when it comes — that is if we haven't blown up the world with atomic bombs by then.'

She laughed grimly. 'I think it's bad luck to

look that far ahead — in any case we'll both be dead by twenty-hundred unless we go and live somewhere like Baden-Baden where we can have regular brine baths and massage.'

★ ★ ★

As Karl and Helga headed north over London's Waterloo Bridge in a taxi, they saw an enormous dome-like structure and, next to it, a strange metal object reaching up into the sky like a gigantic exclamation mark without its underlying dot.

The taxi driver opened a small communicating window behind him. 'That's the Skylon, that is — trade mark of the Festival of Britain. I know that Herbert Morrison wants to give us a pat on the back but that blooming thing alone cost twelve hundred bleeding quid; it'll be scrapped when the festival closes next month.' His head was twisted back but somehow he was still able to steer the taxi. 'We had a laugh down there last Saturday night — me and the missus — dancing in the open-air to Geraldo's Embassy Orchestra, with lights hanging in the trees; just like Christmas it was. And what do you think? Jean Simmons sang 'Let Him Go Let Him Tarry' — then a posh geezer called Noel Coward with a fag in a fag-holder sang

'Stately Homes of England'. The second Battalion of the Scots Guards beat the tattoo better than I ever saw them do it when I were in the British army. No extra charge once you're through them turnstiles, but there won't be no dancing tonight because it's Thursday. Dancing's on Tuesday and Saturday nights, nine-o-clock onwards on the Fairway. Don't you miss it — not if you're still here on Saturday. Well worth a butcher's I'd say.'

Helga said, 'Do they sell meat there too?'

'Sorry love, a butcher's hook — a look — an eyeful. No savvy? — Oh never mind.'

At Dorland Hall in Regent Street they joined a queue at the British Airways enquiry counter to confirm their flight to Dusseldorf on Monday the 27th of August. As Karl re-pocketed the tickets an idea came to him. He said to the girl behind the desk, 'I wonder if you could answer a personal question for me: do you happen to have a pilot working for you called Gatting?'

'Captain Ian Gatting? I used to fly with him before he went transatlantic; he's on Lockheed Constellations now, flies to Idlewild and back on the New York run.'

Karl blinked: *The New York run, could it really be as simple as that?* 'How can I get in touch with Ian Gatting?'

To the girl it was nothing more than routine, she opened a drawer, pulled out pen and paper and suggested that Karl write a letter. 'I'll make sure it's passed on to the Airways Terminal in Victoria this afternoon; they'll deliver it to London Airport and Captain Gatting will read it when he lands. You can keep the pen.' Her smile seemed genuine at last. 'We're rather proud of our biro pens, they can write 200,000 words without a refill — can you hear me? I said you can keep the pen.'

People behind them in the queue were showing signs of impatience as Karl moved away from the desk. He walked with Helga across the hall and they sat together on a leatherette sofa with the sound of Regent Street traffic coming through an open window above their heads. He shook his head. 'I've always known that Ian's ambition was to be an airline pilot. I can't think why I didn't think of this before.'

Karl wrote a long letter to his cousin. He explained about Operation Herod and the mission to destroy the college — and, although he was certain that Robert had told him the truth, he asked Ian to confirm that Andrew was alive and that the Britannia cadets had been absent from the college on the 18th of September 1942. When he had finished writing he sealed the letter in its envelope and handed it back.

Karl and Helga left Dorland Hall and walked down Regent Street. They admired a statue of the Greek God of Love at the centre of a large cross-roads, ate fish and chips in a small café nearby and bought tickets for a continuous variety programme showing at a theatre called The Windmill.

As they settled into the front stalls they could see, on the stage, a tableau composed of five young women with swept up hair, all standing stock still around a Roman pillar — a laurel wreath around each head was their only adornment.

Helga nudged her husband. 'See that one on the left with the dark hair, who does she remind you of?'

Karl narrowed his eyes. 'I know what you're thinking, Helga, but that girl is a lot taller than Anna.'

★   ★   ★

But, two hundred miles away, Anna was not standing stock still. She had slipped out by the back door of the shop while Robert was discussing wine business with his father and was now walking quickly along Duke Street, trying not to draw attention to herself by breaking into a run.

She was breathing hard by the time she found the garage, and knocked so hard on the glass panel of Mr Benson's office door — that it broke across the middle and cut her hand.

24

Anna had the steering wheel in a white-knuckled grip. The accelerator pedal was sandwiched between the cracked plywood floor of the car and the sole of her shoe.

With the engine revving violently in third gear, she roared up the long hill, past the main gate of Britannia College, exhaust smoke and oil fumes blowing past her ankles.

At madcap speed she swerved through Halwell, Totnes and Dartington. Her route was planned: an unfolded map flapped on the seat beside her. Forty minutes to the Venford Reservoir — forty minutes of clamour from Philippa, cajoling, goading, imploring from her place inside Anna's head. That voice had woken her at first light — and had been with her all day, repeating one word over and over again until Anna could think of nothing else as she wrestled with the Riley's slack steering against a buffeting side-gale.

She drove past the Forest Inn at Hexworthy without stopping, sped along the remote tracks beyond: bumping, banging, rattling, bouncing over bumps and potholes.

She stopped the car when she saw it.

A prehistoric circle of dark stone showed itself one hundred yards away to her right — she had already pencilled a circle around it on Ordnance Survey Sheet 175: this was the place. Encroaching grass under the wheels of the car showed that the track was little used. There was a strange pile of smooth boulders close to the prehistoric site, large enough to screen Mr Benson's Riley from anyone who might pass along this track between the time of four-thirty and six o'clock on a Thursday afternoon. She drove across grass to a place behind the stones, parked the car, switched off and withdrew the key. The *tick-tick-tick* of the cooling engine sounded like cracking steel in the hushed shelter of the rock pile . . .

She opened her handbag, grabbed a bottle of perfume and spilled half its contents into her handkerchief, which she held to her face and neck, stinging the cut on her hand, squeezing the damp linen and inhaling deeply until her head began to spin. Streaks of evaporating scent felt like cold fingers closing on her throat. She opened the neck of her coat to allow the heat of her body to produce further heady breaths of *Le Jade* . . .

The savage fragrance made the picture of a room flash into her mind, a room opposite a night-club. The terrifying anticipation of what she was about to do now made her body tremble, like it had just before her first appointment in France with a German officer.

The wind snatched at her raincoat as she stepped out of the car. She fastened the buttons and tightened the belt. Stooping forward against the gale she struck a straight line out across the moor, walking urgently to cover two miles within the time she had allowed herself — breaking into an ankle-twisting trot wherever smoother ground permitted — and all the time the voice of her twin sister clamouring loud and louder without pause: *Revenge, Revenge, Revenge . . .*

With breath snatched from her mouth by the wind, pain tugging her lungs, she made twenty minutes of stumbling progress across the moor to within sight of the trees which showed in the distance, like a dark smudge underlining the horizon. A further ten minutes of steep climbing brought her to the edge of the wood.

In the shelter of trees she leaned back against a smooth trunk. Pine-needles cushioned her aching feet and the slate-grey roof of a farm showed itself in the valley. Away to her right, big brown cows — heavy with milk — nuzzled the ground, searching for the last of the summer grass.

Anna waited. Her pounding heart barely

slackened its pace. She rested there against the tree, watching the minute-hand on her wristwatch make barely visible progress towards the moment . . .

Then she was sprinting across the fifty yard gap which separated her from the paddock fence and the open gate. The gate post, a rotting railway sleeper, had sagged; the gate had sunk to the ground; she struggled with it, closed it, secured the latch for good measure and ran back to the cover of the trees.

She waited again, listening to rustling treetops — and the voice that would not stop. She opened her coat and breathed in a waft of jasmine and lemon.

At exactly one minute past five o'clock she heard the call — faint but clear in the wind.

'*Kommt her, kommt her. Kommt her, meine Lieben!*'

The animals lifted their heads. A large cow with a crooked horn was the first to move towards the closed gate.

'*Komm . . . komm!*'

The other beasts followed but their way forward was blocked. As they began to bunch against the closed gate the leading cow made a bellowing complaint. Carried upwards on the wind the call came again: '*Komm schnell, Film Star, schnell, meine Liebe!*'

The cow with the crooked horn was

pressed against the wooden bars by the rest of the herd — all were now blaring and bellowing in discordant unison.

Anna felt an intense, trembling wave surge through her at the sight of the distant figure of a man as he began to advance towards her. Deep inside the pocket of her coat she closed her fist around the hilt of Alec McGuire's kitchen knife . . .

The man continued to climb steadily up the hill. '*Kommt her, kommt her!*'

She ran from the cover of the trees, bending low, using the bunched cows to screen her from the man. She pushed in amongst the animals, forcing her way between their tightly packed bodies, working forward between sweat-slicked coats, damp muzzles, trampling hooves, until only the cow with the crooked horn stood between her and the gate. Held in the swaying press she saw images of a wounded bull and a spur-raked horse as her perfume mingled with sweet meadow-breath.

The farmer was closer now, close enough to speak more softly. '*Liebe Kühe, gute Kühe!*'

She heard the rattle of the catch and the man's soft grunt as he pressed his body against the bars to lift the gate.

Anna drew the knife and darted forward.

The man saw her. He dropped the gate — but its widely spaced bars offered him scant protection.

Her arm moved like a cat's paw, jarring her wrist as steel hit bone. Her fist bounced off his stomach at the end of the thrust.

The man fell backwards open-mouthed. Air belched from his lungs as he hit the ground. He rolled twice on the slope — and came to rest, stomach-up with the knife's handle standing at an angle from the gap between the lower edge of his waistcoat and the belt of his trousers.

25

On Friday the 24th of August, Karl and Helga bought a couple of five-shilling tickets for the Festival of Britain and boarded a boat from a jetty on the Victoria Embankment. The boatman pointed out features of the festival site on the south bank of the River Thames, but Karl wasn't listening . . .

Could a woman like Anna Stobart really be dangerous — as Robert had once thought . . . ?

'The futuristic Festival Hall is right there in front of you, ladies and gentlemen, it's the only permanent building on the site — some say that London has enough concert halls already but this one uses a heat-exchanger: river water cools the nearby Battersea Power Station — so we reuse that heat to warm the Festival Hall . . . '

That visit to Brixham last year for tea with Anna Stobart: she had been angry all right — but hardly dangerous . . .

'Don't forget to go inside the Festival Hall: indoor plants everywhere and a new style of seating made from bent laminated plywood, projecting boxes, beautiful acoustics. The

Dome of Discovery is that giant mushroom-head of aluminium supported on spindly legs angled around its edge — it's only here for the duration, it'll be scrapped in the autumn . . . '

Her sudden journey to Lisbon last year — why? And what had happened over there? Robert had tried to warn him about something but that telephone line . . .

They walked together between bright pavilions built in every conceivable style of modern architecture, gaudy and geometric. Amongst it all, and looking out of place — the Shot Tower, brick-built, a hundred years old, once used for making perfect spheres of lead by dropping molten metal from a height of 200 feet — but now with a radar telescope fitted to the top . . .

A warning? But Anna seemed harmless . . .

Abandoning the Official Guide Book's suggested route they entered the Dome of Discovery and found an impressive exhibition covering the story of Britain's scientific progress over the past century. Polar Exploration: two life-like explorers clearing 'snow' from outside their hut. Health and Drainage: models of greatly enlarged insects suspended in the air. Helga stood in front of a perfect scale model of Joseph Paxton's Crystal Palace and read from the sign: it was the building which had housed the Great Exhibition of 1851 — but Karl wasn't listening . . .

Why did Robert avoid talking about Anna — even at the lunch party where there had been every opportunity?

Underneath an astronomical telescope, dominating everything, Helga was now looking at a life-sized model of a megatherium with its 'flesh' cut away on one side to reveal the skeleton — she was reading something about Charles Darwin and the mysteries of genealogy . . .

Robert had been working for the other side — Anna would have approved of that.

Together they climbed one of the modern but functional flights of stairs leading to galleries high in the dome. In the Outer-Space Gallery, under a huge relief-globe of the world hanging above them, Helga studied some of Sir Isaac Newton's mathematical formulae; but Karl . . .

Awak: why had Anna been so friendly with him? Why should she have shown such an interest in the farm?

The Transport Pavilion: Karl looked at a scale model of the de-Havilland Comet, the world's only jet airliner, already test-flown and due to go into service in the spring. There were steam engines still working a hundred years after they had been built, cars of every shape and size with panels cut away to reveal how they had been built, motor-bikes, escalators, petrol-powered roller-skates, every imaginable innovation and invention — but . . .

Anna was attractive — but unpredictable, angry but forgiving and, like most women, she was friendly towards Awak. No, she was not, nor ever could be, dangerous . . .

There was evidence of quaint humour in the Lion & Unicorn Pavilion: a life-size model of a long-haired girl called Alice climbing through a mirror with a hundred white plaster doves fluttering silently in the roof above her head. Outside, a fountain tipped water from a chain of buckets into a long rectangular lake alive with waterspouts and gas-flares.

They sat on futuristic chairs, painted lemon-yellow, and ate expensive steak and chips in the Riverside Restaurant followed by coffee at an exorbitant ninepence per cup. They saw Festival Rock being made: lettering running through every stick from end to end. At the Telecinema they wore special glasses to watch three-dimensional films and ducked involuntarily as projectiles appeared to hurtle at them out of the screen.

But it was the Skylon which left the most lasting impression: Karl stood on a brass plate set into concrete immediately below it. The giant aluminium porcupine-quill was exactly vertical, defying gravity, suspended from below, magically, on the thinnest of wires with the point more than one hundred metres above — aimed, at that moment, towards an aeroplane moving steadily southwards under the clouds.

★　★　★

In the sky, somewhere above London, Anna leaned back in the meagre upholstery of a DC3-Dakota aircraft.

She tried to imagine what Robert would do when she failed to return to the wine shop. Poor man — so close to death in Portugal last summer. It was hard to live with that thought: Robert, innocent of any crime. The penalty for murder — even attempted murder — had to be death. However much she loved him now, it could never erase her guilt. He had done his best to prevent the raid on Dartmouth — but he had been overruled by faceless men using Mr Carter as a messenger: guilty men who could never be traced — not now. Sometimes the desire to put an end to it all was almost too strong to resist — but first . . .

Zaunbrecher's death had happened through

good organisation and planning — so had the killing of Albrecht Kauffmann: well planned; on his home ground; *using one's initiative*, that's how Sergeant Cox would have described it — he would have approved if he could have seen how swiftly and decisively the execution had been carried out — but there could be no feeling of satisfaction, no feeling of triumph — not yet — because there was another job still to do before the task was complete . . .

With the steady hum of engines in her ears, Anna tried to picture the farm in France, a place she knew well — she even knew its map reference but that would not be necessary today. She would hire a taxi when she got to Orly Airport. It was going to feel strange, visiting that place again after so long . . .

★   ★   ★

Towards the end of an hour-long taxi ride, Anna recognised a church on the edge of a meadow; a sloping village square paved with flattish cobbles; the smell of fresh-baked bread from the open door of the *boulangerie*. But now the fields were stooked with corn — unlike the ice and snow of February 1944.

The taxi moved along a dusty road leading south. The farm hadn't changed: tall square barn with a roof that looked like a tiled pyramid; turret-like *pigeonnier* with white doves fluttering into slits high in the walls — different of course to the Devonshire farm of yesterday. The house itself was built of stone and white lime-mortar — exactly as remembered, but the gate was new and gleaming white, no longer broken and held together with wire.

Anna told her driver to wait. She got out of the taxi and opened the new gate but as she walked across the yard her mind became crowded with violent images. She paused before knocking; all those carefully prepared questions — what had happened to them?

A young man, thick-set, dark hair, ruddy face, opened the door and waited impassively.

She tried to speak plainly to him but, although French was her second language, she was scarcely able to control the disjointed rush: 'I was working for the Resistance; hiding, trapped in your attic. I have travelled a long way to get here. May I see the attic again? Sometimes I enter that room in my nightmares. A man was standing at the top of the stairs. A shotgun is no match for . . . '

Blood — crimson — dripping off wooden steps . . .

'This house has memories for me. I would like to see your attic room again, the one that overlooks the yard.'

376

A twisted frown: puzzled now, the farmer stepped back from the door, gesturing her into his low-ceilinged kitchen. There was an embroidered inscription in a wooden frame hanging on the wall:

Ah, la belle chose que de savoir quelque chose!

The man went to the door in the corner of the room and lifted its wooden latch. As he led her up the staircase she remembered that too. At the top he reached past her to open a rickety door.

Anna stepped inside.

His voice showed what he was feeling now — some irritation: 'This is the attic. Is this what you want to see?'

She walked to the centre of the dust-filled room, aware of the young man watching her back. She glanced up quickly at the intricate framework of timbers that supported the roof and instantly identified the beam. Remembering the state of the attic floor-joists in her old house in Brixham, she trod carefully across the worm-eaten boards and squatted down by the low window. She needed a moment to collect herself: work out the best way of getting what she needed . . .

Complaining geese skidding on frozen

puddles to avoid the boots of running soldiers in the yard below. Harsh, hysterical commands . . .

Anna got up. She moved to the centre of the room and stood directly below the cross-beam of the central roof truss. The pictures in her head were still vivid, but she would never be able to describe what she had been *feeling* on that wintry day so long ago . . .

The farmer took a step forward. 'What can I do for you, what is it that you want?'

Tell this stranger — if not the feelings — the sights, the sounds, the way it was.

'Monsieur Dessoude fired two shots — he was standing at the top of the steps on the other side of that door. I heard falling bodies on the stairs. Men were shouting. There was a short burst of small-arms' fire. Slivers of wood splintered off that door — look, you can see where it has been repaired. Dessoude was hit. Words bubbled in his throat before he died.'

The man's face froze in surprise. 'Martin Dessoude was my uncle. I knew that he was murdered by the Nazis but nobody ever told me how.'

The years of shunning these things from the mind were over now. Telling about Dessoude's death might soothe the pain, leak

378

it *away from the unhealed wound deep inside . . .*

'Your uncle died firing his pigeon-gun at six German soldiers armed with MP-28 submachine guns. He killed two of them but had no time to reload. What chance did he have with just two barrels of bird-shot? After they had killed your uncle the soldiers came through that door and found me . . .'

She watched his face as she continued. 'You say this man was your uncle? Do you ever wonder what happened to your aunt and your two small cousins who were also in this house that day?'

He looked away. 'Sometimes I wonder about it. Tell me, what *did* happen to them?'

'They were taken with me to Amiens prison and I never saw them again.'

That is enough — that is too far, the pain comes back again. Leave me alone — a few seconds will be enough to retrieve my property and get on with the task that I must do . . .

'I have come to fetch something that I left here.'

His eyebrows lifted. 'You left something — here?'

She glanced up. 'Yes, on top of that beam. If it's still there I'd like to claim it.'

The farmer looked up at the wooden

framework, walked across and reached up. 'This beam, this one here under the joist?'

She nodded.

'Just here?' He was a short man, only slightly taller than Anna, but the beam was low and his hand disturbed a shower of dust which fell shimmering across a shaft of sunlight slanting from the window. 'There *is* something.' He took it down and blew off the dust. 'This is a thirty-eight calibre Smith and Wesson Model 36.' He balanced the revolver in his right hand. 'I killed a man with one of these when I was working for the Resistance just after the Allied landings in Normandy. I should have been in school but killing the Boches was more important than arithmetic in those days.' He swung out the cylinder with a practised thumb, paused a moment, then looked up accusingly. 'Did you know how to use this weapon?'

'Of course I did — and I still do!'

Light from the window glinted on the yellow brass of six live rounds still in the cylinder — percussion-caps still intact.

Challenging her now: 'If this was yours and you knew how to use it, why is it still loaded? Why did you hide it here? You claim that my uncle was trying to defend himself with a shot gun; if that is true he must have been trying to protect you too. What were you doing standing here with a loaded pistol in your hand — then hiding it while Martin Dessoude was giving his life to defend you?'

Anna heard herself translating something from another of the many English quotations that she had learned in childhood: '*He who fights and runs away may live to fight another day; but he who is in battle slain, can never rise and fight again.*'

The farmer shrugged. 'The war has been over for six years, the fighting has finished.'

Anna held out her hand to take the gun.

'*Has it?*'

26

On Saturday morning Karl and Helga boarded another boat and bought threepenny tickets for a trip to Battersea Fun Fair. A bizarre collection of whirring human and animal figures was striking eleven on the Guinness Animated Clock as they stepped ashore.

They took a short ride from Oyster Creek to Far Totting in a quaint railway train pulled by a steam engine called Nellie designed by an eccentric English cartoonist. They rode on the Water Splash and got wet. They risked a spin in the Rotor Cocoon and when the floor dropped away they became temporarily stuck like flies to its vertical walls by centrifugal force. They went for a stroll along the tree-walk, twenty feet above ground, and looked down at a forty-foot paper dragon with smoke blowing from its nostrils.

In the evening they danced under the stars. The Skylon, now illuminated from the inside, pointed into the night like a great splinter of light. A dark-haired singer called Alma Cogan accompanied Geraldo's Embassy Orchestra: *Put another nickel in, in the nickelodeon.*

Three hundred miles to the east of London, a British European Airways DC3 settled itself onto Lohausen's main runway. Anna peered out of the square window with cupped hands to blinker out the light.

Dusseldorf was under a steady slant of rain; it penetrated around her neck as she stood in line for a taxi. Bulldozers working under floodlights laboured, undeterred by the weather, to clear endless stretches of rubble in the city. Square buildings of steel and concrete appeared like dentists' fillings amongst the decay.

From the back of the taxi Anna looked blankly at the scene of rebirth, trying to ignore the voice, and already feeling, perhaps prematurely, like a victorious general entering a defeated city.

Molenstrasse: a narrow residential street near the southern boundary of the city with men on floodlit scaffolding at the far end, too busy and distant to present a threat. Anna waited until the taxi had turned the corner before attempting to enter the house. The windows looked secure at first glance but the front door had a large keyhole and the lock appeared to be an old fashioned mortise-type. For a few seconds she stood still — using a handkerchief to wipe her hands — *was it sweat or rain?*

She could hear the soft-spoken Mr Beckwith: *First probe the lock to establish the position and nature of the protective wards — these are designed to prevent the wrong key contacting the bolt . . .*

The wards: there was no need for him to remind her about them. She undid the flap on the outside of her handbag, found the tool hidden there and carefully inserted it — remembering that Beckwith had a knack of making things sound a lot easier than they really were. With her eyes closed in concentration she twisted tentatively, pushed gently, felt her way around inside the lock to read the invisible layout of the mechanism — which turned out to be not unlike an old-style Strutt's Patent Tumbler but with slightly thinner components.

In three minutes she had found a way through the ward-maze. Beckwith again: *Once you're through them wards, find the spring — usually shaped like a wishbone; it retains the bolt in position. Work on bolt and spring at the same time, that's the key — the key — get it?*

After several attempts the lockpick engaged correctly. She gently tested the force of the spring — it was strong — but she still

384

had reasonable friction on the bolt. Rotate; compress the spring; lift the bolt from its retainer ... another hand to steady the wrist; a little more torsion — but the flattened end of the tool lost grip and the spring snapped down again. It took several attempts before she was rewarded with the sound she had been waiting for ... *CLUNK:* the bolt slid back and hit the back-stop.

★ ★ ★

In London, Karl and Helga had decided to take Anna's advice to spend most of Sunday enjoying the sights. From their hotel they walked across Westminster Bridge and Karl checked his watch against Big Ben, refusing to admit that his Rolex was thirty seconds slow by the midday chime. They walked up Whitehall, trying to ignore the many weed-infested gaps between buildings.

The Cenotaph; Ten Downing Street; the War Office; Horse Guards Parade; Admiralty Arch — by the time they got to Nelson's Column they began to suspect that Anna's true motive had been an attempt to make them admire Britain's prowess in warfare.

Somebody in the hotel had advised them to visit Speakers' Corner so they arrived there after a short taxi ride. An orator, standing in a close-packed audience, condemned government proposals to make seven years' separation acceptable grounds for divorce. The crowd heckled. The orator changed to: '*Where are the two British diplomats, Burgess and Maclean who disappeared from the British Embassy in Washington on June the seventh?*' And, after that: '*What should be done about the secret society called Mau Mau, pledged to drive the British from Kenya Colony with threats of murder, mayhem and mutilation?*'

Monday: a quiet morning at the hotel. After a light lunch, the airport, in good time for Service BE 482, a 38-seater Vickers Viking. Karl and Helga settled back for the two-hour flight to Lohausen, tired but happy.

At a quarter to six the aircraft let down through squalls of rain and made an erratic approach to Dusseldorf. Their taxi-driver complained about the weather throughout the cross-city journey and was unwilling to get out into the wet to help unload the luggage.

Karl found his key. The lock was unexpectedly stiff. He entered their narrow hallway, switched on the light and dropped the suitcases. It felt good to be home. He kissed Helga's rain-wet cheek and opened the door under the stairs.

'I thought you turned off the hot water before we left.'

She looked puzzled. 'That's odd — I'm almost certain . . . anyway, now we won't have to wait before we run a bath.'

Karl picked up the suitcases and started up the stairs. He stopped halfway. Hanging in the air was the faintest smell of something unusual: the fading scent of flowers mingled with some kind of fruit — oranges perhaps, or even lemons, yes, lemons. Helga had never gone in for stuff like that. He breathed in again and now, somehow, the smell seemed familiar . . .

He picked up the bags and continued up the stairs. On the landing the scent was more distinct. It had to be something from Helga's normally limited repertoire still lingering in the air, trapped for two weeks behind closed windows.

Karl ran a deep bath and lowered himself into the scalding water; he lay back and carefully fitted his head between the taps. The heat penetrated. He closed his eyes and thought about unanswered questions: *Where is Andrew now? Has Ian Gatting received my letter? Why did Robert McGuire marry Anna Stobart — of all people, why her?*

He lowered himself further until water lapped his stomach but his thoughts kept returning to the mysterious smell of a particular perfume that, as far as he knew, Helga had never used.

Tea with Anna Stobart last year: dropping his cup on her carpet; the photographs on her mantelpiece — her disapproval when she had found him looking at them. While he had been looking at those photographs, somehow — in some strange way — he had *known* she was standing there on the thick carpet behind him even though he had not heard her enter the room . . .

Brixham! A ripple curved across the bath. Brixham: *that* was where he had first smelled flowers and lemon — on a wet day like this one . . .

Reacting involuntarily to some outside stimulus, his eyes snapped open. A wooden floorboard creaked. In the steamy glass of the basin mirror he could see a woman's face: *Anna's face.* She was standing motionless outside the open door — reflected between vertical streaks of condensation. Her hands were together — holding something in front of her.

Her next step was silent. Although the door

still screened her from him, Karl kept his eyes on the mirror . . .

Two seconds — and she was across the threshold.

Karl hurled himself out of the bath, crashed into the door and trapped her against the wall . . .

She struggled free — and as she did so he saw that she had a gun . . .

Karl caught her by the wrists. She brought a crushing knee into his groin and skilfully broke his grip with a quick movement of her arms. They fell struggling to the floor. The gun went off close to Karl's ear — the mirror exploded in a shower of glass.

Spread-eagled on top, he caught her wrists again but Anna fought wildly: her teeth ripped his forearm as she struggled to point the gun. Broken glass lacerated Karl's body: feet, knees, thighs, elbows . . . A second shot hit the window.

He slammed Anna's right hand against the floor. She screamed. He slammed her hand down again as hard as he could — and kept on banging it again and again until her fingers opened and the revolver spun across the floor.

Helga ran in. She stepped across the struggling bodies, picked up the weapon, pressed the muzzle into the side of Anna's neck and shouted hysterically: '*What are you doing here, what are you doing?*'

Karl scarcely had breath to speak: '*Don't shoot, Helga. Don't shoot; just go downstairs again and telephone the police.*'

★ ★ ★

After treatment in the hospital and statements at the police station, Karl and Helga got home well after midnight. Karl's hands were bandaged so it was Helga who picked up the correspondence that had accumulated whilst they had been away. Two of the letters had English post-marks and, when they were both in bed, Helga opened one of them and read it aloud.

McGUIRE'S WINES and SPIRITS
Duke Street, Dartmouth,
Devon
Telephone: Dartmouth 378

24/8/51

Dear Karl,

I have been trying to telephone you but remembered you were going to go to London so you will see this when you get back home.

I am in trouble. Anna has disappeared and I am at my wits' end. I will inform the police if she isn't back tomorrow but in the meantime I wondered if you might have any ideas where she might be?

Please excuse me for bothering you with this. She went missing yesterday — I hope that she will have turned up by the time you get this.

Please ring me at the shop (phone number above) if you can think of anything. Thanks.

Yours ever,

Robert

Helga said, 'Do you think we should do as he says and tell him what has happened?'

Karl was lying back on the pillow with his eyes closed. 'Don't worry; I'll tell the police about it in the morning.'

Helga opened the other letter.

British Overseas Airways Corporation
London Airport

Hounslow
Middlesex
(Tel: Hounslow: 7777)

24th Aug 1951

Dear Karl,

Just read your letter. What a surprise just when I had given up hope of ever seeing you again. We must meet. I used to fly to Lohausen regularly and know Dusseldorf quite well.

Your account of the raid on Dartmouth interested me. That date (18/9/42) is one that I remember too. I was floating in the Channel with three others in a rubber dinghy on that day — bitterly cold and after four days we were all feeling seedy but had the good fortune to be spotted by a Spitfire pilot returning from France — one of the Czechs I later discovered.

I had another ducking on my way back from Hamburg a year

later — North Sea this time. After two weeks in the drink I was picked up by a Swedish fishing boat — the rest of my crew were dead by this time. I'm married now, Birgita has picked up quite a bit of English and doesn't mind living in Staines one bit and we do manage to get over to Sweden for a holiday once a year (being a civilian pilot has its advantages).

As for Andrew — the Royal Navy rejected him, something to do with his eyesight. He was disappointed about not going to Britannia but that didn't dampen his passion for ships. He is now Third Officer in the *Queen Mary* (c/o Cunard Steamship Co Ltd, 15 Lower Regent Street, London SW1 — should you want to write to him). He would love to hear from you.

You will be sorry to hear that our house in Plymouth took a direct hit and that both my parents were killed — it took me years to get over it — but I must have killed several hundred people myself. I suppose we would all go raving mad if we were to spend the rest of our lives feeling personally responsible for all these horrors so I try not to think about it — as you know, we English call that 'being philosophical'.

Do you remember <u>All for One and One for All</u>? None of us thought we would have to fight each other for six whole years, did we? Funny old world! Time the Musketeers were reunited — how say you?

Well, Karl, that brings you up to date with my doings so I'll sign off.

All the best.

Ian
PS — (Nearly forgot!) My home address is: 7 the Close, Staines. (tel 352).

After reading it again to herself, Helga said, 'What does Ian mean by *funny old world?*'

Karl answered her in English. 'It means strange or unusual; Barbara Carmichael would have said *peculiar-funny*. Didn't they teach you *anything* in those language classes?'

EPILOGUE

Baden-Baden, Germany — Saturday, June the 6th, 2005:

Karl and Helga walked down steep steps leading from their buff-coloured house, crossed the park and entered the beautiful nineteenth century Friedrichsbad Spa. Although both well into their eighties, their legs were strong and this exercise had never caused them any difficulty — in fact it proved everything that Helga had ever claimed about hot brine and regular body toning.

With a crowd of their friends, they bathed naked in scalding mineral water. Helga never felt self-conscious when doing this provided she was wearing a bathing cap to hide the bald patch.

After a vigorous soap-and-brush massage from a woman with arms like trees, they continued their walk to the Kurgarten, an open park at the centre of Germany's favourite spa-town. They sat together under a striped umbrella surrounded by flowers of every variety and Karl ordered a bottle of Guntersblumer, nicely chilled.

Helga, not worrying about lowering the tone of the surroundings, got on with her knitting: a tiny jacket for a great-grandchild. Karl began to read his weekly copy of the English *Daily Telegraph* which he had bought in the shade-dappled Lichentaler Alee on their way down from the baths. It was not so much the news, but a desire to maintain his language skills that compelled him to read an English paper once a week. A simple routine: one that they had been enjoying every Saturday since 1986, the year Karl retired from his career as a schoolmaster.

He moved the bottle to one side and flattened out his paper. Today there was dramatic news from England: the Channel Tunnel had been bombed again but this time hundreds of bodies had been recovered from the wreckage, twenty-seven survivors were in hospital and five terrorists were in custody.

He turned to the magazine section: there was an article entitled 'Britannia Scores a Century' which he read to the sound of a brass-band drifting loud and soft on the breeze. The Royal Naval College in Dartmouth was about to celebrate its centenary on Saturday, the 20th of June: a special parade and a Royal Visit — all very English. A short history of the college named the more illustrious officers who had been trained there but, typically, there was no mention of Operation Herod.

The music stopped. Karl looked up from the page and saw the band conductor chasing a sheet of music sailing on the wind; a pair of black swans, beaks skyward, waddled clear to let him pass.

Karl turned to his wife. 'We haven't been to England since the Festival of Britain and that was fifty-three years ago.'

★   ★   ★

Dartmouth harbour was full of boats: yachts, motor cruisers and speedboats of every shape and size. The fishing boats had gone but the ferry from Kingswear was just the same — a raft-like affair lashed to the smaller vessel which propelled it.

From the outside at least, the Royal Castle Hotel had not changed in fifty-three years — but some alterations inside had made the ground-floor rooms fewer in number but bigger.

In the morning they went to the museum. The curator, a thin woman in middle age, had never heard of Barbara Carmichael. The relief-map of Dartmouth was still there in its usual place; there were many more fossils in the Fossil Room, the same musty smell — but the posters had gone: no more *Wrens saving a man for the fleet,* no *WAAFs serving with the men who fly.* The main feature now was a temporary exhibition of artefacts loaned by a newly-formed local club called Metal Detectives, occupying the central display area and using the same glazed cabinets that Barbara had once used to celebrate five years of peace. Helga was talking about a shoe-buckle marked *Seventeenth Cent* — but Karl wasn't listening . . .

Something had caught his eye — and he was speechless.

A dull film of green had robbed the brass cylinder of its original lustre but there was still some broken thread around the top. Some curling fragments of paper were laid out next to the cylinder and bore faint traces of handwriting: a familiar misformed 'r' was clearly visible — and the curl of a capital 'B' was enough to identify the author. Karl put a steadying hand to the edge of the cabinet and stood there — dumbly — in the sway of an overwhelming feeling of surprise and disbelief.

He turned from the cabinet. Ignoring Helga's *what is it, Deichy?* he went to find the woman on duty . . .

Standing by the cabinet again, Karl tapped the glass. 'Could you tell me where this was found?'

The thin woman adjusted her glasses. 'Funnily enough that's the only exhibit that didn't come from Metal Detectors. One of the Britannia College gardeners found it while he was replanting a flower bed for the Royal Visit; he brought it in last week. We think it's an old cartridge case, very corroded as you can see but you can just make out some letters and numbers stamped into the base. I'll take it out so you can see for yourself.'

She unlocked the cabinet and picked up the object. Handing it to Karl she said, 'The curious thing about it is the tightly rolled paper that we found inside which unfortunately fell to dust when we tried to take it out. It's all a bit of a mystery — those little scraps are all we are left with. We think it must have been some kind of message but we haven't been able to make any sense of it.'

Karl took the brass cylinder from her and slid his thumb over its sharp mouth. *Three quick turns of the handle; the cockpit cover sliding back; reaching into his boot; torrents of air swirling in; khaki figures running towards a Bofors gun parked at the edge of a D-shaped parade ground; a streamer lying in a tangled heap on the floor of the cockpit; the agony of not knowing if his message had been read by the enemy . . .*

He put it back carefully. 'This is a 20 millimetre brass cartridge case: standard ammunition for the Mauser MG151/20 machine gun that German fighter aircraft were fitted with during the second world war.'

The thin woman seemed pleased: 'Do you think you could jot that down for me so that I can type out a proper card? We were pretty sure it was a cartridge case but I don't suppose we will ever find out about the message hidden inside it.'

On the street again they went in search of English beer. The name of the pub was written in bright yellow on a red background: George and Dragon, a colourful strip on a whitewashed gable-end. The room was unchanged — as was the table by the window where once: *Did you leak information about Operation Herod to the Allies?*

Helga took a sip of Diet Coca-Cola: 'Awak would have been interested in your message — found by a gardener sixty-three years late and never read by anybody.'

Karl turned his glass thoughtfully. 'I would never have told him about it anyway. That message was meant to save Andrew and his fellow cadets — it was also an act of treachery against my own comrades — Awak wouldn't have been impressed.'

Helga said, 'It's sad that he died so soon

after he'd made such a good recovery after that dreadful attack. I'll never forget Pauline's letter. I would have liked to have seen Awak one last time before he died.'

Karl drank some beer. 'If last year's breakthrough in cancer research had happened in 1952, Awak would still be with us. I wonder why Pauline never answered any of our letters after that — perhaps she died too, or else remarried and moved away. We might be the only survivors out of all those people we met for lunch at Taylors Restaurant the last time we were here. Robert McGuire must be dead by now — the year of his birth coincided with the start of the First World War, I'll always remember that.'

Helga drank some Diet-Coke. 'And Anna — we never discovered what became of her after she had been extradited to England. Anyway, I think we are being rather morbid with all this talk of death,' Helga counted off the decades on her fingers, 'If Robert was born in 1914, he'd be ninety-one now; lots of people live to be well over a hundred these days — especially if they can be dealt with every week by somebody like Magda with a good brine-bath to follow.'

Karl laughed. 'At least the wine shop is still there, did you notice it as we came out of the museum?'

She shook her head.

'It's changed its name to Vineyards.' He paused for a moment. 'I wonder?'

'What do you wonder, Deichy?'

'Old Robert might still be making his annual trip to Dartmouth for all we know.'

★ ★ ★

At the wine shop Karl said to the man behind the counter, 'We used to know Robert McGuire, son of the owner of this shop. I don't suppose you've ever heard of him.'

'He's upstairs, would you like to see him?'

It was a large room: a bed in the far corner; a map of Portugal on the wall. There was an old man sitting in a high-backed chair watching a golf tournament on television: tight skin across a hollowed cheek; a shaggy mane of white hair. It was Robert.

'Some people to see you, Father.'

'Is that you, Alistair? *People?* What people?' His voice was thin and high, but unmistakable.

Karl stepped forward and said something in German.

Alistair interjected: 'He can't hear you. It's better if you speak into that microphone, it's connected to his hearing-aid.'

But Robert was already out of his chair.

403

'*Karl Deichman!*' Broken veins traced a blue network. '*And Helga — prettier than ever!* I haven't heard from you two in years, not since — not since, well never mind how long it is!'

He put a steadying hand to the back of his chair. 'Alistair, my boy, fetch me Hennesey's swift sensation — *but don't let your mother see!*'

'But Father, the doc . . . '

'Never you mind what that doctor said — be a good lad now and do as I say.'

Refusing help, Robert struggled to pull up two more chairs. His tight skin cracked into a smile. 'Doctors rule my life these days — what's left of it: don't have this; you can't drink that; don't over-excite yourself; *think* your blood pressure down. Young folk think they know it all but my doctor is going to kill me stone dead one of these days. Like Anna, I've never had much faith in that profession.'

Alistair brought brandy and three glasses. He put the tray on a table next to his father with a disapproving glance and left the room. Robert poured shakily, talking as he did so: he had settled in Dartmouth at the end of 1952; his father had become ill. 'I didn't want to leave Lisbon . . . '

There was no further mention of Anna. Robert's conversation drifted wildly and after half an hour he was repeating himself so frequently that Karl couldn't take any more. He was saved by Helga who said: 'Tell us about Anna, we'd like to meet her again.'

'Robert smiled. 'Now there was a woman to be reckoned with! Full of passion, but I never really understood her — there was some kind of barrier always there between us; I never could work it out. As soon as I told her I had been working for the Allies during the war she wouldn't leave me alone. I got back to Portugal shortly after visiting Karl in Plymouth Hospital — and she turned up the next day. She lived with me over there — caused me a lot of trouble I have to say. I had a housekeeper in those days and those two women knew how to fight, jealousy I suppose. Have you ever seen women trying to kill each other?'

He stopped abruptly and changed the subject. 'What became of Andrew — that cousin of yours, the cadet in Dartmouth — and the other one, what was his name, Ian was it? How's that for memory?'

'Andrew never went to Britannia in the end, he joined Cunard and became one of their skippers. Helga and I went on a Scandinavian cruise several years ago; we sat at his table every night for dinner. Ian wasn't so lucky — he was in a Comet airliner that blew up over the Mediterranean in 1954 — metal fatigue they discovered later. He was an airline pilot but on that occasion he was just hitching a ride to Sweden with his wife. Both bodies were recovered — they are buried in Elba. But you were telling us about Anna.'

Robert cleared his throat but waited a little before replying. 'I'm afraid Anna is no longer with us. She was insane but I never realised it. At the Kauffmann trial some fancy barrister insisted she plead insanity, had a pile of medical evidence to prove it. He was right of course. She'd had a tough time of it during the war, used to lie asleep next to me shouting out some name: Sigy-something-or-other.' Robert poured himself another brandy, drank it quickly, and looked away. 'When I got back to England, I used to visit Anna every month — never failed: train from Kingswear, change at Paddington, walk the last two miles from Wellington College Station to Broadmoor — you could do that in those days before they closed two thousand railway stations. From my very first visit Anna begged me to kill her and in the end I obliged. She had always maintained that the punishment for murder — even *attempted* murder — should be death. I know it sounds odd but Anna claimed her attack on Kauffmann was justified, but attempting to kill *me* in Lisbon was a crime because I turned out to be on her side during the war. Silly really, but that's how her mind worked: black, white but no shades of grey.'

'*You* killed her?'

'Officially it was suicide, but I was responsible.' He picked up the brandy and refilled their glasses. 'I never married Anna. We declared ourselves man and wife to suit the conventions of the day — I loved her, I suppose, in a physical way, but we never married.'

'If the verdict was suicide, why do you say it was you who killed her?'

Light from the window caught an unexpected tear leaking from the corner of Robert's left eye; it rolled to a stop halfway down his dry cheek. He turned his head and looked away. 'Every time I visited her in that awful bloody place, she greeted me with the same chilling question: *Have you brought it, Robert dear? Have you? Have you brought me what I keep asking you for? When will you bring it?* She was suffering, you see, and I wanted to help her find peace. We parted with a kiss on the 1st of February 1965 — I associate the whole sorry episode with Winston Churchill's funeral which had taken place the previous Monday. I never saw her again. Lethal pills take about six hours if you swallow them whole — gave me time to get clear. Ironic really: the capsule that killed Anna was the one she tried to use on me in Portugal. Stupidly I returned it to her in an envelope: an act of bravado to show her that I was still alive I suppose. The police wanted to know how Anna could have acquired a lethal dose of poison inside a secure mental institution but for some reason I was never questioned about it.'

Robert's flow stopped abruptly. An elderly woman: slim with long silvery hair, bustled into the room. She picked up the bottle and planted a disapproving kiss on Robert's cheek. 'Nossa Senhora! Que temos aqui, Roberto?' She turned, raising a hand to cover her embarrassment. 'Please excuse me — it is my 'usband. The doctor he say Roberto not to be drinking the brandy.'

Robert took her hands in his and kissed her on the lips. 'These are old friends of mine, Ludo darling, I last saw them more than fifty years ago. They know Ivo and Janet.' He turned to Karl and Helga again. 'This is my wife; we met a long, long time ago in Portugal.'

After she had left the room, Karl said, 'The Kaukys? I'd forgotten about them.'

'Oh yes, they're still around — Ivo and Janet are our closest friends. Ivo is even richer now: when he retired he sold his chain of furniture shops to something called a Nationwide Conglomerate.'

Helga remembered talking to Pauline at Taylor's Restaurant — and her husband: a stooping, prematurely white-haired, chain-smoking man, with an incredible story of how he had escaped from Communist rule. 'We must definitely all see the Kaukys before we leave — a lunch party perhaps. Is Taylor's Restaurant still there?

★ ★ ★

On the morning after the lunch, an elderly couple were seen picking their way up Coombe Road through crowds of people jamming the streets, all hoping to catch a glimpse of Prince Charles and the Duke of Edinburgh. The couple rested on a convenient bench, unoccupied because it faced away from the road. The man was seen to set his watch by the college clock. They got up and pushed through the throng as far as the entrance to the college grounds where four brick pillars supported freshly painted iron-work over the main gate.

A policeman stopped them. 'Excuse me my

friends. Might I see your invitations?'

The man looked blank. '*Invitations?*'

'Access to BRNC is by invitation only. Nobody gets past me without an invitation.'

The old man put on a display of senile confusion: 'This is most unusual. I had no invitation the last time I visited Britannia.'

The policeman was watching a group of rowdy teenagers on the other side of the road and replied without looking at him. 'Is that so? And what, might I ask, were you doing on these premises — *the last time* — that didn't require an invitation?'

'I blew up B-block and my colleague planted a bomb in the quarterdeck.'

The policeman grabbed the old man's arm and forced it up behind his back; handcuffs were produced; urgent messages were shouted into mouthpieces — more policemen — a scuffle; people turned to stare.

A sudden burst of cheering announced the arrival of the royal party. A stretched Rolls Royce — made in Germany — swept in through the gate. The old man's wife, now attached to a policeman's wrist, caught the Duke of Edinburgh's eye through five millimetres of bullet-proof glass.

★　★　★

The following Saturday Helga was listening to a gentle piece of Schubert in the Kurgarten. As usual, Karl was reading his English newspaper.

Helga put down her knitting. 'Deichy darling, do you think we could go to Austria for our summer holiday next year?'

Author's Note

How Much of This Story is True?

Dartmouth Conspiracy is mostly fiction. What inspired me to write it was a true event that I witnessed shortly before my eighth birthday.

Early in 1942 my father, a naval officer, joined the staff of Britannia Royal Naval College in Dartmouth. Our family lived at number five Pathfields Road; the road is now tarmaced and called Townstal Pathfields. I attended Tower House School, now a private house at the top of Townstal Pathfields, about 100 yards from the front gate of our house — it was nothing like the fearsome place depicted in this book.

On the 18th of September 1942, shortly after 11.30 a.m., I was standing at the top of Pathfields Road with the summer holidays almost at an end when I heard — *and felt* — two huge explosions below and behind St Clement's Church. Immediately after that I saw an aeroplane above the church, speeding towards me.

Because I was standing on high ground, the

aircraft — which was flying level — was coming straight towards me. In the few seconds it took to travel the length of Pathfields Road I saw black crosses on the side of the fuselage, a swastika on the tail, and the white face of a German pilot. Two Spitfires (we all knew what they looked like) were close behind. Above the roar of engines I heard — and saw — a lot of gunfire. The three aircraft narrowly missed the top of Tower House and disappeared from view.

My mother, for some reason convinced that all this gunnery was aimed at me, ran into the road: *why hadn't I thrown myself flat on the ground like I'd been taught?*

My father and elder brother were on board the 11.35 pulling out of Kingswear station. The train stopped (Father told me) as soon as the bombing started; he saw bombs drop on the college and ships under attack in the river. My brother, however, was disappointed — he saw nothing because he was told to lie on the floor; Father got down too, and lay on top of him.

Britannia's Christmas Term had been due to start on that day but, shortly before, a circular letter was sent out to all personnel informing them that the beginning of term had been postponed by one week *to phase correctly the Christmas leave.*

More than fifty years later I visited the Public Records Office in London and was able to confirm that six single-seater Focke-Wulf 190s had approached Dartmouth at sea level and had dropped six bombs on various targets. I also discovered, that shortly before the attack, twelve fully armed Spitfires from 310 (Czech) Squadron, based at nearby Exeter, were on formation flying practice above cloud over Teignmouth (following earlier escort duties with an Air Sea Rescue Walrus amphibian). The Spitfires broke off their exercise and dived towards Dartmouth from 8,000 feet; they closed with the Focke-Wulfs but — and here my novel differs from the truth — they failed to shoot down any of the fleeing raiders even though two of the Czech pilots were Battle of Britain veterans.

Britannia suffered a direct hit on the quarterdeck and another on B block. D block also suffered blast damage to walls, roof and windows. The Noss Shipyard belonging to Philip and Son, now a yacht marina, was fiercely attacked, leaving twenty employees dead. A floating crane and the collier SS *Fernwood* were hit while coaling a minesweeper in mid-river with a loss of four more lives. The only casualty in Britannia was Petty Officer Helen Victoria Whittal, my father's assistant, who lived next door to us in Pathfields Road. She was sadly missed; as far as I know she had no twin sister — if she did I am certain she bore no resemblance whatsoever to any character depicted in this book.

Nigel Clarke writes in his remarkable book, *Adolf Hitler's Holiday Snaps*:—

Towards the end of the war, while waiting for the General at a newly liberated Luftwaffe airfield in northern France, Mr Phillips (staff driver to General Horrocks) decided to explore some of the subterranean command bunkers ... The airfield had been hurriedly evacuated and many of the rooms were littered with documents. In one of the bunkers was an operations briefing room, and scattered about were hundreds of photographs of the west of England. Staff driver Phillips filled up his tunic with the most interesting and at the end of the war brought the photographs back to his home in Devon ...

As for the possibility of the Admiralty, or the Air Ministry, having prior knowledge of the raid on Britannia Royal Naval College — I leave you, the reader, to draw your own conclusion, bearing in mind one final coincidence . . .

At the time of the attack, the commander of the college, Captain E A Aylmer, was in his cabin; seated around the table with him was the Headmaster, the Second Master, the Chaplain and two other members of staff. The subject under discussion was *the evacuation of the college in the event of serious air raid damage.*

The first bomb dropped.

The six men dived for cover under the table just as the second bomb hit the north-west corner of the quarterdeck.

As Captain Aylmer emerged from under the table he is reputed to have said: '*At any rate, we were discussing a most appropriate subject!*'

And finally, in the interests of fairness, I give you the final irony: on the 12th of August 1944, a flight of RAF Lancaster bombers scored five direct hits on the German naval school at Brest.

Perhaps Shakespeare should have the last word: *Thus the whirligig of time brings in his revenges.*

James Stevenson

Other titles published by
The House of Ulverscroft:

TO KINGDOM COME

Will Thomas

When the Irish Republican Brotherhood bombs Scotland Yard in May 1884, private enquiry agent Cyrus Barker and his apprentice, Thomas Llewelyn, set out to infiltrate the faction responsible. Working for the Home Office, the duo impersonate a reclusive bomb maker and his assistant, who are willing to help in the plot to blow up London buildings and destroy the monarchy. Accepted by the faction, Barker investigates the identity of the Brotherhood's leader, as Llewelyn becomes involved with an Irish lass with ties to the group. Now the detectives must risk everything to save London from being blown to kingdom come.

THE BLOOD PARTNERSHIP

Seth Garner

Ben Spencer is the ambitious young owner of The Blood Partnership, an online property marketing company. Over the past few months he has become heavily involved with every member of the wealthy property-developing Westlake family — including becoming engaged to beautiful young Caitlin Westlake — and now he's beginning to regret it. Things go from bad to worse when Ben's own family are targeted by the Westlakes. Now he must choose a side, and it seems the only way out is death — but whose will it be?

DARK ANGEL

Raymond Haigh

The Prime Minister and the Home Secretary are scared — very scared. Terrorists, riots, the plague sweeping over the country, these are not the cause of alarm. Their concern centres on the documents held by a biochemist, which implicate the Government in a grave crime. Now, the biochemist is missing, as well as his wife and child. Government agent Samantha Quest is searching for them — but soon she is also being watched and hunted. A trail of death follows. Can Quest find the missing family and protect them from powerful men who will stop at nothing to conceal their crimes?

OCEAN PRIZE

James Pattinson

The S.S. *India Star*, a valuable cargo ship, is abandoned in the mid-Atlantic after suffering an engine room explosion. And Captain Barling of the S.S. *Hopeful Enterprise* has very special reasons for wishing to tow it into port. But is he justified in risking men's lives for the sake of his own desires? Shipmate Adam Loder thinks it is nothing but a wild goose chase, and chief engineer Jonah Madden is worried about his ailing engines; whilst crewman Charlie Wilson is hiding a deeper worry . . . Meanwhile, Barling has more than fearsome gales to contend with as a tenacious rival threatens his chances.

COPPER KISS

Tom Neale

FBI agent Vincent Piper is back in London, and the woman he loves, high-class call girl Celeste Young, is in danger. Her brother has put together an on-line sex blog — but one by one, the girls involved are being murdered, and Celeste is terrified that she could be next. Piper begins his own investigations into the killings. But the line between the good guys and the bad becomes blurred when he realises that the American Government is involved — and these people will do anything to achieve their political ambitions.

WATCHMAN

Jane Morell

Masterminded by the sinister Sarsen, overlord of an Islamic terror network, Operation Zephyr is a suicide mission planned to undermine the morale of the British public and expose the inability of the anti-terrorist organizations to prevent horrendous loss of life. Now the climax is imminent and Jake Messanger is at the centre with his half-sister Gemma in mortal danger. Sarsen has plans for Jake, who is faced with an appalling choice. Can a major disaster be averted?